GREEN
WITH ENVY

A Nick Polo Mystery

GREEN
WITH ENVY

Jerry Kennealy

SPEAKING VOLUMES, LLC
NAPLES, FLORIDA
2013

GREEN WITH ENVY

ISBN 978-1-61232-887-4

For Cookie Picetti
San Francisco just isn't the same
without you and the Star Buffet

CHAPTER ONE

IT HAD STARTED out like a perfect Sunday morning. I was sitting in my favorite booth, the one just beside the front door at the Washington Square Bar & Grill. The ricotta omelet had been just moist enough and the oatmeal muffins still warm from the oven, and Carol, the lovely and efficient hostess, was there to refill my coffee cup every time it got close to the half-empty mark.

I was working my way leisurely through the massive Sunday newspaper and had made it all the way to the comics, smiling ruefully at the latest adventures of Calvin and Hobbes, once again thankful that little Cal would always be around six years of age. Can you imagine what puberty would do to that kid? I was about to turn to see what was happening to Prince Valiant when somebody dropped something that looked like a mechanical spider on the table.

I glanced up to see the gloating figure of Harry Chapman, self-proclaimed "Most famous private investigator in San Francisco."

"Take a look at that, Polo. It's not a fingerprint. More like a signature. Your signature, baby."

Chapman was a tall, good-looking guy with a pound of thick blond hair worn in calculated disarray. He favored well-tailored Italian suits. Today's version was a soft, almost invisible glen plaid.

He was leaning against the wall, his left hand pushing back the front of his suit jacket so that you couldn't help but notice the butt of the SIG-Sauer automatic snuggled against his waist, or the oversized gold cuff links on his white-on-white shirt. The face of his wristwatch was made out of a bright twenty-dollar gold piece.

I picked up the item he'd dropped next to my coffee cup and twisted it with my fingers. I recognized it right away: a battery-operated telephone-line tap transmitter.

"Thanks, Harry, but I never use the things." I tossed it back to him.

He caught it with a well-manicured hand and sat down, uninvited, across from me.

"Listen, Nick, baby. Quit kidding me. I know it's yours." He hesitated, licked his lips, then continued. "What I want is anything you taped off the line. It's that simple. Don't worry, you'll make out okay as far as any money is concerned. We just want the tapes."

"I don't know what you're talking about," I said truthfully. "I haven't done electronic surveillance in years. And if I did, I'd use something a little newer and fancier than that thing. It's ready for a place in the Smithsonian."

Chapman tossed the bug in his hand. "Yeah, you're right there. Old, out of date. Homemade, but still efficient, huh? Just like the ones you used on the Sunset Oil job."

"How the hell did you hear about that?"

Chapman held out his hands. "Easy, baby. After you put the taps in, one of the executives got nervous. I had done a personal job for him. He had me check them out. I told him I would have handled it differently, but it was an okay job. You know, Nick, we all have our different styles, different techniques and equipment. The Sunset Oil job was wired exactly the same as the one we're talking about now. Same cheap homemade bug. You left your signature."

"I'm getting tired of this, Harry. Just where the hell did you find this particular bug?"

Chapman stood up, shot his cuffs, then reached inside his suit coat, flashing his gun butt again, and took a business card out of his shirt pocket and flicked it toward me. It floated down dangerously near the remains of my omelet. "Don't fuck around on this one, Nick. You're messing with the wrong people. You could get hurt. Call me. We can make a deal, and both of us will come out smelling like roses."

He walked over to the bar and ordered a drink. I took a sip of the now-lukewarm coffee. The Sunset Oil job had taken place almost three years ago and was one that I had farmed out. My expertise with electronic equipment is such that it took me almost two months to learn how to operate the remote control on my VCR, and I'm still intimidated by the damn thing.

I went back to the newspaper, but the mood had been broken. Even Snoopy and Woodstock couldn't cheer me up.

Chapman finished his drink and stopped to offer some advice. "Call me real soon on this, Nick."

I watched him walk down Powell Street until he was out of sight, then went to the men's room and used the pay phone to call John Henning.

Henning was a longtime friend and private investigator who was an expert with electronic equipment, and the man to whom I'd given the Sunset Oil job. His answering machine came on, and I left a message for him to call me.

I didn't hear back from Henning, and the next morning I was up early for a long drive to Sacramento to work for an insurance carrier on a civil case involving a small airplane that ran out of fuel and pancaked on the freeway right after takeoff from Sacramento Executive Airport. Getting a statement from a witness to an accident that took place a couple of years ago can be quite a task. People forget the things that attorneys consider important: the color of the traffic light, direction of travel, position of bodies. But not if the accident involved an airplane, no matter how large or small the plane happened to be. It's a memory that seems to be frozen in their minds, and they will happily talk your ear off about the weather conditions, where they first saw the plane, the sound, or lack thereof, of the engines, everything they saw when the bird fell out of the sky. I had little trouble in running down six witnesses who weren't listed on the National Transportation Safety Board's report, two of whom saw the pilot having a couple of drinks in the airport bar just moments before climbing into the little single-engine cockpit.

You might ask just why a lawsuit would develop over an incident where a pilot takes off with a pretty good heat on, the blood alcohol level the coroner found would have gotten the pilot arrested for drunk driving in a vehicle, and the plane runs out of gas less than a mile away from take off. Good question. But that is why we have attorneys. The pilot's family contacted one of these learned gentlemen, who came up with a theory that if the airplane's carburetor had been designed properly, the pilot would have had enough fuel to return safely to the airport rather than crashing on the freeway barely a mile from the airport.

Thus starts the litigation game. The maker of the plane is sued, as well as the people who made the carburetor, who then bring in the people who supplied them with the parts for the carburetor and so on down the line. Cross-complaints are filed, and more attorneys are brought in. Goodly portions of virgin forests are chopped down to handle the tons of paperwork involved, and eventually the trickle-down theory works and someone like me gets hired to dig into it a little deeper.

I didn't get back to San Francisco until late Tuesday night. My answering machine had several messages but none from John Henning. I tried his number and got his machine again and began worrying. Even if John was out of town, he'd be checking his phone messages.

The following morning I tried Henning's number one more time, hanging up as soon as his recorded message came on the line.

Some years ago, Henning had given me a key to his house, "in case anything happens." I rummaged around my desk drawers until I found the key, hooked onto a ring whose red plastic tab was stamped with the logo of a long-closed local car dealership.

Henning was a charter member of the CIA. No, not that one. The Catholic Irish Alcoholics. He would go on the straight and narrow for months or a year, then slip off. And when he slipped off, it was a long, slick ride. His standard routine was to get a case of vodka, the cheapest available. A couple of cases of ginger ale, then a few gallons of vanilla ice cream. He'd start on the vodka until most of it was gone, then work his way through the ginger ale and finally the ice cream. It might take a week. He'd somehow survive, the red of his eyes the only sign of color on his white, furrowed features. Sometimes it would take a few days at the hospital to get him back on his feet, but he always seemed to get there somehow.

Henning's house was in the Mission District, on York near 20th Street, one of a row of old Italianate Victorians, some nicely restored to their original beauty, others with clumsy stucco fronts added. The Henning place hadn't been painted since John's mother died twenty years ago. Flies were dancing around a battered garbage can in the driveway. I walked up the creaking steps to the front door. The key slipped in and turned the lock easily. As soon as I opened the door I knew what was waiting for me. The smell got worse the closer I got to his bedroom. John Henning lay on his bed; what was left of his face was staring up at the ceiling. His right hand was flung up over his head. There was a revolver in it. A swarm of flies were dive-bombing into the wound alongside his right ear. A bottle of Old Crow bourbon, with no more than a couple of shots left in it, was standing upright in the crook of his left arm.

I pulled out a handkerchief and tried to make it back to the front door without throwing up.

CHAPTER TWO

THERE'S A DEFINITE pecking order in responding to a shooting death. First the uniformed cops show up. There were two of them, both strangers to me; the man white, pushing forty, a slight pouch hanging over his belt, the woman black, in her early twenties, maybe an inch over five feet. Her belt, with its holstered Magnum, handcuffs, bullet pouch, Mace can, baton, and radio looked like it would drag her to the ground by the end of her shift.

The man took one look at Henning's body and said to his partner, "Mary, call the medical examiner."

"There's a phone in the kitchen," I told Mary. "I used it to call 911."

"You touch anything else?" asked the policeman.

"No. And I used a handkerchief on the phone."

He tipped his uniform cap back on his head and forced a smile, his lips opening just enough to show the tips of his teeth. He took a notebook from his uniform jacket and started asking me the required questions.

I hurried my answers and headed back to the sidewalk for some fresh air. I leaned against the hood of my car, crossing my legs. They seemed to shake less that way. John Henning had been a good friend. I'd first met him when I was still in the police department. You meet a lot of private investigators when you're a cop. They usually try to buy you a drink, then try to get you to run a criminal or motor vehicles check for them. Henning was the quiet, unassuming, gentlemanly type. He had stumbled across some information that turned out to be very valuable to me on a fraud

6

case I was handling. Henning made no demands, no confidential requests. I quit the department, partially because I'd inherited what I thought was a small fortune when my mom and dad were killed in an airplane crash. I was completely ignorant of inheritance taxes in those days. Something I learned about through harsh experience. The combination of the taxes and the advice of a stockbroker with some "can't lose" growth stocks and limited partnerships had soon whittled the small fortune down to the set of flats my parents owned. So I had to go to work. I figured I'd just put out my shingle and people would be flocking to my door. You know, the kind you see in the movies and read about: beautiful blondes bursting out of Danskin jumpsuits who want their lost husbands found. Big, fat rich guys with bundles of cash. You sit in your office, feet on the desk, and make wisecracks at your prospective clients, who put up with it because they just have to have you handle the case. Wrong. Pick up your local yellow pages and flip the pages until you come to investigators. They're starting to outnumber physicians and real estate agents.

There are several things you're not prepared for when you make the leap from the police department to the outside world. Things like rent, phone bills, stamps, business licenses, Social Security taxes, and the deflating feeling you get when you no longer have complete access to all those wonderful computer data bases.

I was floundering around in a sea of confusion with no clients. Henning stopped by to make a few suggestions, holding my hand gently as he led me through the maze of private enterprise.

The coroner's crew got there about twenty-five minutes later. They were both in their forties and looked alike enough to be brothers: short, thinning black hair and stomachs with fuller measurements than their chests.

They spent no more than five minutes in the room with Henning's body. One of them walked out and went over to the policeman. He had a plastic name tag pinned to the pocket of his shirt. It said "J. Fahey."

"Looks like suicide, Andy," he said to the male cop. "We're going to pack him out of here now."

"Don't you think someone from homicide should take a look at him first?" I said.

He squinted at me, then turned back to the cop. "Who's he?"

The cop read from his notebook. "Nick Polo. A friend of the deceased. He found the body."

"Sorry about your buddy, mister," Fahey said. "But I don't think we need homicide on this."

"I disagree."

That got me a deeper squint. "Oh, you do, huh? Well, maybe I've got a little more experience on this type situation than you do, so why don't you let me handle my job, huh?"

"I'm an ex–San Francisco policeman. I've had some experience with bodies. I don't think this was suicide."

The uniformed cop jumped in. "You should have said you were an ex-cop."

He was right. "How about calling Bob Tehaney down at homicide and asking him to take a look? He knew John Henning."

The coroner's investigator shook his head. "Tehaney is on vacation, pal. It's my decision. We're taking him in now, but I'll tell you what. We'll give it a close look and if anything shows, I'll make it a skull case."

Skull cases are sent up from the coroner's office to homicide for further investigation. They're usually situations when the victim is neither a homicide nor a suicide but a "tweener," quite often drug related, like when two or more guys are shooting up in a room and one overdoses. They don't get a whole lot of attention from the investigating officer.

I watched while they wheeled John's body out of the room and down into the meat wagon.

"Should have told us you were an ex-cop," the young black officer said, shaking her head as we left the house. "We would have handled it differently. Called homicide for you. It sure looks like a straight-up suicide though. How'd you get in? You got a key?"

"No. Front door was unlocked," I said, knowing that if I told her I had a key, she'd confiscate it.

She checked the inside of the door's lock, then slammed it shut.

8

"Not anymore," she said, shaking the door to make sure it didn't open.

Any body coming into the coroner's office is automatically autopsied, unless the victim has been under the continuous care of a doctor for seventy-two hours before dying and the doctor is willing to sign a death slip stating the exact cause of death. The medical examiners were having a busy afternoon. I had to wait three hours before talking to the doctor who performed the autopsy on Henning.

I had killed time, if that's the right expression under the circumstances, by calling the Homicide Bureau and verifying that Inspector Tehaney was indeed on vacation. I asked for Inspector Jim Craley. He was off with a bad back. I then tried for Inspector Frank Fallon. He was in New Orleans picking up a prisoner. I didn't know anyone else there well enough to talk to him. My luck was running bad. But not as bad as John Henning's.

The medical examiner was a thin, middle-aged guy with a sincere smile and a pair of wet brown eyes.

"You Mr. Polo?" he asked. He was still wearing his green smock. There were bloodstains on the sleeves.

"Right," I said.

"Peter Soto," he said, then held out a hand. He must have noticed my hesitation in reaching for it.

"Don't worry," he said, flashing that sincere smile. "I always wear gloves and wash up afterwards. I'm told you found the body and that the victim was a friend of yours. Come on in, tell me all about it."

We went to his office, a small room with a gray metal desk, matching file cabinet, and two wooden chairs. Oilskin charts of various dissected parts of the human body were the only decorations on the wall.

Soto reached into one of the desk drawers, pulled out a portable tape recorder, snapped in a fresh cassette, then looked up and said, "You don't mind if we tape this do you?"

I told Soto I had tried calling Henning for a couple of days, got no answer, became worried, and went over and found him in bed.

9

Soto asked some specific questions, then said, "Is there anything else you'd like to add, Mr. Polo?"

"Yes. I think there's a strong possibility that it wasn't a suicide."

"What makes you think that?"

"I knew John. He was a devout Catholic. Suicide was something he'd never attempt."

Soto shrugged his shoulders. "You never know what's going through a person's mind. He was highly intoxicated."

"That's another thing," I said. "There was a bottle of whiskey on the bed with him. John never drank anything but vodka."

Soto made a sour face. "I saw his liver. If the bullet hadn't killed him, the alcohol might have. If not this time, then the next time he drank that much."

"How long ago did he die, doctor?"

"Oh, sometime Sunday, between noon and ten or eleven o'clock, is the best I can estimate at this time." He blinked those wet eyes at me. "It really does look like he took his own life. Powder burns on his hand. No sign of any struggle, no bruises or wounds other than that caused by the bullet."

"Henning was a private investigator, doctor. So am I. Sunday I learned that he had been involved in a delicate investigation. There is a possibility of foul play."

Soto shrugged and tucked in the corners of his mouth. "I'll make a notation on the report that homicide should do some further investigating into the matter."

"A skull case," I said.

His head snapped up. "Oh, you know about those, do you?"

CHAPTER THREE

I SPENT THE NEXT morning trying to contact Harry Chapman, with, as I like to phrase in my reports to attorneys and insurance firms, complete negative results. Sounds a lot more professional than "I couldn't find the guy," doesn't it?

Chapman's secretary kept feeding me the line that he was "out of town on a case."

I wasted a couple of more hours pounding on the doors of Henning's neighbors, finding out that I'd need Spanish, Filipino, and Chinese interpreters to do a real job of it. The people I was able to communicate with barely knew who Henning was. None of them saw anybody entering or leaving his house on Sunday.

Late in the afternoon I got a call from Inspector Larry Drake of the San Francisco Police Department. Henning's skull case had been dropped in his lap.

Drake suggested we get together for a meeting, and we settled for my place at five o'clock.

I called a couple of friends on the force to get a reading on Drake. The general impression was that he was young, in his mid-thirties, bright, ambitious, and very careful as to just where he stuck his foot, making sure it never ended up in his mouth. "He's the kind of guy," said Paul Paulsen, my old partner, "who, when you ask him the time, he'll tell you, 'My watch says it's three o'clock.' That way if it's the wrong time, you can't blame him, it's his watch's fault."

Punctuality was apparently not one of Drake's attributes. He rang my bell a little before six.

"Polo?" he questioned from the door, pulling out his leather badge holder and flashing his inspector's shield at me, "I'm Inspector Drake. What's your problem?"

He looked older than mid-thirties, close to six feet tall, with drooping shoulders and a sad, hound-dog face. There was gray in his eyebrows and the droopy mustache under his nose but none in the jet-black, carefully combed hair atop his head.

"Come on in, inspector. Can I get you something to drink?"

"No. I haven't got time for that. Why are you making such a deal out of the Henning case? It looks like a straight suicide."

I gave him the same story I'd given to the medical examiner, finishing with, "I know it sounds corny, but I knew John Henning very well. There's no way he would have committed suicide. Come on in the kitchen, I'll get you a cup of coffee."

"No, no. No time for it. I'm up to my armpits in work. I've got that triple homicide at the Chinese restaurant and four jerks that got knocked off in a drug rip-off. I haven't got time to sleep, for Christ's sake. Listen, I know you used to be a cop, and you're buddy-buddy with some of the guys in the department, but I gave the Henning file a good review, and it all points to suicide. If anything interesting pops up, I'll give it another look."

He paused at the door, chewed at the corner of his mustache for a moment, then said, "I wouldn't appreciate it if you started going around putting pressure on to make a big deal out of this. The guy was an alcoholic. He got a roaring heat on and put himself away."

"What about the gun?" I asked.

"Henning's. Owned it for over twenty years. His were the only prints on the weapon and he had powder burns on his hand. And you and I both know that half of the poor bastards that off themselves never take the time to write a suicide note. They just get sick or tired or bored with life and pull the trigger. Open and shut. Take care, Polo. And stay out of the way, okay? Bury your friend and forget about it."

"What about Harry Chapman?"

"The private eye? What about him?" Drake said, glancing at his wristwatch to show me that I was wasting his time.

"Chapman approached me on Sunday. Claimed he had a

12

client, someone important, who had found a bug on his phone line. Chapman thought I had planted the bug, but I didn't. John Henning did."

Drake raked his mustache with the fingers of his right hand. "Listen," he said, with his hand still in front of his mouth, "you PIs are always sticking your dicks in where they're not wanted. But you saw Henning's dump. He wasn't exactly bringing in the big bucks, so I don't know just how many important clients he had. I'll call Chapman, but I'm telling you again, your buddy did himself in. Simple as that." He wiped his hand on his sleeve, then said, "Stay out of it, Polo. I've got more than I can handle now. I don't want to waste my time on a fucking suicide."

He pivoted on his heel and trooped down the stairs, like a man in a hurry to catch a plane.

I closed the door and headed back to the kitchen, taking a vodka bottle out of the freezer and pouring a couple of fingers into a wineglass.

In a way, I couldn't blame Drake. He had more on his plate than he could handle, and a small-time private investigator's death wasn't the kind of case that was going to get him noticed in the department or the newspapers.

Have you ever, purely as a mental exercise, of course, tried to figure out the perfect homicide? All those elaborate schemes: the nontraceable poisons, accidental brake failure, the tricky, fool-proof alibis, all look great on paper or the TV screen. But the one factor that never shows up is really quite simple: do it when the cops are too busy to do much of an investigation.

If your fictitious victim is going to meet his demise in a suburb or rural area, the astute killer plans it to happen when the small police force is tangled up with another killing, or better yet, several killings, and the chief of police or head honcho is out of town or in the middle of a messy divorce case. In some out-of-the-way places the coroner isn't even a doctor, just the local undertaker.

If the victim lives in the city, again the smart, nasty little schemer picks a time when bodies are piling up like speaking engagements for former presidents. Better still to pick a time when not only are the boys in blue busy but the city is in financial trouble and the paper says the mayor is "slashing police department overtime."

Believe me, take away the overtime and a lot of incentive goes out of an investigation. Columbo would never keep coming back for "Oh, sir, just one more question" if the meter weren't running.

Natural disasters like earthquakes or hurricanes throw police departments into weeks of confusion. Cases stack up while they're out attending to lifesaving services. And if our rotten little schemer is really smart, the body will be found in one county while the murderer and his alibi witnesses are in another, forcing the cops to do a lot of traveling. For example, let's say our theoretical bad person lives in San Francisco. The victim's body is found in Vallejo, a town just north of the city. There's a possible suspect, and his alibi witnesses live in San Francisco. The Vallejo cop would have to make a round-trip of seventy miles, over two bridges, every time he wants to talk to our sneaky suspect. The Vallejo cop can call on the S.F. cops for help, and he'll run into someone like Larry Drake, who'd like to help but is too busy to lend a hand.

Most homicide cases are solved the way all cases are solved: The suspect is sloppy. The killer committed the murder in a fit of passion and wasn't worried about leaving any telltale clues, or he was drunk or high on drugs and made no real effort to conceal the crime, or someone simply dumps on him, giving the cops the motive, the opportunity, etc. Now if a really sharp homicide cop, like Bob Tehaney, had the time to look deeper into Henning's death, something might turn up. The killer or killers had to be in the house with John long enough to feed him all that bourbon. Someone might have seen them; they might have left some visible trace. Neighbors would have to be contacted by officers who spoke their language. John's files would have to be checked, to see who this mysterious person was with the bug on his line. Harry Chapman would have to be grilled. Yes, lots to do. And Inspector Larry Drake wasn't going to do any of it. I raised my glass to the ceiling and said aloud, "John, if you really did kill yourself, I'm going to be awfully mad."

CHAPTER FOUR

THE CORONER RELEASED the body the following day. I had arranged a funeral mass at St. Charles, an old-fashioned adobe church in the Mission District.

The Catholic church had wisely modified its stand on the burial of suicide victims. At one time they were banished from a Catholic burial, but now it was deemed that they were not of sound mind at the time the tragedy took place and thus eligible for church services.

The weather matched the occasion: gray and gloomy, with a threat of rain. Attendance was sparse. Besides me there was Jane Tobin, a good friend and a columnist for the *San Francisco Bulletin;* Mrs. Damonte, my one and only tenant, who only knew Henning to nod to but who held a record for consecutive funeral attendance during her eighty-plus years that matched Lou Gehrig's games in a Yankee uniform; a half dozen other souls, all well into an age of cashing their Social Security checks; and a white and black dog that wandered in, strolled up the altar, wrinkled his nose at the smell of incense, and wandered out again.

The service was blessedly short. The priest, a short, balding Mexican-American in his fifties with a perpetual soulful look on his features, whisked through his lines, while Mrs. Damonte, kneeling down beside me, went along with him, though she recited her liturgies in Latin.

There weren't enough pallbearers to give John the traditional lift, so we rolled the coffin on its gurney down the center aisle, me on one side, the funeral director on the other. The hearse driver and the limousine driver gave us a hand loading the coffin into the hearse.

One of the women who had been at the mass approached me on the sidewalk in front of the church. She was a notch or two on either side of sixty, wearing a heavy black cloth coat and a black lace scarf over her hair. She had very pale white skin and bright blue eyes, magnified behind thick glasses.

"Are you Nick Polo?" she asked.

"Yes."

"My name is Laura Bradford. I was a friend of John's." She shook her head. "A terrible, terrible tragedy." Tears started to form behind her glasses, and she put both hands on my arm. "I don't believe it, Mr. Polo. John wouldn't do that to himself. I just don't believe it. They say he was drinking. Is it true?"

"He had an almost-empty bottle of whiskey alongside him when I found the body."

She shook her head, the scarf rustling on the back of her coat. "No. I don't believe that either. John was at last week's meeting. He looked wonderful. Hadn't had a drop in over a year." She wrinkled her nose. "And whiskey. No, I never saw John touch a drop of it when he and I were sharing a bottle or two. Vodka was his demon."

"Meeting? You mean that . . . "

"Yes. AA. We're both recovering alcoholics. Surely you knew of John's drinking? He mentioned your being an old and dear friend."

"Yes, I knew, Laura. Did John say anything about having any particular problems lately?"

"No. He seemed quite happy. Content. He was a good, God-fearing man, Mr. Polo. He wouldn't want to meet our Lord like that. No, he just wouldn't do that to himself."

"I think you're right." I gave her one of my cards. "Please call me. Anytime. I'd like to talk to anyone who saw John in the days just before his death."

She stared at the card. "John said you were a good friend." She looked around the street, back toward the church. "Poor man didn't have many."

The limousine followed the hearse down to the cemetery. Jane

Tobin sat on one side of me, Mrs. Damonte the other. It was a silent trip, the only noise the soft murmuring of Mrs. D. as she said her rosary.

Colma is a little town just a mile or so south of the San Francisco border. It boasts of having a population of over a million under the ground and less than a thousand above it.

Land got too expensive to be used for grave sites in San Francisco back in the 1920s, so they dug up all the remains and replanted them in Colma, which was considered a fairly distant suburb in those days.

Colma has close to twenty cemeteries: They take all comers; there are those specializing in customers of Jewish, Chinese, Greek, Italian, or Serbian descent; and if you happen to want your cat or dog to be comfortable for eternity, there's Pet's Rest, where some of the tombstones are carved in the shapes of bones, birdcages, and fire hydrants.

Our stop was Holy Cross Cemetery. We parked at a round building, ringed with stands of flowers from previous funerals. The priest said a few last words, and John's coffin was left there, waiting for the gravediggers.

As I was helping Mrs. Damonte back into the limousine, someone tapped me on the elbow.

He was a tall, well-groomed man in a dark business suit.

"Mr. Polo," he said, "My name is Arnold Harkins. I was John's attorney."

I shook his hand. "I never heard John mention your name."

"We went to school together at St. Peter's. I hadn't seen him in ages. About a year ago he came to my office and made out a will." Harkins looked at the limousine. "Is there someplace we can talk a bit? I have my car."

"Sure," I told him. I ducked into the limo's door and told Jane and Mrs. Dante that I would be tied up for a while. "I'll be back at my place in time for dinner, Jane. Are you free?"

"Yes, sure, Nick."

"I'll fix you something special," Mrs. Damonte said to me in Italian.

I instructed the limousine driver to take the ladies back home and hopped into Harkins's car, a late-model Chrysler.

I said, "The least we can do for John is have a small Irish wake at Molloy's."

Molloy's was a relic from a bygone era but one that had hung on well for eighty years. The little Victorian saloon was the center for a great many top-ranked bare-knuckle boxing matches in the late 1800s. The fact that it was within walking distance of Catholic, Protestant, and all-faiths cemeteries helped to keep it a going concern.

"Irish coffee, no sugar," I told the bartender, once we were settled on our stools. "How about you, Mr. Harkins?"

"Scotch and soda, please."

We were quiet until the drinks were placed in front of us. I picked up my glass and proposed a toast. "To John Henning, may he rest in peace."

Harkins took a small sip of his drink, then said, "John left half of everything he owned to you, Mr. Polo. The other half goes to the church and Alcoholics Anonymous. There's the house on York Street, his car, and a ten thousand–dollar government life insurance policy. I haven't been able to run the house through a title company yet, so I don't know if there are any liens against it. He named you executor of the estate."

I took a long sip of the Irish coffee, then wiped whipped cream from my lip.

"John didn't have any living relatives," Harkins continued in the same dull tone, "and I guess you were one of his few friends."

I drained my Irish and signaled to the bartender for a refill. "I guess you're right," I finally said. "Not many friends at all. Can you handle the estate for me? Sell the house, the car, whatever there is. I'd like to find out about his bank deposits as soon as possible—checking, savings, any deposits made recently."

Harkins's somber face lit up. "Yes, it would be my pleasure. Selling the house may take a little time. . . ." He paused and leaned closer. "John had a safe-deposit box at the City Savings & Loan at 20th and Mission. I have the power of attorney. I think you should be there when we open the box. How about first thing in the morning? Say ten o'clock. I can have the papers ready by then."

"Sure. I'll be there."

Harkins took another small sip of his drink and glanced at his watch. People seemed to be doing that to me a lot lately. "Why don't you go ahead, Mr. Harkins. I'll get a cab back to town; there are a few things I have to do."

That seemed to cheer him up immeasurably. He shook my hand and reminded me of our meeting in the morning. I worked on my drink and ordered another one, then went to the phone booth and looked up Harkins in the directory. He was listed on the four hundred block of 38th Avenue. The Richmond District. A residential area. Harkins probably worked right out of his house. Who was I to criticize? I did the same thing.

I started talking to myself after the next Irish, then brought Henning into the conversation. Christ, John, you really can pick them. Leaving me half of your property, and having an attorney who doesn't even wait until you're in the ground before he starts running you through probate. Well, he said you were a friend. The money he'll make on selling the house and the other property will end up totaling five or ten thousand bucks, but what the hell. He probably deserves it more than I do. I signaled to the bartender for one more drink and asked him to call me a cab.

CHAPTER FIVE

I HAD THE CAB drop me back at John Henning's house. The police hadn't bothered putting one of their locks on the front door, so there was no problem in getting inside, again using the key John had left me.

The house still smelled of death. I went back to the bedroom. The bedspread was covered with crusted blood. Any effects I felt from the alcohol in the Irish coffees evaporated quickly. I bundled up the bedspread, but the blood had soaked through to the sheets and into the mattress itself.

I opened the bedroom windows, no easy task as the sashes were coated with dust and layers of old paint, but there still wasn't enough fresh air. I opened the kitchen windows, then the door leading out to the backyard. The April showers had given way to a bright, sunny spring afternoon.

The backyard was a tangle of neglected weeds and shrubbery. A rusted wheelbarrow leaned wearily against a rotting wooden fence that looked as if a sneeze from a five-year-old would knock it down. In the middle of all that mess stood an overgrown lemon tree, bursting with bright yellow lemons.

I took off my suit coat, rolled up my sleeves, and went to work, starting with the bedroom dresser, taking my time, going through everything, even unraveling his socks.

His wallet was in the drawer with the socks. It held his driver's license, investigator's license, a Visa card, his Kaiser Permanente Hospital card, a tarnished Saint Christopher medal, a picture of an old woman who must have been his mother, his Social Security card, a dozen or so business cards with his name on them, and twenty-two dollars in cash. John hadn't spent much money on clothes, so the search went pretty quickly. He had been buried in his best suit, a charcoal wool job. There was just a bathrobe, a leather jacket, and a tweed sport coat hanging over two lonely-looking pairs of brown shoes. There was nothing in the coat pockets other than lint, two ballpoint pens, and forty-three cents in change. There was a plain metal key ring with three keys: two for a car, the other for the front door. I pocketed the keys and made a mental note to give them to Arnold Harkins.

The lacy curtains in the living room and dining room were so brittle they almost crumbled when I touched them. The once-white walls were a saffron yellow. I came up with nothing of interest other than an old photo album. It started with pictures of John as a young man, in his army uniform. He aged as I turned the pages. The last photo was of him smiling, leaning against a tree trunk. It looked as if it was taken in the last couple of years. I took it from the album and slipped it into my pocket, then headed to the kitchen.

The china in the cabinets was very old, most of the pieces chipped. The cupboard held three round cartons of Quaker Oats, canned beans, a jar of instant coffee, a box of tea bags, and salt and pepper shakers. John's touchy stomach didn't allow for much in the way of spices.

The refrigerator was pretty bare: a carton of milk that had gone sour, a few eggs, an assortment of cheeses. The freezer was jammed with ice-cream cartons, mostly chocolate. You give up the booze, you have to keep some small vices.

I flicked the switch and a bank of fluorescent lights stammered to life in the basement, which was where John did his work. It was much cleaner than the upstairs of the house. One wall was covered with hundreds of telephone directories, neatly arranged by location and year: Monterey, Oakland, San Francisco, San Jose, Sacramento, half the state. All the books the phone company issued, some dating back over twenty years. In an age of computers and know-everything data bases, it's amazing how handy an old telephone directory can be. It might provide you with a middle initial for that Joseph Miller you've been hired to locate. A common name like Joseph Miller is a lost cause. Just too many of them. But Joseph P. Miller. That narrows it down so you can start digging. There might be a spouse listed: Joseph P. and Yolanda Miller. Just an address helps. You have to have a starting point, and an address, no matter how old, can be the one thing that triggers the rest of the investigation. I'd put John's directories to good use over the years. Mrs. Damonte was not going to be very happy when I carted all the directories down to the basement, an area she deems, along with the garden, her private territory.

On the opposite wall tools were hanging in neat rows above a heavy wooden workbench. On top of the bench were a stack of cassette tapes, a tape demagnetizer, and three metal chests with clear plastic-fronted drawers. They were filled with all kinds of small electronic parts, most of which meant absolutely nothing to me. Some I could identify as amplifiers and transmitters, the basic components of all bugging devices. One of the drawers held four telephone-line bugs identical to the one that Harry Chapman had confronted me with. Henning was an expert at making his own equipment. Give the man fifty dollars and five minutes in a Radio Shack and he could put together almost anything. The workbench drawer held more electronic equipment and a host of soldering tools. There were a half-dozen telephones, the frames opened and stripped of most of their parts.

A beautiful, old, multidrawer rolltop desk stood next to the workbench. I'd have to mention to Harkins that I'd want to keep the desk. It would be a nice remembrance. An IBM-clone computer sat on the desk, a printer on a metal stand alongside. I flopped down into John's high-back typing chair and checked the desk drawers, coming up with nothing of any interest. What was of interest was that there was no business calendar. I knew he kept a daily calendar, a log of his meetings, destinations, that kind of thing. His accounts receivable file was there. I flicked through the copies of his billing invoices. He had roughly two thousand dollars coming to him. The last bill was mailed out almost ten days ago, for a little under two hundred dollars, to an insurance company. Not the kind of client you'd do a bugging job for. I double-checked the desk, but the calendar wasn't there.

Another of John Henning's good deeds was to spoon-feed me

the intricacies of the computer field. I had no trouble turning his machine on; it was a near duplicate of the one he'd help install at my house, same type of machine, same software, same internal telephone modem. I turned the machine on, entered his software, WordPerfect, and punched the button marked List Files.

I won't bore you with a lot of computer language, but basically what John did and taught me to do was type out a report on the computer, print it, mail the original to the client, and make a copy that went into a manila folder and was filed away. The report stayed on the computer disk until it was either erased or moved. The system Henning had worked out was that every six months he'd transfer the files from the computer's hard disk, which is an internal part of the machine, to a floppy disk, which was then stored in a plastic diskette file holder. That way you didn't have to go through a years-long list of file names every time you looked into the computer's hard disk file. Confused? You should have seen Henning trying to drum the system into my thick Sicilian head. If that didn't turn him back to the bottle, nothing would. I'm a low-tech man living in a high-tech world.

So there I sat staring at the screen, which was blank. No files at all. Not a one. I dug through the floppy disk files, which were neatly labeled, six months on each disk, from July 1 to December 31. Nothing for January 1 of this year to the current date. I stared back at the blank screen. Henning might not be the world's best housekeeper, but he was meticulous in his work habits. Someone had gone to the trouble of erasing every one of his working files since the first of the year. Why all of them? Why not just erase the one they were worried about?

Three black metal file cabinets, four drawers high, sat next to the desk. I opened the top drawer on the closest one. There were rows of manila folders, each with a neatly printed tab, showing a name and containing the printed copies made from the computer's files. The first was Albion, Andrew; the next, Anderson, James. There were no dates on the file tabs; John just filed them alphabetically. I slammed the drawer shut. Whoever had gone to the trouble of erasing the computer files surely wouldn't forget to pull the pertinent printed file.

There were two phones on Henning's desk, one hooked up to

the answering machine. It was an extension of the upstairs phone I'd used to call the police after finding John's body, so there was no sense in checking the redial button on that one. The other phone, a gray Radio Shack job, had all the gadgets John loved: speed dialer, loudspeaker, call timer, priority buttons, and a digital display that shows you the date and time of your call as well as keeping track of just how long you've been talking. It was the phone Henning used to make his outgoing calls, leaving the other phone free for calls from clients. I went back to John's workbench, and in a lower drawer found a gizmo he'd shown me just a few months ago—a decodifier is what the manufacturer calls it. It's no bigger than a handheld calculator and can decode Touch-Tone numbers as fast as your fingers jam them out on the phone's keypad. The numbers are printed on the small decoder's screen. You can also hook it up to a tape so that the numbers are printed on paper. Handy gadget if you're tapping a phone line and want to know where the outgoing calls are going to. I pushed the on switch and a small red light came on indicating that the battery was working. I then went back to John's desk and held the decodifier alongside the mouthpiece of his outgoing phone and pushed the redial button. A phone number started popping up on the decoder's screen: 767-8900. The call was picked up on the second ring and a cheerfully recorded voice said, "Good afternoon, at the tone, the time will be exactly . . . " I banged down the receiver before Pacific Bell's Time Announcement Service could tell me what my watch already knew. Oh, these people were careful. Very careful. Just in case Henning's last phone call was to someone who could provide a clue to his death, they made sure that if anyone checked, he or she would run into another blind alley.

Henning's answering machine was one of the microcassette types, with two tapes, one for incoming messages, one for outgoing. I rewound the incoming calls and pushed the reply button. The tape spun around, but no sounds came from it. That was strange. Even if Henning did erase my earlier message, the one I'd left on Sunday after seeing Harry Chapman at the Washington Square Bar & Grill, the last couple, the ones I made when I got back to the city, should have been on there.

I pushed the answering machine's on button and used the other phone to call the machine. Henning's message came on loud and clear. After the beep, I said, "Testing, one, two, three," then hung up.

I rewound the tape again. There was none of that distinctive chipmunk sound you usually get when rewinding a tape with a message on it. I pushed the play button again. Nothing. I flipped open the top of the answering machine and pulled out the incoming-message tape. One of the little goodies in there—I told you electronics weren't my specialty—a chrome thing about the size of a fingernail, was broken and pushed back a half inch or so. Someone had gone to the trouble of fixing it so John's machine wouldn't tape any incoming messages. Why? Why would the killer worry about calls after John was dead?

I was feeling dirty, tired, and hungry, but there was one more thing to look at, John's car, a 1982 Chevrolet that wasn't going to get much of an appraisal from Arnold Harkins.

The glove compartment held two cans of diet Pepsi and some plastic spoons. The trunk yielded a good-sized fishing-tackle box, filled with more of John's electronic paraphernalia, and the usual assortment of tools for changing a tire.

I ran my hands between the seats of the car, along the upholstery, coming up with pens, pencils, paper clips, a few coins, and a receipt in the amount of three dollars and fifty cents. It was a week old and was from a restaurant. The Jefferson Park on Front Street. What the hell was John Henning doing at the Jefferson Park? It was a fairly new addition to the crowded San Francisco restaurant scene. Every week it seemed a place that had once been pretty popular would start to fall out of favor, business would slow, and then someone new would come along, buy it, change the name, gut out all the expensive fixtures and decorations, install slightly different but equally expensive fixtures and decorations, and do all right until the payments on all those alterations took too high a toll on the profit margin, then it was time for someone else to come in and try their luck. The Jefferson Park was located in the Embarcadero Center, a high-rent mixture of office complexes and upscale apartments and shops. It catered to the yuppie crowd and was a bit of a meat market: boy in three-piece suit meets girl in Anne Klein executive dress, and they go to his or her place and make love by the light from the computer. Definitely not the kind of place you find the John Hennings of the world. Unless he was working.

I found a paper bag and stuffed all of the cassettes on the workbench into it, then got out of there.

Mrs. Damonte was true to her word. She had a spinach-stuffed veal breast, some gnocchi, homemade potato dumplings, and a Swiss chard torta waiting for me when I got home. I carried the tray of steaming pots up to my flat, got them safely into the kitchen, then put a call in to Inspector Larry Drake. Surprisingly, I caught him at his desk.

"Inspector, Nick Polo. I went through John Henning's house today. His office calendar is missing, and his computer files have been erased."

"How the hell did you get in there?" Drake said, his tone showing he was anything but pleased.

"The key. I'm executor of the estate."

"Listen, Polo. I told you the man committed suicide."

"Henning was a businessman. He kept a calendar. And there'd be no reason for him to wipe out his computer files."

"People do strange things when they're about to put a bullet in their head, Polo. You know that."

He hung up before I could tell him about the answering machine. I had the impression he wouldn't have been interested anyway.

Jane Tobin showed up twenty minutes later. As we dug into Mrs. Damonte's goodies, I updated her on what I had found at John's house.

"Do you think this Inspector Drake is going to do anything?"

"Nope."

"Where does that leave you?" she asked, using a piece of French bread to mop up the last of the gnocchi sauce on her plate.

"Harry Chapman is still ducking me. Until I can get hold of him, I'll have to do everything the hard way. The only thing I've got is that receipt from the Jefferson Park. I'll have to go through each and every one of John's files. And listen to those tapes I took from his basement, though I'll bet they're all blank. If the killer was cautious enough to screw up John's answering machine, he wouldn't have left anything on that pile of tapes, especially when they were sitting right next to a tape eraser." I reached for the wine bottle. "Who knows? Maybe something will turn up in John's safe-deposit box in the morning."

CHAPTER SIX

ARNOLD HARKINS WAS tapping a well-polished shoe nervously in the lobby of the City Savings & Loan, at 20th and Mission streets, at two minutes past ten the next morning. He energetically pumped my hand and said, "Good morning, good morning. Hopefully this shouldn't take too long."

A guy wearing tan pants and a matching shirt with a half-dozen ballpoint pens in one pocket, and carrying a toolbox, stood next to Harkins. "This is Phil, the locksmith," Harkins said, then came over and lowered his voice. "The charge for opening the safe-deposit box is ninety dollars. I'll give him a check. It will be a probate expense."

Yes, I was sure it would be. I wondered where John had kept his safe-deposit–box key. I hadn't stumbled across it at his house.

City Savings & Loan was one of those outfits that seemed to open a branch in one neighborhood, while closing one in another, every few months. The ceiling was acoustical tile, the carpet a wavy gray tweed, already thinning out in spots around the counters and executives' desks.

A large metal coffeepot stood on a knee-high table, surrounded by Styrofoam coffee cups. A sign Scotch-taped to the pot said, "For our valued customers." Valued or not, I helped myself to a cup.

There were six tellers working behind a walnut Formica counter. Four desks were lined against one wall. The loan officers behind the desks were, like all the tellers, women, ranging from twenty to thirty-five, from short to tall, from blond to brunette.

The only male employee was the manager, a slim, pinch-faced guy who didn't look as if he'd seen his thirtieth birthday yet, with a taste for polyester in his suit and tie. Harkins introduced him as Mr. Fackler.

Fackler's handshake was as limp as the little mustache under his nose.

"You understand," Fackler said to both of us, "that I can only permit you to examine the safe-deposit box for the purpose of searching for a will or military-discharge papers. Nothing else can be touched, and we will not be responsible for opening the box."

Harkins introduced Fackler to Phil, the locksmith, who seemed the strong silent type. Didn't say a word, just nodded his head.

"I can understand the exemption on the will," I said, "but why the military-discharge papers?"

"So survivors can claim burial benefits due veterans," Fackler said matter-of-factly.

I should have thought of that. Maybe John would have preferred being planted alongside his comrades in arms in a military cemetery rather than squeezed in with all those Catholics at Holy Cross. My own preference was to have my ashes scattered around a really good golf course, say like Pebble Beach. Jane Tobin assured me that if she was around to perform the final ceremony, she'd see to it my wishes were carried out. "You'll get there eventually," she told me with a sweet smiling face while making the motions of pulling a lever and then the sound of flushing water. I remembered waving good-bye to a few turtles and gold-fish that way. It hadn't seemed cruel at the time.

Harkins presented Fackler with some documents. "There's the death certificate, the power of attorney form, and a copy of the will in possession, showing Mr. Polo as partial beneficiary and executor."

Fackler examined the papers closely, though the frown on his forehead gave the impression that he really wasn't quite sure what he was reading. He bent his head forward a few times and mumbled something that sounded like "Okay."

He finally said, "Everything looks like it's in order. This way, please."

We followed his dandruff-flaked shoulders past the teller cages and into a small reception area in front of the vault.

Fackler handed us a safe-deposit-inspection request form. Harkins filled in the necessary details and we both signed our names on the bottom of the paper.

"Did John have a checking account with you?" I asked.

"Yes," Fackler said, "I believe he did."

"I'd like to find out if John deposited any money in his account in the last couple of weeks."

Fackler must have been accustomed to dealing with greedy inheritors. He gave me a bored smile. "I'd like to help, but I'm afraid that will have to wait until the probate order. This way, gentlemen."

We walked all of ten feet to the vault. Fackler pointed to one particular box, number 714.

The locksmith took a quick look at it, opened his toolbox, and pulled out a gadget with a red plastic handle and a long tapering blade with a slight hook on the end of it. It looked like a giant version of one of those things a dentist shoves in your mouth while chiding you for not flossing enough.

It's always a pleasure to watch a real pro at work. Phil probed around for just a few seconds, twisted his tool hard to the right, and there was a loud popping sound. He pulled at the safe-deposit box to make sure it was free, then put his tool back in its box and held out a hand toward Arnold Harkins.

Harkins already had the check made out. He passed it over, and Phil left without saying a single word.

Fackler pulled the box from the wall and, carrying it as if there might be toxic waste inside, placed it on a small, metal-topped desk, then before lifting the lid, said, "Remember, we are to look for a new will or discharge papers. Nothing else."

The box wasn't very big, maybe six inches high, a foot wide, three feet long. Fackler flipped open the box's lid. There were several envelopes inside. Fackler picked up the top one. It was a legal-size white envelope, yellowed with age, with the word *Will* neatly printed on it. He passed it over to Harkins. There were a few more documents in the box, and crowded into one corner was a small pile of stones. Green stones. I edged closer as Harkins put on his reading glasses and checked out the will.

"No problem here," Harkins said. "This is dated July 11, 1964, so if there are no more . . . "

He didn't finish his sentence because I had spilled some coffee on the floor and stepped on Mr. Fackler's foot, then backing up, saying "I'm sorry," clumsily knocked the safe-deposit box to the floor.

"God damn it, I'm sorry," I said, stooping to the ground quickly.

"Stop," Fackler screamed. "Stop."

"I'm really sorry about that, Mr. Fackler," I said, picking up the papers and stones and dropping them into the box, which had slid partway under the desk.

Fackler's screams had brought an armed security guard running into the room. The guard was a pimply faced kid in a blue uniform with a Sam Browne belt. He was holding a long-barreled revolver in his hand. I raised my arms up quickly. It's not wise to ever show any resistance to someone with a gun. Especially a uniformed guard who is making a nickel or more over minimum wage and whose only training with firearms was probably watching *Miami Vice* reruns and practicing a quick draw in front of a mirror. I'd rather face a team of trained terrorists then those kids in uniform you see strutting around shopping malls with cannons hanging on their hips. I mean, they are dangerous.

"It's all right, Gerald," Fackler was screaming at the guard. "It's all right. Put that thing away."

The kid pushed the gun in the direction of his holster and missed but finally got it in on the second try.

"Just wait outside, Gerald," Fackler told him. Then he turned his attention to me. "That was very unfortunate."

He bent down on one knee and picked up the safe-deposit box, checked the contents, then dropped back down to the floor. "I'm sure I saw four green stones when the box was opened," he said, his hand brushing the carpet under the desk. He got to his feet and checked the contents of the box. "There are only three here now," he said, his voice pointing an accusing finger at little old me.

"I didn't count," I said. "I think you should have this entire

room checked thoroughly. Those stones, whatever they are, be-
long partially to me." I turned to Harkins. "Can we hold City
Savings and Mr. Fackler responsible if something is lost from
Henning's safe-deposit box?"

"I'm certainly not responsible," Fackler fumed. "You, sir, are
the one who knocked the box over."

I held up my hands in mock surrender. "All right, all right.
We're not even sure if anything is missing. I'll leave it to you and
Mr. Harkins to settle the matter."

I started to exit. Fackler moved to block me.

"I don't think you should leave until this matter is settled," he
said, a note of authority creeping into his voice.

"I'm not at all happy with this morning's transaction. Who is
your superior?"

Ah, the magic word: superior. The bane of bureaucrats the
world over.

Fackler backed away from me, and smoothed his tie with one
hand. "I don't see why that will be necessary. I'm sure Mr.
Harkins and I can settle this here and now. I'll have the room
closed off, and we'll do a complete sweep of the room. If there was
another stone in that box, believe me, sir, we'll find it."

I didn't believe him for a minute.

CHAPTER SEVEN

THE STONE LOOKED quite a bit bigger lying on a piece of white velvet. Gene Chaput picked it up and examined it through his loupe. "Very nice," he said. "Very nice indeed. A little drop of oil."

"Drop of oil?" I said. "You mean it's not an emerald or something valuable?"

When I was in the police department, Chaput was always the man we called in to give his expert opinion on the quality, or lack thereof, of stolen gems. He's a robust, energetic man, whose unlined face and thick dark hair belie the time he's been in the jewelry business. His office always fascinated me. I could spend hours there. It was located on Post Street, in a building catering to the jewelry trade. You had to be buzzed in to the office. Once inside there was a glass-topped counter, behind which was an assortment of rings, earrings, and bracelets. All quality items but nothing you would not find in any top-line jewelry store. It was the customers who came through that door that were the most interesting: from elegantly dressed to barely dressed to those, if not in need of new clothes, at least in need of a stop at the dry cleaner. They came in carrying small bags and envelopes, to have their contents appraised or sold or taken on consignment. Or they'd pick up little packages: small tan envelopes containing a single diamond or a group of precious-to-semiprecious stones: sapphire, topaz, garnet, zircon, ruby, spinel, or a rose-tinted pearl. They'd take their little package and be gone for a half hour or a week. I always wondered just what they did with the damn things. Who were their customers? How were the deals transacted? Who set the final price on gems that flopped up and down in price as quickly and as dangerously as the stock market?

Chaput brought my wandering mind back to the matter at hand. "It's an emerald, all right, Nick. A drop of oil is a term meaning it's from Colombia. The finest. Take a look."

He handed me the stone and his jeweler's loupe. It took some time to get the loupe adjusted to my eye. What I saw was a beautiful green piece of glass.

"See the color, Nick? Deep green, with a very slight blue under-tone. That's a Chivor."

I handed him back his loupe and gave him a confused look.

"Chivor is a mine in Colombia. One of the two major produ-cers. The other one is Muzo. Stones from Muzo have a little more of a warm color."

"You can tell what mine it came from just by looking at it?"

"I've seen a lot of them in my time," Chaput said. "There's no mistaking a Colombian emerald. Much better stone than the African variety."

"Just how valuable are emeralds? Compared to diamonds."

Chaput smiled. "If you're talking about equal-size and quality stones, the emerald would be worth more. Of course it depends on the color, how intense and clear it is. They're the most popular jewelry stone on the market now. The trouble is finding them in any real size. They've been mined since the days of the Incas. An emerald of five or more carats doesn't show up very often. Any-thing bigger than that is very rare. What you have here is a good, marketable-sized gem, right around one carat."

"So what is this particular stone worth?"

"As is? You wouldn't have any trouble getting eight hundred dollars for it. But if you want to sell it, I'd advise you to have it polished and cut. Then you'd be talking about a lot more money. A lot more."

And John Henning had another three of them sitting in his safe-deposit box. What the hell was he doing with uncut emeralds?

"Tell me, Gene, is there much of an underground market in these things?"

"Certainly. In anything valuable. You know that. But especially in emeralds. Cocaine gets all of the publicity in smuggling from Colombia, but emeralds are almost as profitable. They're having gem wars, just like drug wars, down there. Last year a group of bandits interrupted the number one emerald man's birthday party. Killed him and all six of his armed bodyguards. It's a rough business.

"Colombia produces 90 percent of the world's emeralds. And there's no legal cartel, such as there is in the diamond-mining industry, where the De Beers Consolidated Mines controls the amount of diamonds that get to the market. The emerald mines are lucky to get 30 percent of what the mines actually produce. The rest are smuggled out by the *guaqueros*, the treasure hunters."

"Why can't the mines control their inventories better than that?" I asked.

"It's the nature of the way emeralds are mined. The miners bulldoze a hillside, then use dynamite to blast and hydraulic jacks to open tunnels. Then they use high-pressure hoses to clean up the mess and find the white calcite veins that hold the emeralds. They do find a lot of the bigger stones this way, but the rest, the smaller stones, are washed down into the mountains into the riverbeds, where the *guaqueros* are waiting. They are a tough lot. Hundreds get murdered every year. Most by their compadres."

Cocaine, emeralds. I could remember when Colombia came up and all I thought of was poor old Juan Valdez and his overburdened burro, picking those mountain-grown coffee beans, one at a time.

I thanked Chaput for his time and asked him to keep the stone for me.

I stopped back at my place to check the mail and for messages. Naturally, when you are involved in something and need time to work on it, the phone suddenly starts ringing off the hook. There were two calls: both from good steady clients, both needing people located for upcoming trials and depositions.

I opened files on the cases and went to work. You always do as much as you can on a case over the phone or through the computer. I know that doesn't sound glamorous or adventurous; it's much more exciting when the hard-boiled hero goes out and knocks on doors and beats up bodyguards to get his information, but in real life you do the knocking on doors, or whatever, only after you've tried all the other sources.

I put the computer to work, accessing an assortment of data bases, requesting assessor, employment, and civil court checks on the various parties.

The Department of Motor Vehicles tightened up their rules after the murder of an actress in Southern California whose address was sold to a jealous boyfriend by a private eye in Texas. Now if you want to get DMV information with an address on it, you have to be bonded, and the purpose of obtaining an address must be specifically for the serving of a subpoena. You also have to keep records of each of your requests, because the DMV can pop in on you without twenty-four hours' notice, and if you've been using their records for anything but exactly what they're supposed to be used for, you're in a lot of trouble. Fortunately this time I was on the side of the angels.

The DMV records gave addresses that I was able to cross-check with assessor or court records. Another hour or so of digging through telephone books and reverse address directories and dialing directory assistance paid off. I'd located all the necessary parties. I spent another hour at an effort in creative fiction in explaining to my clients just how difficult it was to do the job, then poured myself a glass of wine and dug through the rest of the mail. A couple of small checks and an invitation from an enterprising bunch of con artists in Miami who were providing a five-day seminar on Defensive-Weapons Tactics ("if you don't have your own weapon we'll provide one"), Personal Defense, Crime-Scene Search, and Electronic Countermeasures. The instructors were described as "former CIA field operators and intelligence officers from throughout the world." Unemployed cold war warriors basking in the Florida sun. All for $975. Such a deal. I fought the temptation and tossed the brochures into the wastebasket.

What did tempt me was Mrs. Damonte's *torta* and veal-breast leftovers in the refrigerator.

Jane Tobin called while they were spinning in the microwave.

"How about dinner?" she asked.

"I was just about to eat."

"Oh, and I was going to buy."

"The Jefferson Park at seven o'clock," I said. The leftovers would be just as good tomorrow, and it's not every day that a newspaper person offers to spring for a meal.

"How are you doing on John's case?" Jane asked.

I filled her in on the trip to the safe-deposit box.

"Emeralds," she said. "Somehow I can't figure John Henning collecting jewels. Do you think they're tied in with his death?"

"I haven't the foggiest. I found a receipt in John's car. He had something that cost three and a half bucks at the Jefferson Park."

"I hope that's the price of a full-course meal," she said sarcastically. "See you there at seven."

I looked up Harry Chapman in the telephone book. His office was listed but no residence number. I dialed the office number and got the runaround again. "Mr. Chapman is out of town and unavailable" was absolutely all the lady would tell me.

I knew Chapman lived in the city, so I went back to the computer and accessed the data source that had assessor records. I punched in Chapman's name, and it punched back an address on the eleven hundred block of Filbert Street.

Filbert Street, between Leavenworth and Hyde, is one of the steeper spreads of asphalt and concrete clinging to the hills of San Francisco. The kind the TV and movie boys love to use to film chase scenes of cars and motorcycles, with cameras angled so it looks as if they're filming a paved roller coaster ride. I have no idea just how steep it is, but I remember reading that the grade on a few of the city's hillsides is the same hair-raising scale as Squaw Valley's Siberia ski run. No one with any sense really dreams of a white Christmas in San Francisco.

Chapman's house was a three-story Victorian, painted army green with white and black trim. The door was a glossy black enamel and the brass hardware was bright from a recent polishing. Traces of pink polishing cream were still visible in the front door's keyhole. To the left of the door at eye height was a bright blue sticker showing that the premises were guarded by the ATZ Alarm Company. I pushed the bell a couple of times. I could hear footsteps approaching the door, but it remained unopened. I leaned on the bell again.

The man who opened the door was a big Samoan. I know that may sound redundant, but he was exceptionally large; maybe just an inch or so over six feet in height, but it wasn't his height that struck you at first, it was his width. Maybe he had polished the door so he could slide in. His brown eyes seemed to be squinting against a bright light. He sniffed, ran the back of his hand across his nose, then shoved his hands in his pockets, wiggling the fingers as if he was counting change.

"I'm supposed to meet Harry. Is he in?"

"No," the giant said and started to close the door. I edged my foot over the doorsill, then quickly pulled it back. "Wait, Harry told me to meet him. I drove all the way down from Eureka. Isn't he here?"

"Not here."

"Well, where the hell is he? I don't like to waste my time driving all the way—"

"Not here," was all he said before he slammed the door shut. I leaned on the bell again.

Harry's doorman wasn't happy the first time he opened the door. This time he looked like King Kong after finding out the banana crop was contaminated.

"I tell you Harry's not here," he said between clenched teeth. "Go away."

"Maybe I made a mistake," I said. "Maybe I wasn't supposed to meet him at home. Just where is he?"

He pointed a finger the size of a bratwurst at me. "Not here. You get outta here."

He slammed the door shut again. It was about a four on the Richter scale. I got outta there.

CHAPTER EIGHT

JANE TOBIN WAS perched on the edge of a barstool when I got to the Jefferson Park restaurant.

Lined in front of her were two glasses of white wine and a small pack of dollar bills. She was wearing her working outfit: beige corduroy slacks and a yellow turtleneck sweater under a jacket that matched the slacks. She raked her auburn hair with one hand, the other taking a leather dice cup and slamming it on the bar. She positioned the cup so that the gentleman sitting on the stool next to her couldn't see the roll of the dice.

"Three fours," Jane said, her clear green eyes glistening with anticipation.

Her gambling partner was a young man in a pin-striped suit who looked like one of those guys in the TV ads for whom women buy expensive after-shave lotion: tall, aquiline nose, thick dark hair with that wet, just-out-of-the-shower look.

He glanced down at his own dice, then said in a soft, confident voice, "Three sixes."

Liar's dice. I felt sorry for the guy. Much to my regret I had taught Jane the game several years ago. It's simple, really. You both roll out five dice, shielding the results from your opponent's eyes with the dice cup. Ones, also called aces, are wild, therefore can be anything. The object of the game is to make your partner overbet your combined hands. Or, if your opponent doesn't believe it when you tell him your bet, and he calls and you do have the quoted number, then you win. Say you have two ones and three fours, thus actually five fours in your hand. You count those, along with any ones and fours in your opponent's hand. Say he's got an ace and one four. That would make the combined total of seven fours between you. You make a call of seven fours. He doesn't believe you, so he calls you. You win because the total comes out to your bet of seven fours.

There's a variation of the game you can play using the eight-digit serial numbers on any U.S. paper currency. Jane had a natural talent for the game. Maybe it was because you couldn't believe those shimmering green eyes could be lying. Or maybe it was because the opponent's eyes were wandering up and down her delightful five-foot-two frame, as was the case now with young Mr. Pinstripe. Jane claimed the fact that she inhaled and arched her shoulders back during the times of crucial calls was just a nervous habit.

"Five sixes," she said, then went into a display of nervous habits.

"Six sixes," responded Pinstripe, his eyes nowhere near the dice cups.

"You'd have to have them all, I'm afraid," Jane said, raising her cup high enough to show her hand, three deuces and two fives.

Pinstripe sighed good-naturedly and added another five-dollar bill to Jane's pile.

"Mind if I share the spoils?" I asked, picking up one of Jane's untouched wineglasses.

She flashed her dimples at me, showing not a single sign of remorse over cleaning the young lad's clock.

"Nick, meet Kenny."

Kenny reluctantly pushed a hand in my direction.

"How are you?" he asked with all the sincerity of a dentist saying "This won't hurt a bit."

"Doesn't look like this is your lucky night, Kenny, does it?" I said, putting an arm around Jane's shoulders.

Kenny bounced his eyes from Jane's to mine, finally accepting his defeat like a man, raising his glass in a short toast, then wandering down toward the other end of the bar in search of adventure.

"Looked like a nice kid. How could you do that to him?" I asked, running a finger down her pile of Abraham Lincoln–faced currency. "Forty bucks. He's probably got a payment due on his Porsche. Lucky I got here when I did."

She shook a dice cup at me. "Feel lucky?"

"Yes. But liar's dice isn't a game of luck, is it? Come on, we've got work to do before you feed me."

I led Jane over to a table near the fireplace. A cocktail waitress with a tangle of Goldie Hawn hair came over to take our orders. Her outfit was a short skirt over black-mesh nylons and a white, low-cut peasant blouse.

"I'm fine," Jane said, cradling a glass of wine.

I peered at the small plastic nameplate tag stuck strategically over the waitress's left breast. "Stoli over, Audrey."

"Audrey, God, there's a name I haven't heard in years," Jane said after the waitress trotted away. "Just what kind of work is it we have to do before dinner, Nick?"

I showed her the receipt I'd found in Henning's car.

"You think they'll remember him?" she asked.

"You knew John. He'd stick out in a place like this."

She scanned the room slowly. "Maybe you're right."

Audrey came back a few minutes later, giving me a small napkin and my drink.

I dropped a twenty-dollar bill on her tray. "Keep the change, Audrey. Can I ask you a question?"

Her Barbie-doll eyes grew wary. She looked us both over. "Listen, I don't do—"

"Hey, nothing kinky," I interrupted. "Just want to know if you recognize this man." I handed her the picture of John Henning, then the restaurant receipt. "He was in last week."

She checked the picture first, then the receipt.

"Yeah, three fifty. Virgin mary."

"You remember what he was drinking?" Jane asked.

"The code on the receipt. 6A. That's a virgin mary. The other number, 4, that's my station. Right here." She tilted her head and looked at the picture again. "Yeah, I do remember this old guy. Nursed that one drink all the time. The lady came in later. She was heavy into 19s. Tequila martinis. I kinda thought he was her father or something. She was really slamming down the tequila."

"You wouldn't happen to know the lady's name, would you, Audrey?" Jane asked.

"She was a blonde," Audrey said. "Not too young, not too old." She took a quick glance at Jane but wisely said nothing further on the age matter. "Flashy, kind of, you know. He was kind of plain and drab and she was dripping with all these bracelets, rings, and necklaces. Real good stuff, not junk, you know."

"Was anyone else with them? Did you catch the lady's name?"

"Be right back," Audrey said, swiveling away with her tray held high. I watched her as she threaded her way through a small cluster of tables to the bar. She leaned across the bar and began what looked to be an earnest conversation with the bartender, handing him the photograph of John Henning. The bartender was a dark-haired dude who looked as if he could handle all the chores required of him, including the bouncing of overzealous customers. Audrey pointed a finger in our direction, and the bartender gave me a hard look.

"What do you think?" I asked Jane.

"I think that if dear little Audrey bends over any lower when she serves the next drink, her little boobs are going to fall right out of that blouse."

Audrey bounced over our way about five minutes later, a single drink on her tray. Jane turned out to be wrong on both counts: They didn't fall out, and the view provided proved that they definitely weren't little.

She dropped Henning's picture on the table, then pushed another glass of vodka at me. I got the message and handed her another twenty-dollar bill.

"Any luck?" I asked her.

She went into a sob story about how many people come into the place, you know, and how hard she has to work, you know, and how difficult it is making a living as a cocktail waitress, you know.

I glanced at the bartender while Audrey was going through her "you know" routine. He caught my eye, nodded, then began polishing glasses.

"What about a name, Audrey?"

She placed a hand on her hip and tilted her head to one side. "I don't know her name."

"I don't mean the lady with the jewels. I mean the bartender."

Her eyes twinkled through a maze of mascaraed lashes.

"Winky."

"And what time does Winky's shift end?"

"Same as mine. We're here till closing time."

Audrey trotted over to a nearby table, doing one of her matador dips as she put napkins down and asked a couple for drink orders. The seam of her stockings dived straight down past her thighs, curving calves, and ankles into at least four inches of high-heeled shoes. "Her poor little tootsies must be sore by the end of the night."

"So nice of you to be concerned," Jane said in an icy tone. "What was all that crap about the bartender?"

"Winky and Audrey are playing a little game of shakedown with us. I've got a feeling that he knows who Henning's bejeweled blonde is."

"So what do we do now?"

"We allow you to buy me dinner, then we have a talk with Winky."

"Be careful with him," Jane advised. "A grown man with a name like that must be awfully tough."

We both had orders of ribs and coleslaw, washed down with a bottle of chardonnay and wiped away with several extra napkins. Good, but messy.

Jane went to the powder room to repair the damage the napkins had done to her lipstick, and I wandered over to the bar. The crowd had thinned out. There were just two customers at the far end of the bar. Audrey came by and pressed a small piece of paper into my hand. I opened it. It simply said "Audrey, 555-3911."

Amazing what results you can get from charm and gross over-tipping.

Winky was wearing a heavily starched white shirt, with the cuffs turned up on the inside the way bartenders like to do. A solid-black tie was nailed to his shirt by a tie tack in the shape of a golf ball. He had thick, hairy wrists, one encircled by a gold ID brace-let, the other by a Rolex look-alike. He was about my age, with a thick head of coal-black hair and a deep, eighteen-hole tan. A scar over his right eyebrow and a slightly bent nose gave him a bit of a sinister look.

He gave the bar a quick wipe, then said, "Can I help you?"

"Two amarettos on the rocks."

He made the drinks, placing them down in the exact centers of two cocktail napkins. I put a twenty-dollar bill alongside each drink. "I'm running out of these. Audrey already got her share."

"I never saw your buddy, the guy in the picture," Winky said, deftly picking up the two twenties.

Jane came and slid onto the stool next to me.

"I'd like the name of the blond lady I spoke to Audrey about."

Winky began polishing the already-sparkling bar with his rag. "Man could lose his job giving out information on customers," he said.

"Man could also make some money. A hundred more. That's as far as I can go."

He tugged at one of his sideburns. "You working for her husband?"

"If I was, I'd know her name, wouldn't I?"

He accepted the explanation with a weak smile. "It'd take some work. I'd have to dig up old records. She paid with a credit card."

I waited him out.

"Come back after I get off work. Make it about two-fifteen. Knock on the door."

That left some time to kill. Jane and I nursed our amarettos. I suggested we go to my place or her place and pass the time pleasantly. She claimed she was in a dancing mood. Jane had graduated from the paper's sports page to being a three-times-a-week columnist. She was doing a series on the city's nightlife, so we ended up in what the public relations people refer to as SOMA, the old South of Market section of the city, where old warehouses and small industrial shops had been converted to trendy clubs and restaurants featuring everything from rock to heavy metal to reggae to whatever the latest craze was from South America to, thank goodness, jazz. The final stop was in a basement surrounded by brick walls where a young black kid who couldn't have been more than twenty was doing a credible Miles Davis impersonation on his muted trumpet. The trumpet was about the only thing muted in the club. The crowd was young, half the men in battered motorcycle leathers, the women in abbreviated rainbows of creations that would make Mr. Blackwell drop to his knees and cry. I tapped Jane on her shoulder and pointed to my watch, mouthing the words "It's almost two." There was no sense in saying them out loud. Though her lovely head was no more than a foot from mine, she never would have heard them over the sound of the five-piece band and the chanting of the crowd.

"Wasn't that fun?" Jane asked, once we were out into the reasonably fresh air.

"Terrific," I said, heaving a sigh of relief over the sight of my car, still parked safely in a bus stop zone. My car, sarcastically dubbed the Polomobile by Jane, is a bruised and battered four-year-old Ford, painted a civil service gray, with a big whip antenna. If you look inside you'll see a red "Kojak" light on the front seat and a clipboard holding age-old wanted posters. In other words, cleverly disguised to look like an unmarked police car. Jane hated the thing at first but was gradually won over to its side when she noticed how it could be parked in red zones, white zones, at bus stops, even on sidewalks and seldom acquired a parking tag.

The vehicle's major drawback was that there were times and places when you didn't want to look like you were in any way connected to the police. Judging by the number of chrome-dripping Harleys bunched up on the streets and sidewalks, this could very well have been one of those times. But the natives were friendly. Not a sign of a scratch or flat tire.

Jane stretched out, leaning against the passenger side headrest, which was hollowed out and held a .38 snub-nosed revolver. She was dozing lightly as I drove through the vacant streets back toward the Jefferson Park restaurant. She was even snoring lightly as I parked a half block down from the restaurant's entrance. I climbed out and eased the door shut. Her eyes flickered open briefly at the soft clicking sound. She smiled, folded her arms around herself, and snuggled against the vinyl upholstery.

I tapped lightly on the restaurant's glass doors with my keys. The place was black. I couldn't see a single light inside.

I was about to tap again when someone behind me said, "You trying to break in, stupid?"

There were two of them, both about the same age, mid- to late twenties. One was about six feet, slim, with lank dark hair flopping over his forehead. He was wearing a bomber jacket and black leather gloves. The shorter one looked like a bloated Roberto Duran between fights, all puffy fat over hard muscles. There were balloons of scars over both eyes, and his nose was a lot wider and shorter than the way Mother Nature had created it. He was wearing a dark blue jogging outfit and was bouncing from foot to foot, pounding his right hand into his left palm.

"I asked you a question, stupid," Bomber Jacket said.

"Just waiting to see a friend," I told him, my eyes darting up and down the street looking for help.

Bomber Jacket pulled in his head and edged forward. "You came to the wrong place, stupid."

There's a theory on a situation like this. You're confronted by two men. One has an unmarked face, the other a face that has obviously seen its share of fists. Who's less dangerous? Unmarked, because nobody has ever laid a glove on him? Or his partner, because it's obvious he can be hit?

Personally, I always leaned toward old battered face being the real bad guy. He'd been there. Maybe the other guy was just a watcher.

It looked as if I was right. Bomber Jacket turned to his partner and said, "Get him, José."

I had a good three inches and thirty pounds on José. He moved in close and flicked out a left jab. I saw it coming and ducked. The next three jabs I didn't even see, but I certainly felt them. Bam, bam, bam. Nose, chin, nose. It might have been a right that caught me in the solar plexus; I didn't see that coming either. José was a real pro.

The air whooshed out of me, and I fell to the ground. Bomber Jacket didn't think I should be getting any rest breaks. He started kicking me with sharp pointed leather shoes and shouting, "Get up, pretty boy. Get up."

I didn't really take his "pretty boy" comment to heart. Ernest Borgnine would have looked like a pretty boy in comparison to the two of them. I struggled to my feet, put my hands in a defensive position, and managed to block José's first two punches, even landing a solid right to his forehead before he hooked in two good lefts to my ribs and a right to the side of my neck as I was going down.

Joe Louis, the greatest of all the heavyweights, fought Max Baer back in 1935. Baer was no match for Louis, and Joe knocked him to the canvas several times. After the fight, a reporter asked Baer if he could have gotten up after that last knockdown and Baer replied, "Yeah, but he would have just knocked me down again."

I had the same feeling about José. He had earned all that scar tissue in the ring. Getting hit by a professional boxer is a lot different than getting tagged by a drunk on the street. Their hands are trained to twist just enough upon contact to drive their gloves deep into the opponent's flesh. Bomber Jacket wasn't about to let this fight end on a technical knockout. If this went on any longer my only chance would be to let José hit me until his hands broke.

Bomber Jacket bent over at the waist and spit at me. "Get up, you chicken shit—"

I grabbed his leg just above the ankle, moved my right hand down to his foot, and put all my strength into twisting the leg and foot in different directions. I could hear the bone snap just before he screamed and fell down alongside of me.

"Get out of here," I yelled at José, "or I'll break his fucking leg off."

He didn't pay much attention to me, but Bomber Jacket's screams got to him. "Do what he says! Do what he says! Get me a doctor!"

I applied more pressure on the foot, and Bomber Jacket screamed loud enough to wake the dead. But not Jane Tobin. I kept looking at my car, hoping to see headlights. Hear a horn.

"Let go of him, or I'll kill you," José said, over bomber jacket's continued moans and screams.

"Take off, José. Fast. I want to see you at least two blocks from here, then I'll let your buddy go." I applied more pressure to the foot, and Bomber Jacket in no uncertain terms told José what to do. "Get the fuck out of here, man! Get me a doctor!"

José backed away slowly, as if going to a neutral corner in the ring. "I'm going to get you for this," he promised me, before swiveling on his heel and jogging away.

"What's Winky's last name? Where do I find him?" I asked, my eyes on José's retreating back.

"Get me a doctor, man. You broke my fucking leg!"

"Just one of them. Where do I find Winky?"

"Man, he just told us to scare you, nothing serious. Help me, man."

"You tell me where I can find him, I'll call an ambulance." I looked at his leg. Blood was seeping through his Levi's. "You might bleed to death if you don't get help soon."

"Winky Harris. He lives out on London Street. 945 London."

I got to my feet, trying to cause as little damage as possible to his leg as I crawled out from under him. I ran back to the car, looking over my shoulder for the possible return of José as I stabbed the key in the door. Jane was lying down across the front seat, snoring lightly.

I snuggled against her, got the car started, and drove away, stopping at a pay phone on Embarcadero and dialing 911, advising the operator to send an ambulance to the Jefferson Park restaurant.

Jane came out of her coma when I got back into the car. She stretched, yawned, took one look at me, and snapped wide awake.

"Nick. What happened to your face? You're bleeding."

It was an opening I couldn't pass up. One of the all-time clichés. "You should see the other guy."

CHAPTER NINE

I GAVE JANE A capsule review of what went on while she was blissfully knocking out the z's.

"What are we going to do now?" she asked, patting a handkerchief gently under my nose to help stop the bleeding.

"We are going to drop you off at your place, then I'm going out to see Winky Harris."

"You know where he lives?"

"I persuaded the guy with the broken leg to give me his address."

"Well," she replied in a determined tone, "I'm coming with you."

I took the handkerchief from her hand before responding, "Only if you promise not to go to sleep again."

London Street was located in the Excelsior District, or Outer Mission area, known by the natives there as the Outa Mish.

A linguistic expert had once done an article on the speech patterns of the various districts in San Francisco. For some unknown reason a goodly portion of those from the Excelsior spoke with a distinct New York accent. I had several friends born and raised in the Excelsior who had gone through life being asked, "What part of New York you from?"

At one time the area had more Italians then North Beach. Now it was a nice, fairly quiet, multinational residential district. The names of the streets were a European smorgasbord: Vienna, Italy, France, Madrid, Naples, Edinburgh, Lisbon, with Persia, Amazon, and Brazil thrown in for good measure.

I parked under a streetlight in front of the address bomber jacket had given me for Winky Harris. It was a typical stucco-front, twenty-five-foot-frontage, single-family dwelling. Like its neighbors, it had been the victim of a graffiti artist. The poor, misguided chap who wielded the spray can in an attempt to express his bottled-up hostilities had apparently been absent from school the day the teacher taught the class how to spell the dreaded "F word." He left out the letter *c*.

I reached behind Jane's neck and pushed in the side of the headrest and extracted the .38 belly gun.

Jane made a clicking noise against her teeth. "Has that been there all the time?"

"I would have told you, but I was afraid it would keep you awake."

She aimed a left at me that looked every bit as vicious as one of José's. I caught her hand and held it. "Jane, this is serious. Stay in the car. Keep an eye on me. If I get into the house, and I'm not out of there in five minutes, blow the hell out of the horn."

Her face was set in her "I'm a reporter" look.

"Jane, you can really help me the most by staying in the car right now."

"Be careful, damn it," she advised as I got out of the car.

The front steps were terrazzo. An outside fixture threw a pool of yellow light that enabled me to sidestep the old newspapers littering the steps. I mounted them slowly. The front door was weathered gum wood, the varnish cracked and peeling. There was a small, diamond-shaped window in the middle of the door. I peered through. A light was coming from what looked like the kitchen. A radio or phonograph was playing soft Latin music. There were two locks on the door, one a sturdy-looking dead bolt, which meant that picking both of those locks would be a chore, unless I drove home and got the proper tools. I gave the knob a try. You never know.

Mr. Harris had locked his door. There was an old-fashioned, wood-framed window adjacent to the door. The window was divided into four glass panels, each about two feet square. I ran a finger alongside the old puttied caulking around each piece of glass. It broke off in my hand. I took a penknife from my pants pocket and began digging into the putty. It fell away in inch-long sections. When all the putty was removed there were just four little U-shaped staples holding the glass in place. I pried the staples back and carefully slid out the entire section of glass.

The Latin music was still going strong. I laid down the glass on Harris's dusty welcome mat, then reached in the window, undid the upper latch, and slid the lower portion up slowly, inch by inch, my eyes staring into the house, ears listening for anything other than violins and mariachis.

I looked down to the car, waved at Jane's rather nervous-looking face, and crawled through the window and into the house, gun in hand. I was in a dining area; a big wooden table, a matching hutch against the wall. There was a living room to my left; French doors led to another small room to my right. Straight ahead was a small breakfast area off the kitchen. The house was so small that the kitchen light splashed out enough illumination to keep me from falling over the furniture.

A Formica table sat in the middle of the kitchen. The table was littered with liquor bottles: Scotch, bourbon, vodka, tequila. Harris took his work home with him. A plastic ice tray, the ice melted halfway down, sat alongside the bottles.

The music got louder as I went through the kitchen and into a hallway. Over the music came grunts, moans, and unintelligible murmurings. One vice squad officer, who had maybe busted a thousand prostitutes over the years, when called to court always testified that "I heard the sounds of intercourse and entered the room and found the defendant engaged in a sexual act."

A smart defense attorney challenged him one day as to just what were the sounds of intercourse.

The cop delighted the jury with a series of loud, enthusiastic grunts, groans, moans, and wheezes. The judge was impressed enough to let his description stand as expert-witness testimony. He was known for the rest of his career as a "fucking expert."

While no expert, I could see that the two people on the king-sized bed were definitely engaged in sexual activities. They were both naked. Audrey, the cocktail waitress, lay on her back, eyes closed, blond hair fanned out on a pillow, while Mr. Harris's head bobbed up and down between her legs.

I coughed loudly, then said, "Did you know that in some states oral sex is still a criminal offense?"

Harris's head snapped around, and he let out a snarl, legs dangling over the bed searching for the floor.

"No, no," I said, quickly striding to the bed and shoving the gun at his face. "Stay right there."

Audrey was squirming around the bed, reaching for the bedspread to cover herself.

A robe of rough-textured white toweling lay on the carpet. I put a toe under it and kicked it toward her.

"What the hell do you think you're doing here?" Winky Harris demanded.

"I'm not feeling too good, Winky. A couple of your friends worked me over pretty good."

"I don't know what the hell you're talking about," he said, crossing one leg over the other and placing his hands behind his head. He was acting amazingly cool under the circumstances.

I walked over to him and bounced the butt of the revolver lightly against the top of his skull. "I'm sore, I'm tired, and I'm pissed," I told him. "I want the name of the blond woman who was drinking with my friend in the photograph."

"I'm telling you—"

I brought the gun butt down a little harder this time, hard enough to make him wince.

"For God's sake tell him, Winky," Audrey whined, wiggling off the bed and holding the bathrobe in front of her as if it were a shield. "You know her. It was Sharon Rochard. What's the big deal?"

"Thanks, Audrey," I said. "Why don't you go outside. A lady named Jane is waiting in my car. Tell her I said to forget about blowing the horn."

"Hey, I don't have to—"

"Shut up," Harris said sharply. "Do what he says!"

Audrey turned her back to us while she struggled into the robe. She padded by me barefoot. Without her stiletto heels she was barely five feet tall. She bumped into the wall on her way to the door.

"Without her contact lenses she'll be lucky to find your car," Harris said.

"Your two friends weren't very good."

He shrugged his tanned shoulders. "Busboys."

"Pretty rough characters for busboys."

"One's an illegal, the other's a doper. They came to work a week ago, they'll be gone in another week. You know how it is."

I didn't, but I nodded my head in agreement.

Harris said, "All I asked them to do was scare you off. Nothing heavy. If they got carried away, I apologize."

"Why were you so anxious to scare me off?"

"Mind if I smoke?" Harris asked.

"Your house. Your lungs."

He slid up to the front of the bed and grabbed a pack of unfiltered Camels from the bed stand, then used an old Zippo lighter to get it going. He exhaled a stream of smoke and appraised me through the haze.

"I know the lady you're looking for."

"Sharon Rochard. Nice name," I said.

"Yes. Nice lady. Very nice. She's married. Very married. To a lot of money. I don't think she'd appreciate someone like you asking a lot of questions. Her husband might get the wrong idea."

"I take it you and Sharon have been close friends on occasion."

"Yes. Just a few times. Like I said, she's a nice lady."

"How do I get hold of the nice lady?"

He took another deep puff on his cigarette. "I'd rather not tell you."

"You just work at the Jefferson Park, or do you have a piece of it?"

"It's mine," he said.

"Then think of it this way, Winky, my friend. I've got the gun. I also know the whereabouts of your two busboys. One is in the hospital now and will gladly spill his guts out about what happened tonight. And what happened was that you hired two men to commit felony assault on my person. I can have you arrested. You may beat the rap but not until you've spent a small fortune on a defense lawyer, and you may not have much money to pay that noble gentleman because you'll have to hire another attorney after I bitch to the Alcoholic Beverage Control Department. They can take away your liquor license over something like this. So all things considered, you're not in a position to refuse to answer any questions. Now, I'm going to find Sharon Rochard anyway, I just want you to make it easy for me."

Harris laughed through a smoker's cough. "You should have gone into sales. You certainly know how to close a deal. She lives with her husband somewhere in the East Bay. I don't know the address."

"Husband's name?"

He stabbed out the cigarette butt in an oversized ashtray in the shape of a golf ball. "George Rochard."

The name rang a small bell. "The jeweler?"

"I guess so. We didn't talk much about her husband when we were together."

"Have you got her telephone number?"

Harris shook another smoke from the pack. "No. She came in to see me. I never called her."

"If you're bullshitting me, I'm coming back." I waved the barrel of the gun down toward his groin. "You can count on it."

Harris crossed one leg over the other, nodded casually, then said, "Send Audrey back, will you?"

I found Audrey in the backseat of my car in an animated discussion with Jane. She narrowed her eyes almost to closing again when I climbed in the front seat.

"Hi, again," she said.

"Hi to you. Mr. Harris is requesting your presence as soon as possible."

"Okay, okay," she said hurriedly, then turned to Jane. "See what I mean? Bartenders. They're all bastards. But at least you know that going in. The weirdos that come in the bar, who's to know what they are? You can't be too careful nowadays."

She got out of the car and groped her way up the steps of Harris's house.

"You girls have a nice chat?" I asked Jane as I turned the motor over and pulled the car away from the curb.

"She was telling me about the life of a cocktail waitress. It'll make a good column."

54

"Well, I'm glad I didn't take that beating for nothing," I said in a voice begging for sympathy.

Jane slid over and patted my knee lightly. "Poor baby. Tell me where it hurts."

CHAPTER TEN

IT HURT ALL OVER in the morning when Jane nudged me awake by putting a steaming cup of coffee under my sore nose.

"I've got to get going, Nick," Jane said, looking amazingly perky, dressed in a fresh corduroy outfit, this time the turtleneck a periwinkle blue. "Give me a call later." She gave me a cheerful smile and trotted off to work.

I glanced at the clock alongside her bed. Eight-thirty. I eased out of bed, one agonizing muscle at a time, shuffled to the bathroom, and looked in the medicine chest's mirror. I winced, closed my eyes, swung the mirror open, and gazed at the jammed shelves, my grateful fingers digging out a plastic bottle of Anacin.

I popped a couple of pills into my mouth, made a cup of my hand, and drank in a quart of water aborigine style.

Outside of an aching back, aching ribs, aching neck, throbbing nose, and headache, I was ready to face the world. But not that bathroom mirror again. I got dressed, took a quick look into Jane's refrigerator. The results showed why she ate out so much; I decided to head for home.

The venetian blinds to Mrs. Damonte's downstairs flat fluttered as I walked by. I stopped and knocked on the door.

Even though she knew it was me, she opened the door just a crack. Maybe it was because she knew it was me.

I thanked her for the meal she'd prepared for Jane and me after John Henning's funeral.

Her ancient face cracked into a brief smile. "You in a fight?" she asked in Italian. Mrs. D. speaks Italian almost exclusively. The exceptions are "nopa," her all-American negative response; "bingo," her personal favorite; and, finally, "shita", when something terrible happens, like the price of olive oil goes up a few cents.

"Come in," she commanded. "I fix."

I walked in carefully, out of fear. Fear that I'd slip on the highly polished floor or fear that I'd scuff the glossy oak surface and get on her "shita" list.

The first whiff you get when entering Mrs. D.'s domicile is cleaning solvents. She should have been an admiral in the Italian navy. If it doesn't move, clean it, then paint it or wax it. But the wonderful smells of garlic and spices take over as you get near the kitchen. Fresh bunches of rosemary, oregano, and thyme were soaking in the kitchen sink. Mrs. Damonte grows a large variety of herbs in our backyard, in enough quantity to supply several top-notch North Beach restaurants. I say ours because, legally, I own it. Mrs. D. figures I have as much right to the grounds as do the unlucky snails that creep in from neighboring yards. I won't tell you what she does with them.

"Fix us a drink," she told me, while she went out to the back porch.

Mrs. D.'s morning drink is a shot of rock 'n' rye, a foul-tasting concoction of whiskey and herbs.

I found the bottle and two shot glasses in the kitchen cupboard, poured a full one for her and a drop for me.

I smacked my lips, holding my almost-empty glass up for her inspection when she returned, carrying an old jelly jar filled with a cloudy, evil-looking liquid.

She handed me the jar and proclaimed, "Rub in, morning and night."

"Will do," I said, upending the shot glass.

She took her glass and downed the shot in a gulp.

"You and lady at funeral. Not getting—"

"No, no. We're just good friends," I told her.

Mrs. D.'s biggest fear is that I'll get married and my wife will move in and try and take over the flats. Since Mrs. D. figures she'll outlive me and the flats will somehow revert to her, my love life is of major importance to her.

She nodded her head in agreement. "She's too old."

"I wouldn't tell her that," I advised, picking up the jelly jar and tracking my way carefully to the front door.

Once in my place I got a pot of coffee going and rummaged through the refrigerator, deciding to go with Mrs. Damonte's leftover torta.

I showered, shaved, and felt reasonably human. I uncapped Mrs. D.'s magic elixir and took a whiff. It smelled like a salad dressing. I had no idea what was in it, but the old Italian witch doctor had mixed up some concoctions that had done me a lot more good than the antibiotics and pills my doctor prescribed, so I followed her directions and rubbed the lotion into my now-various bruises and contusions, then splashed on enough after-shave to hopefully cover up the smell.

I dressed casually in slacks, button-down shirt, and sweater and went to what was my bedroom as a child and I now used as an office. I turned on the computer and printer, accessed an assessor-records data base, and input the names of George and Sharon Rochard.

The computer went through a series of electronic burps and gargles, then the laser printer went to work and began shuffling out the results.

George Rochard was listed as the owner of two properties:

> 10486 Eagle Nest Road, Danville
> 1449 Saddle Lane, South Lake Tahoe.

The Danville property was listed as a single-family residence, built in the last year. Rochard had paid $1,790,000 for fifty-four hundred square feet of living area, five bedrooms, four and a half baths, a swimming pool, and a spa. His annual taxes were listed at just under twenty thousand a year.

The South Lake Tahoe property must have been just a shack in comparison, purchased three years ago for a paltry $700,000. The computer printout showed a swimming pool and spa again, but only three bedrooms and three baths. Sometimes you just have to make do.

I dug through a file cabinet and pulled up maps for Contra Costa County and the Lake Tahoe area.

The Eagle Nest Road address was in Blackhawk, an upper-scale suburban residential park built on five thousand acres under the shadow of Mount Diablo, in Contra Costa County, some twenty-five miles east of San Francisco. The area contained two championship golf courses, acres of tennis courts, equestrian trails, and an establishment that bills itself as "The Bloomingdale's of Supermarkets." It's become a tourist attraction. A tuxedoed young man plays show tunes on a Yamaha grand piano, while clerks, dressed up like English butlers, wear cellular phones on their hips for the complimentary use of the patrons. They roam the aisles to help the cashmere-and-denim shoppers push black-and-gold carts and finger the zucchini under the luminous glow of crystal chandeliers. The concierge who greets you at the entrance can advise you on just where to find the caviar and truffles. For more detailed questions, he will turn you over to the registered dietitian, who will direct you to the sommelier if you want to know just what vintage burgundy goes with those Kansas City T-bones. What the hell, the rich have to eat too.

The Tahoe map showed that the property was located roughly halfway between the Heavenly Valley Ski Area and the state-line casinos.

I wasn't surprised to learn from telephone information that both the Rochard numbers were unlisted. I called what we in the private-investigation field like to label "a contact" at the phone company and requested the number for the Blackhawk property, which for a not-inconsiderable fee the contact quickly provided.

"Rochard residence," said a female voice with a heavy Latin accent.

"Mrs. Rochard, please."

"Who is calling?"

"Umm, this is Louis at the beauty salon," I ad-libbed. "Sharon was due in for an appointment half an hour ago."

"Oh, she must have forgot. She's at Lake Tahoe."

"Oh, no. And I had something I wanted to speak to her about. Do you have the number for her at the lake?"

Once in a while you run into a trusting soul who believes what you tell him or her no matter how silly it may seem. Or maybe in Blackhawk hairdressers make long-distance house calls. She supplied the number and even thanked me for calling.

I tried Lake Tahoe. No answer. No reason for there to be one. There were lots of reasons to be out of the house in Tahoe, day or night.

I went back to the map. The Lake Tahoe airport looked as if it was no more than five miles from the Rochards' place. The drive of some two hundred miles would take over five long, boring hours.

While I was debating with myself whether to take the car or fly, the phone rang. It was the attorney, Arnold Harkins.

"Mr. Polo," Harkins said in a brisk, officious tone, "I've done some preliminary work on John Henning's estate. There is a loan against his house, but I think we'll be able to net it out for something like seventy thousand dollars, half of which of course will be yours. That and his life insurance policy and personal effects should have you ending up with, after probate costs, somewhere in the vicinity of thirty-three to thirty-five thousand dollars."

"Did you find out anything about John's banking activities for the last ten days or so before he died?"

"Not yet, but I don't think that there will be any large additions or subtractions to the figures I quoted you."

It's a disease. They all talk like that. "Listen, Mr. Harkins, I'm not that interested in the money aspect of it. I want to find out who John was doing business with before he died. I'd appreciate it if you could put a rush on finding that out."

"Well—"

"Naturally I expect you to add the extra work to your billable hours."

Billable hours. It has the same effect on attorneys that "Shazam" had on Captain Marvel. That "Do you take this man . . . " has on a Gabor.

Harkins coughed to cover up his salivating. "I'll get right on it, Mr. Polo."

With my newfound wealth there was no point in worrying about the cost of a flight to Lake Tahoe, which turned out to be a pretty heavy $342. There are two ways to get to Lake Tahoe from San Francisco. Fly to Reno, then rent a car for the hour or so drive to the lake, or fly directly. I chose a direct flight and was luckily booked, due to a late cancellation.

Worse than the price was the airplane. American Airlines was the only carrier serving Lake Tahoe out of San Francisco International Airport. The airplane was a Fairchild turboprop F27, a shaky-looking, high-winged little metal-skinned, two-engine contraption that looked too squat and scrunched up to make it off the ground. There was no flight attendant, and the plane only held some twenty passengers. No flight attendant, thus no coffee, tea, or small bottles of purely medicinal alcohol. Had I known, I'd have brought a flask. I don't have a real fear of flying, as long as the plane has no fewer than four engines and flies directly over flat land—flat unsettled land where the plane can make an emergency stop if one of those four engines decides to go on strike.

The guy sitting next to me looked like an unsuccessful rodeo cowboy: long, lean, continually massaging his elbows, neck, and knees. Once we were in the air, he tipped his stained Stetson back on his head, reached into his Levi's jacket, and pulled out a half-pint bottle of Wild Turkey.

"Here, partner," he said tapping my shoulder with the bottle. "Take a pull. You look like you could use it."

The flight took less than an hour, and between the two of us the bottle was long gone before touchdown. I had the window seat and killed time in between sips by watching the engines and searching for spots where the pilot could put the plane down. The mountain peaks were covered with pure, wedding-white snow. Below the snows were thick forests of ponderosa and Jeffrey pines and red fir trees.

We started the landing approach and before I was finished with three Hail Marys and an Act of Contrition the plane coasted to a stop at the small Tahoe terminal. I thanked my flying companion for his hospitality and headed for the car-rental counter.

The bright, sunny-faced clerk gave me a choice of a Ford sedan or four-wheel-drive Bronco. There were still patches of snow close to the terminal, so I took the Bronco.

The Rochard house—calling it a cabin would be an injustice—

was a two-story peaked-roof affair. A bubble skylight, looking like a giant doorbell, sat right in the middle of the roof. There were no fences protecting the front of the house or separating it from its neighbors, which were a good hundred yards away on either side. The grounds were blanketed with junipers and old pinecones that had survived the winter. A late-model, mint-green Mercedes was parked in front of the garage. The front-door knocker was tarnished brass in the shape of a lion's head. I put it to work, but there was no response. I used my hand on the door and got the same results.

I walked over to the Mercedes. The hood was cold. I tried pounding on the door again. Still nothing. I went back to breaking and entering basics number one. The knob turned and the door swung open. Never a good sign.

"Hello, Mrs. Rochard," I called out, poking my head through the door.

The inside was decorated in Swiss-clock Tyrolean, with carved wooden beams painted in reds and blues and greens. The walls were flagstone, the furniture Hansel and Gretel.

The kitchen was all oak cabinets over a blue tile floor.

The stairs leading to the upper floor were polished oak on top; the risers were painted lavender, and every second one had a circular painting of a flower. Even though I was wearing rubber-soled shoes, I kept my feet to the edges, wondering why anyone would choose to paint pictures on their stairs as I cautiously made my way upward, shouting a "Hello, anyone home?" every few seconds.

The master bedroom walls were varnished knotty pine. A saddle leather–covered hope chest, studded with brass, stood at the end of the bed. The wool rug was in a fawn-skin pattern. I felt as if I was tiptoeing over Bambi as I went into the bathroom. Nothing there but a pair of women's pink pants, a matching sweater, and a lacy pair of bikini panties and bra in a shade of pink just a little brighter than the sweater and pants scattered haphazardly on the white tile floor.

I went back downstairs. Mrs. Rochard was apparently out enjoying the good life and just too lazy to lock up the house after herself.

There was a humming noise coming from the back. Through the windows of the kitchen's double Dutch doors I could see the swimming pool. A few yards away was a large gazebo, circling a hot tub. A blue towel trailed over the side of the tub.

I unlocked the Dutch doors and went outside. The humming sound was the noise from the hot tub's motor. The tub was terra-cotta fiberglass, with an outer wrapping of redwood slats. An almost empty bottle of Monte Alban tequila sat on the edge of the tub, next to a glass with pictures of poinsettias decorating it.

The tub's water was bubbling away. A big toe, polished in a pink that was a close match for the clothes on the bathroom floor, floated in and out of the bubbles. It took longer than it should have to figure out the tub's control buttons, but I kept punching away until the motor went off, shutting down the jets that ringed the tub, and the water cleared. It was hard to tell if the woman on the bottom had been young, old, pretty, or not. Blue eyes stared up from a puffy white face, the head arched oddly against the side of the tub. I couldn't understand what had kept her under like that, then I noticed her blond hair had been pulled into the tub's suction drain.

CHAPTER ELEVEN

SHERIFF ERIC COLVIN was a soft-spoken, weathered-faced guy a year or so on either side of sixty; well over six feet in height, broad shouldered. His khaki uniform was starched and creased in all the right spots. The gold badge over his heart looked as if it got a polishing every day. He was wearing one of those Smokey the Bear–type hats, and he had on a pair of yellow-tinted aviator glasses. He had a pimple on the bridge of his nose, right about where the glasses rested. A chrome-plated, ivory-handled revolver in an oxblood holster hung at his hip. For such a big man, his handshake was mushy and boneless.

"Private investigator," he said, taking off his glasses and examining my business card as if it were the fifth card drawn to an inside straight. "San Francisco, huh?"

He didn't sound overly impressed. I took my old gold-plated San Francisco Police Department inspector's badge that I hadn't turned in when I left the department from my pants pocket and flashed it at him. "Ex–San Francisco cop, Sheriff."

His eyes brightened a bit. "Ah. You look young to be retired. Bad back?"

"Among other things."

His right hand went to the small of his back. "It's all that goddamn driving around all night that does it. What happened to your face?"

"Had a losing argument with a door, Sheriff."

He grunted, then said, "What brought you up here?"

We were sitting in the two yellow and green–striped vinyl and

64

aluminum chairs alongside the Rochard swimming pool. Steam was rising off the pool's sparkling blue water.

"I wanted to see Mrs. Rochard about a case I'm working on."

"You're not going to pull that confidential-client shit on me, are you, Polo?"

"No. It's an insurance case. She was a witness to a major automobile accident."

Colvin took off his hat. He had a thick head of curly gray hair, interrupted by a bald spot at the back. His scratched his fingers on the bald spot.

"So you must have had an appointment with Mrs. Rochard, huh?"

"No, not really."

"Came all the way up here on just the chance you'd run into her?"

"I called her home. The maid, or whoever it was who answered the phone, told me she was here."

A fly buzzed by his ear, and he waved it away with a flapping motion of his hand. "So you called up and made an appointment to meet with her, huh?"

"No, Sheriff. In my line of work it's sometimes better to just knock on the door. You try and make an appointment, they usually find a way to avoid you."

Colvin gave a noncommittal grunt. "Seen 'em like that before," he said, gesturing with his chin to the hot tub, where two members of the county medical examiner's office were pulling the woman's body from the tub. "Mostly kids. Get in the damn tubs when their folks are away. Go diving down the bottom, sitting under the water, holding their noses. Hair gets caught in that suction, and, man, they just can't get away. Crying shame." He went through the hat-off, scratching-his-head routine again. "New hot tubs are different. The filter-return suction is up top. Probably some lawsuits filed by the families of the people that got killed made them change it. Damn shame. You ever see Sharon Rochard before?"

"Never."

"Then you don't really know that's her the boys are yanking out of there now."

"No. I sure don't."

"You know her husband?" he asked.

"Never met the man."

The fly buzzed Colvin's ear again, and he slapped the palm of his hand against his head, mashing his ear. "Must have a lot of money, this Rochard. How big you reckon that swimming pool is?"

The pool was oblong. Some twelve to fifteen feet wide, twice again that in length. The bottom of the pool was white concrete, the sides done in a turquoise tile. One of those automatic pool sweeps was methodically sweeping the bottom. "Good sized," was the best I could come up with.

"Yeah. Heating that sucker costs a fortune this time of the year." He glanced over to the house. "Nice place. You been inside?"

"Just to call you people. The front door was open."

"Was it, now? Convenient for you, huh?" Colvin placed his hands on the chair's small aluminum armrests and pushed himself to his feet. "Looks like she's out. Let's take a look."

The medical examiner's team had placed the body on a collapsible metal gurney. They saw the sheriff coming and snapped back the sheet covering the corpse.

Her skin was a grainy white, the consistency of cookie dough, the face puffy and wrinkled at the same time. What the homicide boys call "the washerwoman effect." The body oils had literally been boiled out of her skin.

"Had to cut off some of her hair, Eric," one of the medical examiners said to the sheriff. "Damn stuff is wrapped in those pipes pretty good."

I joined Colvin in looking down into the hot tub. It had been drained to make removing the body easier. The suction drain was a round hole maybe two inches wide, with a piece of wire mesh in the center. Strands of blond hair were tangled in the mesh.

The sheriff leaned over to get a better look. "Bet the poor lady tried to pull away, couldn't. You think you could pull away if your life depended on it, don't you? Damn motor is probably no more than one and a half horsepower. Don't sound like much, but that's a pretty good pull." He leaned back and wrinkled his nose. "That and the liquor would do it all right, don't you think, Polo?"

"I guess so," I said, looking at the body again. There was no blood around the area where the hair had been cut away.

"Either that," the sheriff continued, "or it's a hell of a smart way to murder someone. Tell me again just when you got here, will you?"

I told him my story, showing the sheriff my airline ticket with the departure time from San Francisco and the arrival time at the Tahoe airport. "Rented a car and came right over here, Sheriff."

"You packing a gun, Polo?"

"No."

"Being a private eye and an ex-policeman and all, I just thought you might be. I'd appreciate it if you'd stick around for a day or so."

"I've got a lot of work waiting for me back in the city," I said.

"Just till tomorrow. Need a statement from you. Follow me back to my office. I have to get ahold of the lady's husband. Make sure we got the right person."

It was another hour before Colvin was finished at the Rochard house. I got in the Bronco and followed him to the sheriff's office on Johnson Boulevard.

A secretary with hair so black it had hints of blue in it typed out my statement. A brass nameplate on her blouse gave her name as Anona. I wondered if she was Indian. Lake Tahoe had been in the heart of Washo Indian lands. It was considered a sacred place then. The lake must have been loaded with fish in those days. Commercial fisherman had come in the late 1800s, and by 1915 the trout that had been there had been harvested and shipped to restaurants on both coasts. Now the trout were almost extinct. Lumber mills came in and started doing to trees what the fisherman were doing to the trout, and the denuded hillsides had scars that haven't healed yet.

Anona transcribed my report on a computer, printed it, and handed it to me to read.

"Looks fine," I said, passing the document back to her.

She nodded her head. In the forty-five minutes it took to put the statement together, the longest string of words I got out of her was "Repeat that, please."

She kept to her silent ways, crooking a finger at me to follow her down a hallway to Colvin's office.

He was behind his desk, leaning back in a swivel chair, his hands locked behind his head, zip-sided boots planted firmly in the middle of the desk.

"Thanks, honey," he said, accepting my statement from Anona's outstretched hands.

Colvin went over the statement, rocking back and forth in his chair as he read it. He looked up at me from under bushy eyebrows, smiling as a proud parent might after his child finished off a difficult word in a spelling bee. "This the way you want to leave it?"

"I could add what I had for breakfast and what I drank on the plane, but I didn't think you'd be interested."

"Hmmmph," he snorted, pulling his feet from the desk and dropping them to the floor. "Got a place to stay?"

"No. Not yet."

He reached for one of the three phones on his desk. "Friend of mine, Jack Drago, used to work for us, runs security at The Granada. I can get you a good deal there." He gave me that parental smile again. "Professional courtesy. We cops have to stick together, don't we?"

It seemed like the number of motels and fast-food franchises had doubled along Lake Tahoe Boulevard since my last visit. McDonald's, Wendy's, Burger King, all the major players along with a bunch of small operations with neon signs of burgers, shakes, and ice-cream cones that blocked the view to the lake itself. I rolled down the Bronco's window. The smell of fried foods overpowered the scent of pines. I bumper-to-bumpered along for a couple of miles, getting stalled at a stoplight in front of Harvey's. There are a couple of small casinos in South Shore, but the biggies, The High Sierra, Harrah's, Caesars, The Granada, and Harvey's, call themselves Resort Hotel Casinos.

Just after World War II Harvey Gross, a butcher in Sacramento, built a log cabin with a single gas pump out front and a half-dozen slot machines and a craps table inside and had the missus putting out some of her fine home-cooked meals.

By the late seventies Harvey's had developed into an eleven-story hotel-casino. A gentleman decided that old Harvey had made too much money. He wanted some of it, so he made up a very sophisticated bomb; 750 pounds of dynamite he stole from a Pacific Gas & Electric plant was housed in a quarter-inch-thick steel metal box the size of a refrigerator with four antidisturbance arming switches. He delivered it to the casino, then told the police what was inside his little creation, and if he didn't get several million dollars in cash, he'd blow the damn place up. Negotiations didn't go very well, and this early venture capitalist pushed the button and over fifty pounds of high-speed dynamite packed in-side that metal box exploded. The portions of the building that weren't blown up eventually had to be torn down. Had the idiot seen what Harvey had in mind as a replacement, he might have changed his mind.

Now the massive hotel was eighteen stories high, twice as deep as the old place, with more than seven hundred rooms; it looked as if it belonged in Los Angeles or Vegas but not in Tahoe.

The Granada was just three blocks and a ten-minute exhaust-sucking crawl away and wasn't much smaller than Harvey's. I dropped my Visa card at the registration desk in front of a sour-faced clerk, a young man in his twenties with skin the color of an orange from an overdose of a quick-tanning lotion. The clerks in the hotels are usually sour-faced because they know the keno runners and cocktail waitresses are making four or five times as much as they are.

"Oh, we were expecting you, Mr. Polo," he said without look-ing at me. "Just a moment, please." He picked up a phone, and I heard him ask for security.

He began punching my credit card number into the hotel's computer, and by the time he had the paperwork done a man with linebacker shoulders dressed in a khaki uniform similar to that of Sheriff Colvin came to the desk and introduced himself.

"Jack Drago, Mr. Polo. Eric asked me to take care of you." He had droopy eyes and looked a little like the actor Robert Mitchum, after old Bob had been roughed up trying to save Jane Russell from Raymond Burr, in Burr's nasty, pre–Perry Mason days.

He gripped my hand hard enough to show that if he felt like it, it would be no problem to crack my knuckles.

"Where's your luggage?" Drago asked.

I held up my little carry-on tote bag that held nothing but a change of socks, underwear, and a toilet kit.

"Traveling light, huh?" Drago said, then turned to the clerk and asked him for my key.

The key was a piece of light blue plastic, slightly smaller than a playing card, with an arrow on one end under the notice "This Side Out." The back side showed a diagram of a doorknob with instructions on how to insert the card into the lock, then wait for a green light to show before entering the room. If a red light should appear, the card ordered you to wait another three seconds, then try again.

"Call me old-fashioned," I said, "but I still like the old, heavy brass keys."

"These save the hotel a fortune," Drago said, leading me to the elevator. "Electronic room keys. Cost about six cents each. When you check out, they rekey the door by a computer, make up a new card key. All the information is on the brown piece of magnetized tape on the back of the card."

"You people in security must have a master card," I said while we waited for the elevator.

"Oh, yeah. We do, so does housekeeping and engineering."

"That's a lot of master keys floating around."

An elevator hissed open, and a flood of serious-eyed people filled with gambling fever exited.

Drago waited to continue the conversation until we got to the eleventh floor and the last of our fellow passengers got off at his floor.

"Yes, a lot of cards," he agreed. "Every one is numbered, and that ever-present computer keeps track of the time and number of every card that enters a room."

"Housekeeping must love it," I said. "They can time just how long it takes for the maid to do her labors."

"Yeah, they stop to watch a soap opera and the computer knows."

My room was on the hotel's west side and had a magnificent view of Lake Tahoe and the snow-capped mountains beyond.

Drago said to be sure and call him if I needed anything. I thanked him, knowing full well that he was going to pass along anything he thought might interest Sheriff Colvin. Professional courtesy strikes again.

The room, actually a suite, was done in earth tones—oranges, browns, and all the shades in between. A small refrigerator-bar sat alongside the TV. It was stocked with airline-size bottles of all the popular liquors, as well as pony bottles of champagnes and wines and an assortment of peanuts and snacks. I inserted the blue card key and within seconds the hotel's computer knew that I was fond of Stolichnaya vodka and Planters unsalted nuts.

I poured the icy vodka into a glass and carried it over to the window. I remembered reading that Lake Tahoe was more than twenty miles long, a dozen miles wide, and at its deepest point touched bottom at some sixteen hundred feet. A lot of water. Enough to cover the entire state of California with over a foot of water. And since the state was suffering from a series of droughts, and seeing what man had already done to the lake, flooding the state with it was a possibility that was probably floating around in the mind of some harebrained politician in a parched area in Southern California. No wonder I was rooting against John Wayne in those old movies now. The wrong guys went to the reservations.

CHAPTER TWELVE

EVEN WITH ITS ever-increasing environmental problems, Lake Tahoe is one of the world's premier locations to gambol and gamble. In the winter there's the skiing, in the summer great golf courses, nature trails, gorgeous natural scenery, and casinos that offer the whole enchilada: baccarat, roulette, craps, poker, the increasingly popular Oriental games like Pan, and the casino's favorite, slot machines.

Little old ladies hobble around, tilted to one side because the arm they use to pull that handle has developed biceps big enough to challenge Hulk Hogan in an arm wrestling match. If you're tired of parachute jumping, skydiving, or jumping off those rocks in Acapulco to the ocean below and really want to face a dangerous challenge, just try finessing one of those slots away from those unsmiling, clench-jawed senior citizens carefully nursing coin after coin in the everlasting search for a row of sevens or cherries to pop up in front of their eyes.

In the old days you put in one coin, pulled the handle, and waited a few seconds to see the results. But someone, I don't know who, but he was immediately inducted into the Con Man Hall of Fame, came up with the idea of expanding every single play at the slot machine from one coin up to four or five. Four or five ways to win with each pull and, of course, to lose. You can still play just one coin, but if all those sevens or pictures of sports cars come up on the line just above yours or the one below or diagonally, you kick yourself all the way back to the tour bus for not shoving in those extra coins.

The Granada had several restaurants, the most popular being the Grand Granada Buffet, where you could stuff yourself an unlimited amount of times with a variety of hot entrees and desserts. Nice food, but I would have had to stand in line alongside families of people who survived on one big daily meal so the rest of their vacation money could go where it belonged: in the slot machines. They shuffled slowly ahead, eyes never leaving the numbers popping up on the keno board. I settled on the Vista Room and had two perfectly done lamb chops. The whole meal was excellent, highlighted by the extra efforts the waiter put into mixing up the Caesar salad at my table. Bullfighters in Mexico City in July didn't work up that much of a sweat. He looked at me triumphantly after swirling away with the anchovies, oil, raw egg, and finally grinding fresh Parmesan with the enthusiasm of a ten-year-old ripping open packages on Christmas morning. I think he expected me to clap. I made up for my silence by leaving a big tip.

The casino cashier was only too happy to cash my check for three hundred dollars. The blackjack dealers were even happier to relieve me of the money. I tried a few keno games, then made the obligatory deposits at the progressive slot machines whose total payoff was over a half million dollars. What the hell, someone's got to win on the things. Everyone has an equal chance. Miracles do happen. When I finally put my plastic key card into my room door I had fourteen cents in coins in my pocket.

First thing in the morning I called room service and ordered breakfast, then showered, shaved, and rubbed in some of Mrs. Damonte's magic lotion. The stiffness was just about gone from my back, neck, and shoulders, and even the bruises looked better than they did yesterday.

I had drained the last of the coffee from the thermos pot when the loud knock on the door came.

"You weren't very truthful to me, were you, Mr. Polo?" Sheriff Colvin said as he pushed his way past me.

"Come on in, Sheriff," I said graciously.

Colvin's eyes darted around the room. Unless he had some unusual interest in unmade beds and dirty breakfast dishes, there was not much to catch his interest.

He took off his hat and flipped it on the bed. "You told me you left the police department because of a bad back."

"No, that's not what I told you. You brought up the back."

He flipped open the top of the coffee thermos, saw it was empty, went to the phone, and called room service. "This is Sheriff Colvin. A pot of coffee and some raisin toast, no butter, to room 1417," he ordered.

"Nothing for me," I said, but by then he'd already hung up.

"Look, Polo. I don't like being jacked off by some hotshot private eye from San Francisco." He dug a piece of computer printout paper from his shirt pocket. "You quit the department, then a year later you're arrested and do time in a federal penitentiary."

"True," I said. "But there's no connection between the two events."

"Oh, no?" He plopped down in a chair alongside the small, round dining table, leaned back, and locked his fingers behind his head. "You know a Lieutenant John Lynch down in Frisco?"

"Yes," I nodded. Lynch was a good cop. And a pretty good friend.

"I called him. He helped me out on a case once. Told me about you finding this suitcase with some half million dollars in it belonging to some drug dealer. Turning it over to an attorney. He the one who hired you?"

"The dealer was his client."

"Yeah. Split the money with the attorney, who then got cold feet and turned you in."

"Wasn't very nice of him," I agreed.

Colvin must have really needed a cup of coffee. He upended the pot and watched a few drops dribble into my cup. "Ever think about just keeping the whole bundle?"

"Every night I was in prison."

Colvin liked that one. He chuckled for a good minute.

There was a knock on the door, and a waiter carried in a tray with Colvin's coffee and toast. I signed the bill while Colvin went to work on his breakfast.

"You know a man name of Moana Tagaloa?" He pronounced

the name slowly, rolling each vowel around his mouth before blowing it past his lips. "Samoan, I guess."

"Never heard the name before," I said truthfully, though my mind was picturing the giant who'd answered Harry Chapman's door. I waited for the sheriff to drop the other shoe.

"Private investigator, like you," Colvin said. "Only not like you, he's dead."

I poured coffee into my cup. Colvin watched carefully, as if I were a chemist concocting an exotic formula. "Like I said, I never heard of the man."

Colvin reached for the coffeepot, replenished his cup, then put the pot on the far side of the table, out of my reach. "ID on him showed he was from Los Angeles. Found his body in the woods near Zephyr Cove."

He saw the confused look on my face.

" 'Bout fifteen miles from here. In the wonderful state of Nevada, so he's not my problem. Kind of coincidental isn't it? You coming up here, finding one body, then another one pops up, this one a private investigator. Never did like coincidences. You look better this morning, Polo. Those bruises are healing real nice. You don't move quite as stiff as you did yesterday, either."

"When did they find the body?" I asked.

"Daybreak."

I pointed to the bed. "I was right there. Sound asleep."

He smiled unpleasantly. "Any witnesses?"

"Just the hotel computer. I came in a little after midnight. No one was in or out of the room until the waiter brought me breakfast an hour or so ago. But I assume you've already checked that."

He dunked his toast in the coffee. "Assume. Nice word. Yeah. I checked. Smart boy like you could probably figure a way around that door, if he wanted to."

"I'm not that smart, sheriff. Any news of the body in the hot tub?"

"Nah. She drowned all right. Water in the lungs. No marks. No signs of a struggle. Coroner can't peg a time of death. The temperature gauge in the tub showed 101 degrees when I got there. Coroner can't even tell how much alcohol she consumed. Tried Casper's Law, but it's useless."

Casper's Law was a method medical examiners used to get an approximate time of death by measuring the core, or internal, body temperature with that of the ambient, or outer, temperature, and dividing the two figures. "Any of the neighbors see her?"

Colvin swallowed the last half piece of toast in two huge bites. "Nope. I don't figure it to be a suicide, though."

"No note?"

"No. Half of them don't leave notes anyway. But no jewelry on her. Women her age, when they go they usually put on all their best bangles. House was full of necklaces, rings, bracelets. Nice stuff. All she had on was one ring. Big diamond."

I hadn't noticed the ring.

Colvin answered my thought. "Hands were so wrinkled and puffy I didn't see the damn thing until the coroner showed it to me."

"So you're going to treat it as an accident?"

He leaned forward on the chair and rubbed his hands together briskly, as if to get the circulation going. "Not much choice, is there?"

"If it was an accident, you'd think once she got to the bottom of the tub and her hair was sucked into the pipe, that she'd struggle. That there would be some hair pulled from her scalp when she tried to get away. When I looked at the body, I didn't see any sign of that."

"Neither did I, or the coroner." He poured more coffee, then locked his eyes on mine. "Yes, sure is a coincidence you coming up here. Finding one body, then another turning up while you're safely tucked away in bed here. Course we can't tell just when the lady died. And I haven't seen the full Nevada report on the private investigator. I don't know how or when he died. You got an alibi for your time in San Francisco day before you got up here?"

"Yes, in fact I do."

"Someone who can verify where you were day and all night?"

"Yes. A reporter. Jane Tobin."

Colvin arched an eyebrow. "Lady reporter?"

"Very much so. Look, I was surprised as hell to find that body in the hot tub, and I never heard of this man from Los Angeles. People die all the time, Sheriff."

76

"Yep," he concurred. "I'd be out of business if they didn't." Colvin put his palms on his knees and pushed himself to his feet. "We got in touch with George Rochard. He was down in San Diego opening a new store. He'll be up later today. Go home, Polo. You smell like one of those guys that trouble follows around. Get out of my territory."

Maybe it was just Mrs. Damonte's snake oil Colvin was smelling, but I followed his suggestion, packing my bag and checking out of the hotel. I called the airport. The next flight to San Francisco was three hours away. I cashed another check, turning in a twenty-dollar bill for quarters and used the hotel's pay phone to call San Francisco.

"Chapman Investigations," a pleasant voice answered.

"Let me talk to Harry," I said, deepening my voice.

"Who shall I say is calling?"

"Moana Tagaloa."

A few seconds later Chapman came on the line. "Hey, Manny, baby. How are you?"

"Not good, Harry. Not good at all. Manny baby is dead."

"Who the hell is this?" Chapman asked, his voice low and razor sharp.

"Nick Polo, Harry."

"What the hell—"

"And your client's wife, Harry. I found her body yesterday. In her hot tub. It wasn't a pretty sight."

It was a wild shot, but it had all the accuracy that Errol Flynn's arrow did in *The Adventures of Robin Hood* when Errol sent that quiver slicing through the arrow already stuck directly in the middle of the bull's-eye, cleaving it in half and thus winning the hand of the fair maiden. Actually I think Basil Rathbone had him thrown in a dungeon, but eventually good old Errol got the girl.

Chapman finally got his mouth working again. "What the hell are you talking about, Polo? Where are you?"

"Lake Tahoe, Harry. I came up to see Mrs. Rochard about the job she hired John Henning to do for her. The wiretap, Harry."

"Listen," Chapman said, his voice barely above a whisper now. "Stay away from me, Polo."

"What was Tagaloa doing for you, Harry?"

"Nothing. Nothing at all. I know him, that's all. I don't know what the hell you're talking about, Polo. Stay away from me!"

The line went dead. I dropped in some more quarters and called San Francisco again.

"You just caught me, Nick. I've got to go down and testify in court," said Inspector Paul Paulsen, my former partner.

"Paul, I need a favor."

"What else is new?" Paulsen responded sarcastically.

"A driver's license photograph." I gave him Tagaloa's name. "I think that's how it's spelled, Paul. He's from Los Angeles, somewhere in his early thirties."

"You want a rap sheet on him, too?"

"Anything you can get, without leaving your fingerprints all over the computer, Paul. This guy is an ex–private investigator. The ex just happened. They found his body up in Lake Tahoe."

"California side or Nevada side?"

"Nevada."

"Good. That makes it easier. If he died in California my request might be tagged and sent to the investigating officer. What is the reason for my request, by the way?"

"Dinner. House of Prime Rib on Van Ness Avenue."

"Tonight?"

I could almost hear him rubbing his stomach. "Tonight," I agreed. "About seven. Bring the picture, will you?"

"Bring your credit card, Nick. I'm skipping lunch."

CHAPTER THIRTEEN

I GRABBED A CAB at the San Francisco airport and had the driver wait for me while I went to Gene Chaput's shop and picked up the emerald, then went to my flat.

I tried calling Harry Chapman again but couldn't get by his ever-efficient secretary. His home number wasn't listed, so I had to go throw fifty dollars at my phone-company contact again to get the number. No answer. Chapman was taking deep cover, and the way things were going, I couldn't blame him.

I never had much love or respect for Harry, but I couldn't see him involving himself in a murder. I showered, shaved, changed clothes, adding a holstered .32 revolver to my wardrobe. It felt uncomfortable on my hip, even though it was one of the lightest weapons available.

Paul Paulsen was waiting for me in a booth at the House of Prime Rib. Paul's a big, ginger-haired, freckle-faced man who always seems to have a smile on his face. He waved a friendly hand at me, and I joined him.

The restaurant is a throwback to the days when cholesterol was unknown and red meat was considered a health food. The beef is carved from a cart wheeled to your table and fills most of the plate. Huge baked potatoes came with a choice of being smothered in real butter or real sour cream.

Paulsen's hand was wrapped around a highball glass.

"Nice place," he said.

A tuxedoed waiter appeared, and I ordered a glass of the house red.

Paulsen took an envelope from his jacket pocket and handed it to me. "Here's the stuff on Tagaloa," he said.

I upended the contents of the envelope onto the table. There was a faxed copy of Moana Tagaloa's driver's license. The face glaring back at me in the small one-inch-square photograph certainly looked like the man who had answered Harry Chapman's door.

The printout of his driving record showed he was forty-two years of age and lived on Haskell Avenue in Van Nuys.

"You'll find the rap sheet interesting, Nick," Paulsen said, wiggling his empty glass under the waiter's nose when he brought my glass of wine.

The rap sheet was interesting indeed. There were more than a dozen arrests. I scanned the coded and abbreviated rap sheets, deciphering the computer shorthand for aka, VC, PC, asslt. bdy hrm. There were a half-dozen arrests for possession of controlled substances, all discharged by the DA for "questionable search and seizure," and an equal amount of batteries and assaults with a deadly weapon. The government had wasted a lot of paper and manpower on Tagaloa. I couldn't find one conviction.

There was a notation seven years ago showing he was an applicant with the Bureau of Collection and Investigative Services.

"Drugs and assaults. Nice guy," I said, my hand searching for my drink.

"What's your interest in this character, Nick?"

I told Paulsen the whole story over dinner.

"So what are you going to do now?" he asked, eyes searching for the dessert cart.

"I don't know, Paul. What do you think Inspector Larry Drake will do if I drop this information in his lap?"

Paulsen listened to the waiter recite the dessert possibilities with rapt attention. "I think it will be the cheesecake," he finally said with all the gravity of a jury foreman announcing guilt or innocence.

"Drake probably won't do much, Nick," Paulsen said after a small, exploratory bite of the cheesecake. "What have you got really? Was Henning actually working for this Rochard lady? Any proof other than what this bartender told you? And what about Mrs. Rochard? Are we sure it was her in the tub?"

"No, but the odds against it are off the board."

"So it is her. But was it accidental? This Tahoe sheriff, what's his name?"

"Colvin. Eric Colvin."

Paulsen took a bigger bite of the cake, chewing it slowly as if he hated for it to pass from his teeth down his throat.

"Colvin. Don't know him. Any good?"

"Seemed to be a competent guy. If Mrs. Rochard was killed, it was a real professional job." I tapped the pocket on my sport coat where I'd put Moana Tagaloa's rap sheet. "Tagaloa looks like he could fit the bill. No one gets arrested that many times for assault unless he's stupid or he's being paid to rough someone up."

"And not one conviction," Paul said. "He's a pro."

I pushed my untouched cheesecake to Paulsen's side of the table. He was right. The real pros don't serve much time. "He's the kicker all right, Paul. He was at Harry Chapman's house, then he winds up dead a few miles from the Rochard place in Lake Tahoe."

I took out the small emerald and rolled it, marblelike, across the starched tablecloth to him.

"I found that in John Henning's safe-deposit box. There were three more just like it. Rochard runs a chain of jewelry stores."

Paul picked up the stone, rubbed it between his fingers, then rolled it back to me.

"All interesting stuff," he agreed. He took my full dessert plate, placing his empty one in front of me, so the waiter wouldn't think he was a little piggy. "But unless you can tie it together somehow, Drake isn't going to work up a sweat over it."

"Any suggestions?"

Paulsen held his fork up in front of his face. "Maybe some cherries on top," he said, then put the fork back to work.

"Just club soda," I told Winky Harris when he approached me.

Harris fixed the drink, then set it in front of me.

"You look a lot better tonight," he said, his eyes scanning my face.

"A lot better than Sharon Rochard does now."

The frozen smile on his face started to thaw. "What did Sharon say?"

Before I could answer, a group at the end of the bar called down orders for drinks.

Audrey hopped by with an empty tray, spotted me, and came over, greeting me like a long lost friend. "Hi, where's Jane tonight?"

"Somewhere else."

"Did she say anything about doing that story on me?"

"She asked me to help her on it, dig up a little background on you?"

"Really?" she said, her mascaraed eyes suddenly blinking rapidly. "Really?" she repeated.

"Would I lie?" I asked.

She settled her drink tray on the bar and adjusted the elastic bands on her blouse. "You guys. You'd all sell your grandmother's tombstones for a quick feel."

"You must have a basement full of tombstones."

Her blue eyes lost some of their innocence. "What's that supposed to mean?"

"It was a compliment, Audrey. I mean men must be falling all over you all the time. The night my friend was in here—the man I showed you the picture of—did you notice a big Samoan hanging around?"

She blinked and put a finger at the edge of her right eye. "Damn contacts. I tried going for the soft ones, but they just don't work for me. What did you say? Samoans? We don't get many Samoans in here. I think the last time—"

Winky Harris leaned across the bar and tapped her on the shoulder. "What do you need?"

"Manhattan up, two V.O. and waters, and a gin over with a slash of 7UP," she recited in a bored voice.

Harris went about making the drink order. Audrey edged up to me. "You know, I like you, but I wouldn't want to make a move if you're going with Jane. She's a real class lady."

"Yes, she is," I agreed. "But we have an arrangement. Just friends. We see other people when we want to."

82

"Yeah, I bet," she snorted. "You and every guy that comes in here has an arrangement." She went over and picked up her filled drink order.

"What did Sharon say?" Harris asked, ignoring a call for his services down at the end of the bar again.

"She's dead. I went up to Lake Tahoe and found her dead at the bottom of her hot tub."

"Jesus Christ," Harris said, loud enough to stop the conversation of the people at the bar. "You kidding me?"

"No. It should have been in tonight's paper. If not, it'll be in the morning's."

Harris shook his head rapidly from side to side as if he was trying to dislodge a insect that had settled into his hair. "Jesus, that's the shits. She was a nice lady."

"How well did you really know her?" I asked him.

He stared at me with flat eyes for a full minute. "Not well. We dated a few times, that's all."

The boys at the end of the bar were getting rowdy. Harris wiped his hands on his pant legs and went down to serve them.

I waited, rattling the ice cubes in my glass. I had the feeling someone was boring holes in my back. I swiveled on my seat and saw little José, standing at the open kitchen door. He was rocking back and forth on his heels. I made a gun out of my hand and pulled the mock trigger, then used the same hand to pull back my sport coat and show him the holster. He just kept glaring. I mouthed the words "green card." Still he stared. Guns didn't worry him, and he didn't read lips. If he ever became a citizen, George Bush wouldn't get his vote.

Harris came back to ring up the drink order on the cash register.

"Did you ever see Sharon with a big Samoan?"

Harris screwed up his face. "Samoan? No. Like I said, I just saw her a couple of times."

"Were you ever up to Tahoe with her?"

"No. She really die in the tub?"

"Hair got caught in the suction."

"Was she . . . was she drunk?"

I pushed my empty glass over to him. "Couldn't tell. She was in that hot water too long." I handed him one of my business cards. "How about Harry Chapman. Ever see Sharon with Chapman?"

"The private eye that's always in the paper? No. Like I say, Sharon was a nice lady, but it was just fun, you know what I mean?"

"Sure. Just fun." I left him staring at his shoes. Audrey gave me a wave, circling her index finger around as if she was dialing a phone, and said, "Call me."

I waved back and looked toward the kitchen door. José was nowhere in sight. I kept my hand on the butt of the .32 all the way to the car.

CHAPTER FOURTEEN

I SET BOTH THE coffee maker and the alarm to go off at a quarter to six the following morning. By ten after I had showered and filled a thermos with coffee. I made a quick stop at Dianda's Bakery for some calorie-dripping pastry confections with apricots, picked up a morning *Chronicle* at the stand on Green and Columbus, and fifteen minutes later was parked up the street from Harry Chapman's house.

The *Chronicle* had a brief story on Sharon Rochard's death, headlined "Jeweler's wife dies in hot tub tragedy."

There was no mention of the possibility of murder, and the body had been released to the family, which meant that old Sheriff Colvin was not going to treat it as anything but an accident. A funeral was scheduled for tomorrow.

By nine-fifteen I had a lap full of pastry crumbs, ink-stained hands from the paper, an empty thermos, and an urgent need for a men's room. There had been no sign of life, coming or going, around Chapman's house.

I climbed out of the car, grateful for the opportunity to stretch, and hiked over to his place. The fog was gone already, the light-blue sky cloudless. Sparrows were zooming in and out of the ficus trees planted in front of Chapman's front steps. I rang his doorbell for several minutes. The door was very solid, and the leaded windows nearby looked to be locked. I stared at the ATZ burglar alarm company's decal in disgust.

I checked under the doormat and an adobe clay flowerpot filled with bright yellow mums. No key.

Chapman's Victorian was attached to the houses on either side, so there was no way to get to the back, except through his garage door.

I drove to his office, which was located at Pier 9, at the foot of Davis Street. A working tugboat was tied up alongside the dock, its mooring lines creaking like an old spring mattress as it rocked lightly in the murky green bay waters. A polished brass plate the size of an envelope announced the door to Chapman's office. Another sticker from the burglar alarm company was stuck on the wall next to the door. At least it wasn't locked. The furniture was all chrome and black leather Eames chairs. The walls were painted a frosty white. Black metal–framed Andy Warhol prints of Liz Taylor and Liza Minnelli bracketed a Danish-modern walnut desk. Chapman's secretary was a coolly attractive, olive-skinned brunette with ashen gray eyes. She wore a double-breasted jacket and matching skirt in black-and-white mini-houndstooth check. She looked all business, and she looked like she knew her business.

"Is Harry in?" I asked casually.

"Not at the moment, sir."

I waited for further information. She let me wait.

"Do you know when he'll be in?" I asked.

She wasn't volunteering anything. "Who are you, sir?"

"George Rochard."

Her beautiful face folded into a disappointed frown. Wrong name. No doubt she'd seen Rochard. And no doubt Rochard didn't often dress in faded Levi's and a hooded sweatshirt. Of course he didn't pull too many early morning surveillance jobs, either. "George Rochard suggested I see Harry," I said hurriedly, then lowered my voice to an almost hush. "It's about Mrs. Rochard."

She still wasn't budging. "Such a terrible thing, wasn't it? Who did you say you were, sir?"

"Polo," I admitted. "Nick Polo."

Those gray eyes turned a steely color, and she picked up a pen and scribbled down my name on a notepad. "I'll be sure and tell him you were by, Mr. Polo. Where can he reach you?"

I gave her my number. "Thanks very much, Ms. . . ."

"Parker," she responded, somewhat reluctantly. I got the feeling she hated giving anything away. Even her name. Whatever failings Harry Chapman had, his secretary was not one of them. She protected him like an offensive line protects a Super Bowl quarterback.

There were two messages on my answering machine when I got back home: one from Sheriff Eric Colvin in Lake Tahoe, the other from Jane Tobin.

I called Colvin first.

"I thought you might be curious about that Samoan private eye fella, Mr. Polo."

"Anything interesting?" I asked.

"Well, he's got cards in his wallet saying he was a private investigator, but I called Sacramento. They pulled his license years ago."

"Maybe they were old cards," I suggested.

"Yeah, maybe. Died of an overdose. Cocaine. Medical examiner said his nose was about to fall off. That's why he switched to using a needle, I guess." I could hear the rustling of papers, then Colvin said, "Official cause of death a cerebral hemorrhage. All that cocaine caused a great discharge of blood into his brain. I wonder if there's any pain that way? Probably too high to feel anything."

I remembered Moana Tagaloa's glassy eyes and his wiping his nose when he answered Chapman's door.

"Had a good-sized stash with him," Colvin continued. "Couple of ounces in the car, which was a rental from Reno. Picked up the day before you found Mrs. Rochard."

"I see her funeral is tomorrow, Sheriff."

"Yep. Mr. Rochard was pretty insistent on having the arrangements done right away. Can't say I blame him too much."

"So you think it was an accident?"

"Nothing to prove otherwise." He paused. "Right now. That Tagaloa fellow. I checked his record. Not a nice boy."

"Oh?"

"Rough character. You sure you never ran into him before?"

"I don't get down to Los Angeles very often, Sheriff."

"Nice evasive answer. Tagaloa had almost two thousand dollars in cash in his wallet. Lots of other junk, pictures of girls almost in swimsuits, a couple of rubbers. That kind of thing. And a business card of another one of you San Francisco private eyes. John Henning. You know him?"

It took me a while to respond. "I knew him, Sheriff. Henning died recently. The police say it was a suicide."

"Lot of that going around, isn't there, Polo? Keep in touch."

Colvin hung up without saying good-bye. I went to the kitchen and poured myself a stiff Jack Daniels. It was a waste of good whiskey. It might as well have been Mrs. D.'s rock 'n' rye. I didn't taste a drop.

I called Jane at the paper, but she was out of the office.

I walked the three blocks to the North Beach Library and dug the Los Angeles phone book out of the reference section and flipped through the yellow pages until coming to "Investigators." There were seven pages, some with large ads showing the investigator's picture, others with drawings of blinking eyes, men in trench coats, scales of justice, bull's-eye targets, and for some reason several with eagles, wings spread, talons clenched. About half of the ads had the investigator's state license number, the others did not, and it was a reasonable guess that half of those were unlicensed. If you ever do find yourself in need of a private investigator, I'll give you a tip. The bigger the ad, the more reason for skepticism.

Tagaloa just had a plain old listing, under the name Tagaloa and Company, with an address on Sunset Boulevard. I copied down the phone number, then looked him up in the white pages. Same address and number.

I stopped at the Bohemian Cafe for a meatball sandwich, then waddled up the hill to my flat.

I called the *Bulletin*. Jane Tobin was back at her desk.

"When are you going to repay me for that dinner at the Jefferson Park?" she asked in a mocking tone.

"Can't tonight. I've got a stakeout."

"Is it on the Henning case?"

"Yes. Don't know how long it'll take."

"I'll join you."

"Jane, it'll be long, boring, cold, dull."

I realized the opening I'd given her before the last word was out. She jumped right in.

"Like most of our dates, Nicky. What time do you start?"

"About six tonight." I gave her the address.

"You bring something to drink. I'll pick up the eats."

I dialed the Los Angeles number for Tagaloa and Company, expecting to hear an answering service or a recorded message. The phone was picked up immediately as though they were waiting at the other end.

"Tagaloa and Company," said a strong male voice that sounded amazingly like that of the Samoan I'd met at Harry Chapman's doorstep.

"Mr. Tagaloa?" I asked.

"Yep."

"Then this must be a long-distance call. Moana Tagaloa died in Lake Tahoe a couple of days ago."

"Who are you?"

"Sheriff Colvin."

"What's your number? I call you right back," he said quickly.

I remembered that the area code for Nevada was 702, so I gave him that and the first seven numbers that popped into my head. "Just who are you? There are still some questions about Mr. Tagaloa's death."

"I call you," he said firmly, then disconnected loud enough for me to pull the phone from my ear. Whoever he was, he was smart enough not to talk to someone on the phone without checking out his ID. I dialed the number again; it was busy. I wondered briefly what part of Nevada he would get connected to.

"You were right," Jane admitted. "This is boring." She leaned over my shoulder and pointed to a lighted window in the house next to Harry Chapman's. "Someone keeps walking back and forth behind that shade. I bet they think we're up to something kinky."

We were sprawled in the back seat of my car amidst wrappers from McDonald's. "There's not enough room to be kinky here."

Jane picked up her third cheeseburger and began to demolish

it. I poured some Sterling Vineyards zinfandel into a paper cup and handed it to her.

"But what if that person thought we were doing something kinky and called the police?"

"I already called the cops. Gave them my license number and told them I was on a surveillance."

She took a sip of the wine, swished it around her mouth, and smiled. "That's nice."

"Yes. A perfect complement to cold, greasy hamburgers and limp french fries."

She pouted. "You don't like McDonald's? That's anti-American."

"The Japanese will probably buy them out any day now. Sushi burgers. Might be an improvement."

"What are you going to do when you see Chapman?" she asked in between bites.

"Talk to him."

"That's all?"

"He's tied into it. I think I can scare him into talking. He's the only connection I've got right now."

"So we sit and wait," Jane said, balling up the hamburger wrapper and napkin then tossing it over the front seat in the general direction of the now-empty McDonald's bag she'd brought with her a couple of hours earlier.

We sat and waited. I told her about Sheriff Colvin's call and Henning's business card showing up in Tagaloa's wallet. We discussed the various aspects of that for a while, then passed the time with small talk about movies, political scandals, and rumors on the sex lives of various sports celebrities.

By nine-thirty there was still no sign of Chapman, and Jane was fidgeting in her seat.

"Tinkle time," she said.

"Why don't you take off. I'm going to stick it out until midnight."

She didn't need much encouragement. "Okay," she said, gathering up her belongings. "What about tomorrow?"

"Mrs. Rochard's funeral."

"My, my, you certainly know how to treat a girl to a good time. Two funerals and an exciting stakeout all in a week."

"You don't have to go to the funeral. In fact I don't remember inviting you."

She patted my cheek gently. "What time?"

"Funeral is at eleven, over in Danville."

"I'll pick you up at ten." She wrinkled her nose and looked around the car's interior. "We'll take my car. I've had enough of this one for a while."

I watched her in the rearview mirror as she hiked up the hill to her little white VW convertible. She gave a toot of the horn and a cheery wave as she drove by me.

I picked up the remains of our gourmet meal and climbed into the front seat. My mind wandered around, trying to figure out just how a rich, fashionable, high-rolling-type lady like Sharon Rochard would hook up with a private eye like John Henning. She seemed much more likely to call upon an investigator with one of those gaudy phone book ads. Henning was like me, he abandoned the yellow pages to get away from the crazies that called in the middle of the night wanting their spouses tailed, or the ones that are sure their neighbors are from deep beyond the friendly skies and are shooting death rays at them. So how did she make contact with Henning? What did they have in common? An attorney could have recommended John to her, but the Rochards seemed the type to use attorneys who shunned three-piece suits and conducted most of their work around the pool or at the golf course. Besides, if I was right about Henning tapping phones for Mrs. Rochard, she certainly wouldn't use one of her husband's attorneys. Or would she? According to Audrey, the cocktail waitress, Mrs. Rochard belted down Tequila martinis like they were water. She was attracted to Winky, a bartender, and when I found her in the hot tub, there'd been a bottle of tequila on the tub's rim. So she liked booze. And Henning was a recovering alcoholic. Another blank. The emeralds in John's safe-deposit box had to come from Mrs. Rochard. Payment in lieu of a check or cash. At least that was the way it seemed now. But I'd been in this racket long enough to know that nothing is ever really the way it seems to be.

Would Tagaloa be stupid enough to kill Henning and shove

91

one of John's cards in his wallet? Where the hell did he get the card? From Sharon Rochard? Just before he killed her? But John was already dead by then.

I waited until eleven, turned the motor over, and drove out in search of a rest room, settling for a Chevron station near Fisherman's Wharf. I drove by Chapman's office. There was no sign of life, just the creaking of piers, barking of seals, and moaning of foghorns from the bay. I parked a block away and began searching the streets for the proper tool for the job I had in mind, settling on a fist-size rock near the railroad tracks.

The wind was picking up, whitecapping the gunmetal bay waters. I got within fifteen feet of the door to Chapman's office, went into a windup that would never cause Roger Clemens a moment of worry, and heaved the rock at the window alongside the door.

The crashing sound was partially muffled by the wind, but it was loud enough to make me hurry back to the car. At least there was no ringing alarm. Chapman no doubt had a silent system wired directly to the alarm company. I turned on the engine, got the heater going, put the car in reverse, and backed up half a block.

It took almost ten minutes for the first black-and-white police car to get to the scene. A partner joined it minutes later, and finally a light-blue sedan with a red light on the roof and the emblem ATZ ALARMS printed on the doors arrived.

The black-and-whites hung around for fifteen minutes, then took off. A minor incident. They'd make out a quick, one-page report, more for insurance purposes than anything else. Chapman would no doubt contact his carrier to take care of the loss. I felt a tiny bit of guilt at the costs incurred. Then I remembered my premium payments and the guilt washed away quicker than a campaign promise.

Just to be safe I backed up a half block, got a pair of binoculars from the trunk, and waited.

It wasn't long. A burnished silver BMW sedan, one of the big ones—I can never get the models straight or the numbers right—pulled in behind the alarm-company sedan.

I focused in the binoculars. The grim, unsmiling face of Ms.

Parker was visible above the steering wheel. In the passenger seat was Mr. Chapman himself.

They both exited the car, leaving the motor running and the headlights on. Chapman was wearing a trench coat tossed over his shoulders. Parker was neatly turned out in gray slacks, a matching sweater, and a black beret. I had the feeling that she woke up in the morning looking like the ladies do in the movies: hair neat and makeup on.

They disappeared into Chapman's office, coming out a few minutes later, Chapman waving his arms at the poor alarm man like a soon-to-be-fired Yankee manager disputing a close play at home plate with the umpire.

Parker stood by, arms folded across her chest, finally tapping Chapman on his trench-coated shoulder and gesturing toward the car.

There wasn't much traffic, so I was able to let the BMW stay a block or so ahead of me as it wound its way around the deserted streets, past barricades and over metal-plated ramps, remnants of the ongoing repairs resulting from the October '89 earthquake. There was an article in the paper the other day pointing out the fact that the two great bridges, the Golden Gate and the Bay Bridge, were both completed in only four years. Four years. It was going to take the masterminds of city and state agencies that long just to decide what they might do to the various buildings and roadways hit so hard on the evening of the quake. It wasn't the disaster itself that had killed off all too many restaurants and small businesses. It was the bumbling bureaucrats and their passing the blame and an empty hat that was drying up some of the best parts of San Francisco. The city wizards wanted the state to pay for everything; the state naturally wanted the federal government to open its wallet. They all know it's the same wallet in the long run—ours. But their only concern about the long run is getting elected again. So now too many of the shops that make a city a city are dying: the dry cleaner that replaces the buttons they break, the coffee shop where the waitress greets you by name and tells the cook to start on your "usual" before you order it. The shoe-repair place that gives you a free shine when putting on new heels and soles, the bookstore that stocks a few copies each of thousands of different books, rather than thousands of copies of a few books. And in their place we get franchise shopping mall retailers, with cash registers that don't have numbers, just pictures of soft drinks, hamburgers, or french fries, so as not to confuse the help who are in a constant daze wondering why they're working for peanuts when they should be rock stars. Instead of the mom-and-pop grocers, who go down to the produce mart at three in the morning to pick out the cream of the crop and who encourage you to take a bite of the peach to see how sweet it is, we get mini-supermarkets with plasticized food, wrapped, sealed, and stamped with a bar code so the clerk can run your order through without once looking you in the eye.

Pleasant thoughts about dictatorship flashed across my vision as I slowed down for the various bumps and metal plates spanning the ever-enlarging potholes.

Parker was an efficient driver, never going even a mile over the speed limit and using her turn signal at every opportunity. I followed her out Sacramento Street, to Van Ness, then straight west on Geary Boulevard. The fog thickened block by block, turning into a heavy mist. Parker turned left on Masonic. She made a few more left turns, finally pulling into a driveway on the one hundred block of Fortuna Avenue. Fortuna was a two-block affair on the border of the fast-remodeling Western Addition area of the city and the more prestigious Laurel Heights section, filled with two-unit flats, all with bland stucco fronts and aluminum windows. Functional and easy to maintain was the kindest thing you could say of them.

I doused my headlights and coasted to a stop, watching as Chapman got out of the car, slamming the door behind him. Parker followed, and they disappeared into the front of the building. Moments later the lights went on in an upper-floor window.

The terrazzo steps were slippery from the fog and mist. Parker's front door had another of those ATZ decals, one of those small peepholes. I wondered if Chapman owned stock in the burglar alarm company while I banged my hand against the door. The metal plate on the peephole slid open, and I heard Chapman yell, "Shit."

"Open up, Harry. I want to talk to you."

I could hear the scraping of the door chain over Chapman's mumblings. He swung the door open and gestured me inside with his nasty looking SIG-Sauer automatic.

"You son of a bitch. It was you, wasn't it? You son of a bitch."

Chapman had discarded his trench coat. He was wearing a royal-blue jogging suit and high-topped running shoes. The shoulder holster looked ridiculous against the shiny jogging-suit material.

"Put that away, Harry. You're going to hurt someone, and it might be me."

Chapman seemed to have a one-track mind. "You son of a bitch," he repeated, waving the gun around like a conductor leading "The Battle Hymn of the Republic" on the Fourth of July.

"Calm down, Harry," Parker said, patting Chapman gently on the shoulder. "My neighbors downstairs are light sleepers."

"Shit, Elaine, I'm telling you, this . . . "

"Call me a bastard instead of a son of a bitch this time will you, Harry," I interjected. "And Elaine, tell him to do something sensible with that gun."

Chapman stared at my face, his eyes drifting down, charting a course to my jugular vein.

"That wasn't very nice of you, breaking our office window like that, Mr. Polo," Elaine Parker said, turning on her heel and retreating into the living room area. She sank gently down onto an overstuffed black leather couch. The room looked as if it was done by the same designer who did Chapman's office—sleek, modern, a little hard looking, with bone-white walls dotted with acrylic paintings. No Andy Warhol here, just jagged rainbow slashes of color portraying nothing but what was in the artist's mind.

"Office window?" I said innocently, brushing past Chapman and flopping down at the opposite end of the couch.

Parker studied me through half-closed eyes. "Yes, the alarm company said the window was broken at eleven-forty-nine."

Eleven-forty-nine. Not ten to twelve or around midnight. She had it down to the minute. I rubbed a thumb under my chin. "Eleven-forty-nine. Why, I don't think I was within a stone's throw of your offices at that time."

Her sleepy cat's eyes opened fully for a moment, then went back to half-mast.

"Not very funny," she said. "Now that you found us, what do you want?"

I turned to face Chapman. He was poised like a tightrope walker about to edge off the platform. At least the gun was now pointed at the floor.

"I just wanted to talk to you, Harry. About Moana Tagaloa. And Sharon Rochard." I looked at Elaine Parker. "Both of them are dead. Both died in Lake Tahoe. Did you know that, Elaine? Tagaloa was a houseguest of Harry's a couple of days ago, and ⸍ Mrs. Rochard was a client. Now they're both dead. Just like my friend John Henning."

No reaction from her. I might as well have been reading her the weather report.

Chapman reacted, though. He was back on his son of a bitch kick. "You're full of shit. Completely full of shit," he yelled, then took three quick strides across the room and shoved the gun inches from my nose. "Get out of here, you son of a bitch."

Harry's eyes were dancing around in his head. His breathing was hard and labored, but the gun barrel didn't seem to move a fraction of an inch.

I got up very slowly. "Take it easy, Harry. We have to talk. You know that. Why don't you put the gun away and we can—"

"Leave now, Mr. Polo," Elaine Parker said in a calm, well-modulated voice. "I'll set up an appointment for you and Mr. Chapman in the near future."

How's that for cool? Her boss looks as if he's ready to come unglued, waving a deadly weapon under the nose of a man who she damn well knows just busted their office window and she's going to arrange an appointment in the near future.

I flicked my eyes away briefly from Chapman's gun and gave her a tight smile. "I'll look forward to hearing from you."

CHAPTER FIFTEEN

"You mean after all that, you didn't learn a thing?" Jane Tobin asked, pulling her car over to the side of the road opposite the tollgates on the Bay Bridge and within sniffing distance of the East Bay sewage-treatment plant.

It was an area designated for towing cars that had broken down on the bridge. Jane's little convertible was running fine, the only problem, from her point of view, was that the top was up and that now, since we were almost to Oakland, the skies had turned blue. When Jane saw blue skies the top had to come down even though at this time of the year your skin started turning a similar hue. Los Angeles is for convertibles. San Francisco is a hardtop town.

There must be an unwritten law in the Volkswagen sales manuals that says that their convertibles will only be sold to attractive young women. The next time you're driving down the freeway and are bored with trying to decipher personalized license plates, check out the VW ragtops. Nine out of ten of the drivers will look like models on their way to a photo assignment. Jane being no exception, a couple of cars driven by middle-aged good samaritans, including a Highway Patrol cruiser, slowed down with ideas of lending a helping hand, only to speed up again when they saw me already on the job. It took no more than a couple of minutes to lower the top, and we were on our way again, maneuvering onto and off of freeways with designated numbers such as 80, 580, over 880 to 980 and finally to the lowly number 24, all of this in a matter of a few miles. The morning traffic reports were beginning to sound like a breakdown of Einstein's theory as the con-

97

fused reporter advised the even-more-confused commuter what routes to take and which ones to avoid due to the inevitable "overturned big rig." Maybe it's the irresistible pull of nostalgia, but I'd be willing to bet that until just a few years ago I'd never heard of one of those big monsters overturning. Now, not a day went by when a couple of them weren't overending, spreading their loads—which more than likely were, in the deeply serious voice of the announcer, "possibly toxic"—across all lanes of traffic.

Even though the commute hour was over, the roads were still bumper-to-bumper as Jane pointed the Volkswagen's nose in a more or less easterly direction. We got past the heavily industrialized sections of Oakland, the view now of the thickly wooded Berkeley Hills. The gleaming, ocean-liner white bulk of the Claremont Hotel blinked in the sun shortly before we disappeared into the Caldecott Tunnel. Traveling east you enter the narrow, ceramic-tiled tunnel in Alameda County and exit in Contra Costa County, a sudden change of at least five degrees in temperature and ten percent in property taxes.

The sky was almost all blue now, and Jane gave me a smug smile as I fiddled with the car's radio dial, the Dave Brubeck version of "Maria" turning into a mass of static now that we were out of range of KJAZ's transmitter. I ran the dial on both the AM and FM bands, finally giving up, and plowed through Jane's glove box in search of a cassette.

"You never answered my question," Jane said, brushing away strands of her copper-colored hair that crossed her sunglasses like out-of-control windshield wipers. "You didn't really learn a thing from Chapman or his secretary, did you?"

"It sounds more like an accusation than a question. I did learn something last night. Harry Chapman is scared to death."

"Of who?"

"Not me," I said, saddened by the revelation that Jane had somehow become a hard rock fan. Her glove box was filled with cassettes showing pictures of young men and women in black leather costumes of various sizes, who looked like they could scare gangs of Hell's Angels away from a free drug party. They had names like Judas Priest, The Sisters of Mercy, The Cult, War Zone, and Lizard Lickers.

"They're for a story I'm doing," Jane explained. "Some of them are pretty good."

I took her word for it and settled for silence. We played the highway numbers game again, this time turning south on 680. The hills that weren't covered with new housing tracts were still a rich green, freckled with bright yellow mustard weed and oak trees. Soon the sun would turn them brown, and assayers and surveyors would plod the trails once roamed by mountain lions and deer, mapping out the blueprints for yet another tract of homes.

They are having their way. Not the good theys, as in, they say that falling in love is wonderful, or the theys that say big bands are coming back. The bad theys, the ones that aren't going to be happy until every inch of livable space from Marin County to San Jose is paved over. And when that dark day finally comes, the Northern California theys will send the signal to the Southern California theys. First one who paves his way to somewhere mid-state, like Bakersfield, wins the game.

The Woodland Chapel and Crematorium was located over a dry creek in the little town of Danville. Jane nudged her car under the sheltering protection of a massive oak tree. We trooped along across a raked gravel walkway with a group of well-dressed people, all white, middle-aged, the men in dark suits and ties, the women in well-cut dresses of subdued colors, all smiling those sad little smiles people do at funerals, not really sure if the person they're smiling at is a relative of the deceased.

The chapel itself was of redwood, dome-shaped, the walls lined with multicolored floral sprays. We took a seat in the rear.

Sharon Rochard's casket sat squarely in the center of the altar at the front of the chapel. The lid was closed. I remembered how the poor woman had looked when the sheriff's men had pulled her from the hot tub. No doubt she had once been a beautiful woman. I was ten or so when one of my aunts went sobbing up to the coffin, tugging at poor Uncle Julio's sleeve, trying to pull him out of the box and almost succeeding. Ever since I've been an advocate for closed coffins at all funerals. The thought of a deceased loved one's rigid features being slathered with lipstick, makeup, and hair spray just so the survivors could say, "She hadn't looked that good in years," made no sense at all to me.

Most of the guests dutifully strode up to pay their last respects. A tall man with dark hair shot with gray, in a pin-striped charcoal suit, greeted each one with a slight bow of the neck and a handshake. His back was to me, so I couldn't get a good look at him.

Mrs. Damonte would have been disappointed. No long sermons. No rosary. Just a simple, ten-minute ceremony by an elderly gentleman in a shiny blue suit.

Jane leaned over and whispered in my ear. "That was quick. Where do they do the—" she hesitated, rolling a hand over as she searched for the right word, finally settling for, "burning of the coffin and everything?"

"Right here on the premises. Maybe we should have put the convertible's top up."

She looked at me with blank eyes.

"The ashes will hardly show on the white paint, but it'll play hell with the upholstery."

Jane dug two sharp fingers into my ribs just as the blue-suited minister made an announcement: "Mr. Rochard thanks you all for attending our services this morning and asked me to invite you all to his home for refreshments."

We stood outside as the subdued crowd made their way to their cars. No sign of Harry Chapman or anyone else that I recognized.

Jane got behind a series of Mercedes and BMWs, and we wound our way past a couple of golf courses, through the security gate guarding Blackhawk, the caravan eventually pulling into the curving driveway of a large, rambling house built to resemble a French château, all pale gray, with a mansard roof. Jane parked alongside a shoulder-high privet hedge bordering a tennis court.

The path leading to the house was lined with graceful poplar trees. A family of quail played follow-the-leader across a lawn the size of a small airport runway.

"All it needs is a moat," Jane said, her high heels snapping firmly on the tile walkway.

We followed an anonymous group into the house. An ancient Italian marble fountain with a muscle-bound gentleman carrying a jar over his right shoulder sat in the middle of the terrazzo floor. At one time water had dripped out of the jar. Just looking at it got me thirsty.

A cantilevered staircase led upstairs. Richly woven tapestries followed the bend of the stairs, and high overhead were frescoes of muscle-bound men, possibly related to the water-jug chap, locked in either combat or early S & M foreplay.

We followed our leaders through a massive dining room out to the back of the house. Tables had been set up alongside a lap pool, some hundred feet in length but only ten feet wide. I looked down into the sparkling blue water. It didn't appear to be more than four feet deep. The decking on each side of the pool was glazed ceramic tile, in a blue that almost matched the water.

"Food at last," Jane said, marching right to the tables, picking up a plate and shoveling up portions of potato salad, raw vegetables, and slices of turkey and roast beef.

A suntanned young man in chinos and a heavily starched blue shirt came by with a tray of champagne glasses. I grabbed a couple of the glasses and waited for Jane, surveying the crowd, again coming up with blanks.

"Aren't you supposed to be doing some detecting?" Jane asked, relieving me of one of the glasses.

"Yes. I'm going looking for George Rochard."

"I'll circulate, see if I can pick up any juicy gossip," she said, looking down at her nearly empty plate and glancing back at the serving tables.

The food and wine had loosened things up, and the after-funeral silence was gradually building up to cocktail party volume.

"Seen George?" I asked several times, finally getting an answer from the man with the drink tray that he was, "probably in his study."

The next problem was locating the study. I kept knocking softly on doors and opening them a crack, finally hitting pay dirt.

A distinguished-looking gentleman in a charcoal-gray pin-striped suit coat was sitting behind a desk, telephone against one ear, the palm of his hand against the other. He looked up at me briefly, then lowered his voice and continued his conversation.

Whoever the decorators were, they liked yellow. The walls were a soft lemon color, with white-trim scalloped moldings around the ceilings. Oil paintings covered the wall: A life-size eighteenth-century–looking character dolled up in red velvet was sitting down on a rock, holding a book in one hand, a painful expression on his face, possibly due to the rock. Single flowers, landscapes, scenes of horses pulling sleighs through the snow, a serious-looking woman playing the harp. The carpeting was yellow and red fleur-de-lis. Two paisley-print overstuffed chairs bracketed the fireplace.

The man hung up the phone and stood up. He was well over six feet, his hair was thinning in front and carefully sprayed in place. He wore a pair of gold-rimmed glasses over ball bearing eyes.

"Can I help you?" he asked, his voice hard and belligerent.

"Mr. Rochard?"

"Yes."

"I'm Nick Polo."

"Polo?" His eyebrows knitted together. "Do I know you? Were you a friend of my wife?"

"I never spoke to your wife. But I found her body at Lake Tahoe."

"Ah, that's where I heard the name," Rochard said, his voice dropping almost out of hearing. He took a deep breath, then squared his shoulders. "The sheriff said you were an investigator. Sharon was a witness to an accident of some sort."

"I'm a private investigator, Mr. Rochard. So was John Henning."

The name seemed to have no effect on Rochard. He said nothing. I waited him out.

"I'm sorry," he finally said, "but I don't know the name. Is he investigating the accident Sharon witnessed, too?"

"No. I found his body, too. I think he was working for your wife."

Rochard shook his head side to side violently. His cheeks and double chin wobbled, but the hair spray did its job. Not a strand moved.

"Sharon would have no reason to hire a private investigator, Mr. Polo. None at all."

I reached in my pants pocket for the emerald and dropped it in the center of Rochard's desk. "Henning had a bunch of these in his safe-deposit box. He was seen with Mrs. Rochard a few days before he died. I think she hired John to do a job for her."

Rochard stared at the emerald.

"It's called a drop of oil, isn't it, Mr. Rochard? Colombian."

Rochard reached out slowly for the gem. His fingers were long, the nails well kept. He picked up the emerald between his thumb and index finger and brought it close to his glasses, then he placed it in his palm, rolling it around as if assessing the weight. "Where did you say you got this?"

I held out an open hand toward him and he rolled the emerald like a dice across the desk toward me. "From John Henning's safe-deposit box, Mr. Rochard. Henning was a specialist. His specialty was electronics. Bugging telephones. That kind of thing. There were several tapes in the box also. They were labeled with your name."

Rochard flinched back as if I'd struck him. He opened his mouth to speak but nothing came out.

"John Henning was murdered, Rochard. I think your wife was too. I think—"

The door burst open and a middle-aged woman in a pearl-gray dress stormed into the room. "George, what are you doing in here? The guests are asking about you. Don't you think you should be out there. After all—"

She stopped when she saw the expression on Rochard's face. His complexion had gone gray and sweat was cascading down his forehead.

"George, dear. Are you all right?" She swiveled to face me. "Should I call a doctor?"

"No, no need for that, Martha." Rochard took a handkerchief from his back pocket and mopped his brow. "Martha, this is Mr. Polo. Mr. Polo, my sister Martha, down from Seattle. Mr. Polo was just leaving. We'll have to continue our conversation later."

"Sure. Have Harry Chapman set up an appointment." Rochard's sister stepped in between us, so I wasn't able to see the expression on his face.

CHAPTER SIXTEEN

JANE TOBIN WAS chatting away merrily with a group of five or six women sitting around an umbrella-topped table by the swimming pool.

She waved a glass of champagne at me and smiled, then dove back into the conversation. George Rochard came upon the scene, still looking quite shaky, his sister supporting him by his elbow. I caught Jane's eye, made a motion as if I was holding a steering wheel and mouthed the word "car." She nodded her head a few times, then turned her attention back to her newfound friends.

I made my way back to Jane's VW, sorry now that I hadn't made a stop at the buffet table or at least grabbed another glass of wine.

The winds had kicked up and clouds were scudding across Mount Diablo. The sound of grunts, skidding rubber-soled shoes, and smacks of a tennis match wafted over the privet hedge. I walked around till I found an opening in the hedge. The young man who had been serving drinks by the pool had taken off his blue shirt and was batting the ball across the net to a dark-haired man in his thirties. The fact that a funeral reception was going on just a lob ball away didn't seem to bother them at all. Both looked to be in good shape, with perfect tans. Dark Hair was wearing white shorts, with matching wristbands and a headband to keep his long dark hair out of his face. He picked up a tennis ball, bounced it on the cement several times, held it out in front of him, ready to serve, racket slowly coiling behind his head. He froze like a statue, then slowly turned his head to look at me. His dark eyes didn't look friendly.

I gave a noncommittal smile. He continued to stare. I guess he didn't like an audience. I stood my ground, and finally he went into action, going through the pattycake on the ground with the ball, racket back, then coming through with a ferocious swing, making a loud grunt as the ball met the racket strings. The ball took a wicked curve and was out of bounds by a good yard. He performed a mini–John McEnroe impression, slamming the racket to the ground and shouting obscenities. "Shit" and "bastard" were thrown in with some Spanish I didn't understand. He pulled another ball from his back pants pocket and gave me the death-ray look again. I took the hint this time and went back and climbed in Jane's convertible, leaning back against the headrest and letting the sun's rays coax me into a nap.

The sound of the car door opening brought me back to life.

"Find the gathering a little boring, did we?" Jane said, sliding behind the wheel.

She looked awfully cheerful and smug. "What did you find out?"

Jane maneuvered the car out onto the street before saying, "I found out quite a lot, Nick. Sharon Rochard wasn't exactly a favorite of this particular social set. She was George Rochard's second wife. His first wife, Helen, died of cancer six years ago. He met Sharon in Las Vegas. She'd been a showgirl, of all things."

Jane checked the dashboard. "Damn, I've got to stop for gas."

"So let me guess. As soon as Helen was in the ground, George was jumping Sharon's bones."

"Right. They were married within six months of Helen's funeral. It didn't sit too well with Helen's friends. That's why there weren't too many teary eyes at the funeral."

"The job description 'Las Vegas showgirl,' covers a lot of sins," I said.

"Oh, she was in the shows all right. A dancer. Though I got several broad hints that dancing wasn't the only thing she did."

Jane took an off ramp by the town of Dublin and found a Chevron station. While the car was being filled up I used the pay phone and checked my answering machine for messages. One call, the calm, efficient, well-modulated voice of Elaine Parker informing me that the time of her call was 11:06 A.M., and that "Mr. Chapman would like to meet with you this evening. Please call and confirm. Thank you."

I called. I confirmed. "Where does Harry want to meet?" I asked Ms. Parker.

"Would you be free for dinner this evening?"

"Yes."

"Seven o'clock, Lascaux on Sutter Street."

There was the click of the line being disconnected before I could say thank you.

The idea was to make Lascaux look like a cave. A very clean, nicely lighted, and carpeted cave. You walked down a short flight of stairs. The walls and ceilings were all of rough-cast adobe, looking like they had been carved out of a New Mexico hillside. It worked. You had the feeling that a whistling line of laborers in dusty overalls and flashlighted helmets, with pickaxes over their shoulders, would come chorusing through any minute.

The maître d' smiled as if I had given him the winning numbers for next Saturday's lottery when I told him my name.

"Certainly, Mr. Polo. Right this way, please."

Harry Chapman was sitting at a table against the far wall, across from the open kitchen and rotisserie, where he had a good view of everyone entering the restaurant.

The maître d' pulled my chair out, wished me a good evening, and promised that a waiter would be by very shortly.

Very shortly indeed. I'd just planted my butt on the chair when a waiter appeared.

Chapman held up his glass. "Another Chivas. What do you want, Polo?"

I ordered a club soda, and after the waiter was out of hearing, Chapman leaned across the table. His speech was already a little slurred.

"Sorry about last night, Nick. I was a little wound up, I guess."

"I guess."

Chapman swallowed what was left of his drink, then began crunching the ice cubes with his teeth. He seemed to want me to start the conversation. I let him wait. Silence. It's one of the first things they teach you in any interrogation class. Silence is your number one weapon. Draw the other person out. Let him do the talking. Sit. Keep your face blank and stare him right in the eye. It was amazing how much you could get out of a suspect by just keeping quiet. Someone who's worried about being charged with a crime is nervous to begin with. He's been devising his stories, figuring out just what questions you might ask him. He had built elaborate walls of half-truths around the spots where he was most vulnerable. He wanted you to ask those questions. He needed to have them asked.

Once on a homicide case, Paul Paulsen and I were sure we had the right suspect. It was a husband who had murdered his wife, and we were pretty sure he was guilty, but we had no real proof. He was an intelligent man, good job, mid-management in a large financial corporation. He appeared to bend over backward to be cooperative, mentioning several times that he wanted to help, that he didn't need an attorney present, that all he wanted to do was help us capture the person who had killed his wife.

Paul and I sat across the table and just stared at him, answering his pronouncements with a nod or a grunt. The silences between his outbursts got longer and longer. You could almost see the wheels spinning in his head. "How could they know?" "What do they know?"

We knew nothing, but after less than half an hour of being ignored, he broke. I can still remember his confession. "All right, all right. I did it. I killed her. But how did you guys know?"

"You told us, stupid," was Paulsen's thankful reply.

"Listen," Chapman finally said, only to go silent again when the waiter brought our drinks to the table. His eyes shifted around the room as I took a sip of my drink, wishing I could change places with him. For all I knew Elaine Parker was within listening distance. While I ran strictly a one-man shop, Chapman would have up to a half-dozen or more employees, any of whom could be at the next table. And though his boasting of his expertise in electronic surveillance was vastly overblown by the gullible local press, he knew his business, so he could have a microphone planted anywhere under his light tan suit or in the briefcase lying snugly against this leg.

We went back to our wait-and-see game, with Chapman taking numerous small, birdlike sips of his drink. This time I broke the ice.

"Shall we see what looks good, Harry?" I said, reaching for the menu.

"Fuck the food, Polo. I want to know what the hell you're up to. Give me some bullshit line about Tagaloa being at my house. Then you break my office window. Who the hell do you think you are?"

I took a sip of the soda water, watching Chapman's eyes. They bore right back into mine. It was even money now that he had a tape recorder in the briefcase. "Not me, Harry. I never broke your office window."

"Bullshit," Chapman said hotly. "It had to be you. And what's this crap about Tagaloa being at my house?"

"I rang your doorbell a couple of days ago, Harry. He answered. Then he turns up dead in Lake Tahoe, along with Sharon Rochard. And guess what your buddy Tagaloa has in his wallet? One of John Henning's business cards."

Chapman bowed his head and pinched his nose. "You straight about Tagaloa being at my place?"

"He didn't give me a name, but he was a great big Samoan."

"When was this?"

I gave him the date and time. He grimaced, picked up a fork, and ran his fingers across the tines, dropping it suddenly as if he'd pricked a finger.

"These bastards don't trust anybody," he said through clenched teeth. "Not anybody."

"I read somewhere that they do great things with duck here," I said.

"Fuck the duck." Chapman's drink was down to the bitter end, and he was swirling the cubes in his glass. "I hear you went to the funeral today."

"I was surprised you weren't there. Rochard must be a good client."

"What's this shit about emeralds and some tapes?"

I rolled the emerald from Henning's safe-deposit box across the thick white linen table cloth. Chapman stared at it but seemed reluctant to touch it.

The waiter came back and recited the liturgy of the restaurant's daily specials. He changed my mind about duck when he mentioned they had fresh sturgeon. Chapman grunted that he wasn't hungry and ordered another drink.

"Anyone can buy an emerald," Chapman said, picking up the stone and casually tossing it back to me.

"Sure, but a whole bag of them, Harry? That gets expensive."

"How many?"

"I didn't make an exact count. And I haven't listened to the tapes yet."

Chapman scanned the room again. "How do I know you're not bluffing?"

"You don't," I said, studying the wine list.

"I'd need proof."

"No problem."

The waiter brought my dinner salad. Chapman looked as if he was going to keep to his Scotch, so I ordered a glass of chardonnay.

"When?" Chapman demanded.

"We haven't discussed compensation yet, Harry."

He smiled for the first time. "Make us an offer we can't refuse."

"No, no. You start the bidding. I'll let you know when you're getting close."

That didn't seem to set too well with Chapman. "What do you want, Polo? What the fuck do you want?"

"When I discuss price, I don't want to do it with a middleman."

He turned his head to one side, the cords in his neck taut. "I think you're bluffing, Polo. Just a pure bullshit bluff." He stood up and straightened to his fullest height. "When you can convince me that you've actually got something, give me a call."

"What about dinner? I thought it was your treat."

He pursed his lips in a gesture of contempt. "Call us even. I had to pay the deductible on the broken office window, you bastard."

CHAPTER SEVENTEEN

As soon as Chapman left, I switched seats, taking his still-warm chair so I could see if anyone was paying attention to me. Once I had a client, a bright young attorney, who got too rich too fast and started sticking bigger and bigger spoons of cocaine up his nose. He once asked me to run checks on thirty-two vehicle license plates of cars he thought were following him. Thirty-two. I tried talking him out of it, but he came up with a rather plausible explanation. "Just because I'm paranoid, doesn't mean someone isn't following me."

Lesson learned. A little paranoia doesn't hurt. Especially after John Henning, Sharon Rochard, and Moana Tagaloa all died under what I considered to be unusual circumstances. Three dead bodies and nothing there to get the police to treat them as homicides.

The rest of the diners seemed interested in nothing but their companions and the food and drinks set in front of them. I ate leisurely, running the conversation with Chapman through my mind.

Since the message on my answering machine from Elaine Parker had come in at precisely 11:06 A.M., well before I had my talk to George Rochard at his house, Chapman had wanted to see me even before I flashed the emerald at Rochard. What was the original purpose of the meeting? Because he was pissed at my breaking his office window? Chapman looked as if he had the wind knocked out of him when I dropped the word that the big Samoan had opened the door to his house. If I had to bet, I'd say he was really surprised. What the hell was the connection between Tagaloa and Chapman? And the two of them and George Rochard?

George Rochard looked every part the grieving widower, but he'd gotten in contact with Chapman right away about the emerald. That's the only way Chapman could have known about my conversation with Rochard. Or was Chapman playing his own game? Could he have Rochard's house bugged now? I debated that part over dessert, pecan pie. No, Chapman wouldn't be bugging his own client's house. Or would he? Chapman found John Henning's antique transmitter. Where? Rochard's house? Or his office? The bug had to be the connection between Sharon Rochard and John Henning. What else could there be?

I ordered an espresso and continued my depressing one-way conversation. Sharon Rochard and John Henning. How did they get together, damn it? And if my reading of Chapman was right, how did Moana Tagaloa break into his house? The alarm system could be bypassed by a real professional burglar, and while Tagaloa showed plenty of exposure to the cops on his rap sheet, none of it was burglary related. It didn't fit. Something was out of kilter. Could Chapman have been working for Sharon Rochard? Was George Rochard the one who hired Henning? Maybe George thought Sharon was playing nice-nice with the help, or some of her old friends from Vegas. I drained the last of the espresso from its cup while thinking that one over. It didn't hold together, either. George Rochard was even less likely than his wife to hire a private investigator like John Henning. How did Sharon Rochard hook up with you, John?, I silently asked my dear departed friend as I signaled the waiter for the check.

The answer to that last question came, as they often do, from an unsuspected source.

The kitchen phone rang the next morning just as I finished loading up the coffee machine.

"Mr. Polo?"

"Yes."

"This is Laura Bradford."

I tried to place the name.

"John Henning's friend. We met at the church."

"Oh, yes. Laura. How are you?"

"Just fine, thank you." Her voice was very earnest, businesslike. "You asked me to call you if I heard from anyone who saw John before he died."

"Yes, I remember. Did you find anyone?"

"No, John hadn't been around to his usual haunts, Mr. Polo. No one that I've spoken to saw him for almost a week prior to his death. But that's not why I'm calling. It was the picture in the paper."

"Picture?"

"Yes, that woman that died in the hot tub in Lake Tahoe. I don't know if it means anything, but she used to come to a few meetings. I saw John talking to her once."

"Meetings—you mean . . . "

"Yes. AA meetings, Mr. Polo. We meet at 1010 Valencia Street every Wednesday night."

"And this woman in the picture, Sharon Rochard. You're sure she was at the meetings?"

"Positive. Very attractive, in a hard sort of way. She looked like she was very wealthy and from what the papers say, I guess she was."

"And she and John Henning were friendly?"

"Yes, nothing romantic I'm sure," she said with a nervous laugh. "John just liked to set newcomers at ease. A lot of first timers will go to a chapter well away from where they live, you know, so their friends won't find out."

"How long ago was this, Laura?" I asked.

"Oh, months ago. She only came to two or three meetings. That happens a lot, too. People drop in and drop out."

"Did she seem friendly with anyone else at the meetings?"

"No, poor woman," Laura Bradford said softly, "she looked like she really needed help, but she kept her distance, always in the back of the room, ready to slip out the door when she felt the need."

"Did John ever mention anything about his conversations with her?"

"No, not a word."

I told Laura nothing really new had developed on the case and thanked her for calling.

A piece of the puzzle solved. I poured a cup of coffee and sat at the kitchen table. They met at an Alcoholics Anonymous meeting. John was just the kind of guy to come over to a frightened first timer. Gently pat her on the back, reassure her. Probably give her one of his business cards.

I leaned back in the chair and smiled, feeling somehow as if I'd accomplished something worthwhile. Nothing major, but at least some progress. Sharon Rochard hires John. He hooks up his bugs. They meet at the Jefferson Park. Was that where she paid him off in the emeralds?

The doorbell rang. It was Jane Tobin. No cords and turtlenecks this morning; she was decked out in a crisp white linen suit with black ribbon borders.

She pirouetted around as she stepped into the flat.

"Very impressive," I said. "Change of life-style?"

"No, I'm doing a column on the fashion industry. There's a brunch this morning at the Fairmont, showing off the new West Coast designers."

Fashion designers. Recycling pirates. White hemline crime. Take a snip of this from twenty years ago, add it to a snip of that from thirty years ago, expand any details that were slim last year, or trim those that were wide five years ago, sew them all together and, "Voilà, the new spring collection!"

I brought her up-to-date on last night's meeting with Harry Chapman and my conversation with Laura Bradford.

"Chapman sounds a little spooky. What are you going to do?" she questioned, opening the refrigerator and taking a quick inventory.

"Make him spookier. He wants proof, I'll have to give it to him."

Jane grabbed a tightly wrapped hunk of aluminum foil. She questioned me with her eyes.

"Mrs. Damonte's *buccellato*," I reluctantly admitted, a sweet anisette-scented bread, filled with raisins that are soaked in grappa before going into the batter.

Her eyes brightened and she carried her prize over to the sink, unwrapping the ring of bread and slicing off two hefty pieces.

I looked at the kitchen clock. Almost eight-thirty. "I thought you were going to a brunch at the Fairmont?"

"I am," she agreed, returning to the refrigerator for butter. "But you know how those things are. Runny scrambled eggs, undercooked sausage, and mushy croissants." She slathered butter on the *buccellato* and popped it into the microwave.

"Just how are you going to prove to Mr. Chapman that you have something that you don't have, that you don't even know ever existed, and that you aren't sure what it is supposed to be?"

The microwave alarm pinged.

"Is one of those slices for me?" I asked.

Eyes like a doe startled by headlights. "Oh, did you want some?"

I nodded, and she sawed off two more slices and went through the buttering routine again.

"John had a few emeralds in his safe-deposit box," I said. "I'm going to add a few more."

"How many, Nick? Surely the people who owned those missing emeralds will know exactly how many were taken."

Good point. "I'll have to think about that."

Jane reshuffled the *buccellato* slices in the microwave, bringing the first batch to the table. She took a bite, rolled her eyes heavenward, then said, "How old?"

"The *buccellato?* Made yesterday."

"No, not the bread. Mrs. Damonte."

"She'll never see eighty again, but I don't have the nerve to ask her her age."

"What a woman. I'd like to do a column on her. Think she'd mind?"

"Ask her."

Jane nodded noncommittally. She had started her career as a sportswriter, one of the first of her sex to break down the sacred barrier of the all-male locker room. She'd put up with macho juveniles who swore, made gastral noises, and did everything but put a Hula Hoop on the end of their manhood and spin it around to get her to cast her eyes down in that forbidden direction. She was gradually and grudgingly accepted after the players got to know her and her work. She then moved on to a three-times-a-week column, tackling everything from the arts to politics and crime, the latter subjects both singularly and when they were all too often connected. None of it fazed her. But Mrs. Damonte intimidated her for some reason. Probably the same reason she intimidated me. My father was a big man, broad shouldered, with muscles hardened from a life as a bricklayer and cement mason. I can still remember him creeping downstairs to ask Mrs. D. for the rent, almost apologizing as he held out his palm for the bills Mrs. D. would slowly lay in his hand one by one, as if they were all family treasures he was confiscating. If she had slowed down in any way, it was in the laying out of the rent money. Snails climb redwood trees faster than Mrs. Damonte parted with cash.

The final score was three slices of *buccellato* for Jane, one for me. She left with a smile and a glaze of butter on her lips. We made a date for later in the evening.

I went to my office and called Arnold Harkins. He didn't sound all that happy to hear from me.

"These things take time, Mr. Polo. I'm moving as fast as I can on it."

"No problem, Arnold. I just wanted to trouble you for the name of the locksmith."

"Locksmith?"

"Phil, the one who opened John's safe-deposit box."

Harkins obviously considered the request a strange one, but he asked me to hold for a moment. I could hear him rummaging through papers before he came on the line and gave me the address and phone number.

"Was there something wrong with the safe-deposit box?" Harkins queried.

"No, no problem. I just needed a locksmith, and he looked reliable." I thanked Harkins and hung up before he could start making like a lawyer and asking unanswerable questions.

I called the number Harkins had given me. The strong silent image old Phil had projected at our meeting at the City Savings & Loan came through over the phone, also. He answered all my questions in one or two words: "Yep." "Nope." "Sure." "Why not?"

Why not, indeed. I next called Gene Chaput. He could have a grouping of twenty emeralds available in his office by noon.

The notepaper I'd taken to the library with the telephone number for Moana Tagaloa was skewered on a brass spindle on the edge of my desk. I twisted my neck so I could read off the Los Angeles number. The phone was answered on the second ring by a recorded voice: "We're out. Leave a number."

The voice sounded heavy, tough, much like the voice of the Samoan gentleman who met me at Harry Chapman's door.

If Tagaloa's answering machine was similar to mine—inexpensive, efficient, and guaranteed to break down after a year's service—it would have a call-back feature, so that you could enter a digital code over the phone and the messages on the machine would be played back to you from wherever you were calling from. The digital codes were usually a two- or three-number cipher, say three-two or two-one-three. A small, enterprising electronics firm sells a handy little gadget called the Super Speedy Dialer. One of its purposes is to let you dial one telephone number and if it's busy, the dialer will keep calling it for you until the line is free. The machine dials the electronic telephone numbers at speeds you could never achieve with your index finger. Another feature of this gadget is that, after you are connected to the number you've dialed, and after the answering machine's message has been played, you can program it to random dial, so that it floods an answering machine with so many numbers so fast that it breaks into the answering-machine's access code in a very short time.

The other way to break into the code is to punch away at the ten numbers on your phone as fast as your little fingers will fly.

I called Tagaloa's number back and set my hands to work, the fingers moving like George Shearing doing an Irving Berlin melody.

Somewhere between "Blue Skies" and "It's a Lovely Day Today" I got lucky. Tagaloa's tape started rewinding. I switched on the Sony microrecorder hooked up to the phone line and sat back to listen.

"Hello, this is John Figone at Wells Fargo. It is Wednesday at 3:00 P.M. I was sorry to hear about Mr. Tagaloa. Please call us as soon as possible regarding your account."

"Hello. Hello? Listen. Eddie. Call me, damn it. We've got to talk."

The last caller left off the hello part. "Call as soon as possible."

The next sounds coming back to me were those of my pounding on the phone keys.

I disconnected and ran back the tape, fast-forwarding through the banker's call. It was the second call that interested me. Harry Chapman. No doubt about it. The banker's call took place at three yesterday afternoon. No telling when Chapman called, other than it was after three yesterday. He sounded agitated as hell. Maybe it was after our meeting. After I told him about Tagaloa answering his door.

I replayed the third call. Male, not too old, not too young. Strong, dominating voice. Sounded almost sinister. Or was I reading too much into it?

I popped the cassette out of the recorder, put it in the center drawer of the desk, and put in a fresh tape.

Eddie. Who the hell was Eddie? Tagaloa's partner? Whoever he was, he wasn't going to be very happy when he played back his messages. A few seconds of listening to my Berlin chimes and he'd know just what happened. And he wasn't going to like it. So the trick was to find out just who Eddie was.

I went to my Rolodex and flipped to the M's. I keep the listing under M for money, because money is what this man is all about. He charges you a lot of it for finding out just how much other people have by hacking his way into bank computers. I don't know how he does it. I don't want to know.

He answered the phone in his usual cheery manner, a long dissolving grunt.

"And the rest of the day to you, sir," I said cheerfully. "Nick Polo calling."

Another grunt.

I gave him Moana Tagaloa's name, his office address, and phone number.

"You got a social?"

"Yes." I dug up Tagaloa's rap sheet and read off his Social Security number. "I'm in a hurry."

"Costs more that way."

"I know. I'd like to know everyone who has access to the checking account. If you run across a Visa or MasterCard, run that too."

"Costs more. A lot more."

"Money is no problem," I said for what must have been the first time in my life. "Fax it up as soon as possible."

Another grunt, then the connection was broken.

CHAPTER EIGHTEEN

GENE CHAPUT PULLED a chamois pouch from a drawer, loosened the strings, and emptied a pile of balls of orange-colored paper onto a display board covered with gray velvet. He began unwrapping each packet to reveal an uncut emerald similar in size to the ones in my pocket. "Emeralds are always wrapped in orange stone paper," Chaput explained. "Sapphires in brown and diamonds in blue, the pale blue that Tiffany now uses for everything from its jewel boxes to the carpeting on the floors."

"Any problem getting hold of this many stones, Gene?"

Chaput splayed out his hands. "No, Nick. They all came from within the building."

"Can I use a desk in your back room?"

He picked up the tray, and I followed him around the display counter and into his back office. A desk against one wall looked as if it would be perfect.

"Sorry to trouble you like this, Gene."

"No problem, Nick."

He watched with professional curiosity as I placed the long, gray metal safe-deposit box I'd purchased from Phil the locksmith on the desk. It wasn't a duplicate of the one at City Savings & Loan, but it would do. I opened the top of the box, arranging several envelopes; the top one, with the printed words JOHN HENNING—WILL was easily visible. Stacked alongside were three thirty-minute cassette tapes, the name ROCHARD hand-printed in red ink. I fanned out the tapes so that the corners of the bottom two would show.

I explained my problem to Chaput. "I want to show a large amount of emeralds alongside the tapes, Gene. I want to take some photographs and have whoever looks at the pictures think that there can be any amount of stones there. Any suggestions?"

He took the chamois pouch from his pocket and waved it at me. "Yes, why not stuff this with paper, the end of the pouch open, the gems spilling out."

It was much the same idea I had. "Would George Rochard carry around emeralds in a pouch like that?"

Chaput's eyebrows shot up at the mention of Rochard. The Rochard jewelry store was no more than a block away from Chaput's office. He shook his head. "Could be. Chamois is more or less a standard material. Soft leather has been used to convey precious stones since Biblical times."

I thought about it, but not knowing just how or in what manner the emeralds were delivered to Rochard, I decided on using just an envelope. Chaput dug a regular 8½-by-11 manila envelope from his desk, and I crumpled up a bunch of Kleenex tissues, stuffing them into the envelope, then laying the envelope alongside the tapes while Chaput arranged the emeralds carefully, the final effect looking like a haphazard spill, jewels tumbling out of a horn of plenty.

I took a small Rollei camera, loaded it with high-speed 1400 ASA film, and began clicking away. Careful not to make the pictures look too professional.

When I was through, Chaput began wrapping the stones back in their orange-colored sealers. I gave him a hundred-dollar bill.

He passed it right back to me. "Not necessary."

He was one of those stubborn Frenchman, so we finally settled for me buying a pair of gold earrings for Jane.

"Good choice," Chaput said, slipping my selection into a red-velvet jewelry box that looked as if it was worth more than the earrings. "I don't like to pry into your business, Nick, but you mentioned George Rochard."

"You know him?"

"I know everyone in the business."

A customer came in and Gene signaled his handsome son, Mark, to handle him, then led me back to his office.

He sat on the edge of his desk, folded his arms across his chest, with a serious look on his face. "Tell me about Rochard."

"The emerald. The first one I showed you. It's one of four I found in a friend's safe-deposit box. My friend was a private investigator. I think George Rochard's wife hired him to do a job and paid him off in the emeralds."

"Sharon Rochard? She just died."

"So did my friend, the private investigator."

Chaput screwed up his eyes and made a wry face. "Antoine Rochard, George's father, was a wonderful man. He learned his trade in Paris. He was a master at setting stones. He opened his trade here in San Francisco and did very well. The wealthy didn't just buy their wives or girlfriends a diamond ring or brooch or necklace, they bought them 'a Rochard.' George came to work for his father. Poor old Antoine had a love of the good life. Too much wine, too much rich food." Chaput's eyes twinkled a bit. "He died of a heart attack in his early seventies. Legend had it that he was with a young woman at the time of his death. George was over forty by then. He inherited a fool-proof business. All he had to do was keep the staff Antoine had assembled, open the doors to his shop, and count his money. But George had the modern disease. Expand. Sell volume, not quality. It was sad to watch the business change. There had been"—Chaput rolled his hand in a Gallic gesture—"rumors that he was close to bankruptcy. This was a couple of years ago. But things changed suddenly. His creditors were paid off, and he began his expanding ways again, opening stores in shopping malls up and down the coast."

"Any rumors on why the sudden change?" I asked.

Chaput shrugged and smiled as only the French can. "The usual rumors, Nick. There are always rumors in this business."

"Could the rumors have anything to do with smuggled gems?"

"When you find a jeweler in trouble, that is always one of the rumors. *À bon chat, bon rat,*" he said in liquid French.

I was struggling with the translation.

"To a good cat, a good rat," Chaput said.

* * *

I dropped the roll of film at one of those one-hour-development shops near Chinatown, found a phone booth while I was waiting, and called Harry Chapman's office.

Elaine Parker answered in her crisp, no-nonsense voice.

"Tell Harry I've got that proof he needed."

Parker didn't need an explanation. Apparently Chapman had told her of our conversation.

"He'll be very interested in seeing what you have, Mr. Polo. When can we see you?"

We, not he, I noticed. "When will Harry be available?"

"This afternoon, if that is convenient. Say two o'clock?"

"I'll be there."

I grabbed a roast beef sandwich and a beer at Lefty O'Doul's bar and got back to the photo store at the appointed time, only to be told that it would be another fifteen minutes. It was more like thirty, but I didn't complain. It's a miracle to me that they can churn the things out as fast as they do anyway. I bought more film and reloaded the camera while I waited.

I legged it back to the car, just in time to see a meter maid peering into the front window.

The term most commonly used is "flashing the tin," though my inspector's badge was gold, not tin. The police department supplies you with your first badge when you enter the department. If you get promoted and want something a little fancier than the chrome jobs the city gives you, you have your own made. It's more or less standard procedure for your comrades in arms to present you with the fancier edition at your promotion banquet. That way the badge is yours, not the city's, and when you retire you keep it. If the first Dirty Harry movie had run another five minutes, after Clint Eastwood shot the bad guy, saved the kid, and threw his badge into the water, a realistic scene would have been of Clint taking off his shoes and socks, rolling up his slacks, and wading into the water and going looking for that gold badge.

The meter maid, a thin, twentyish brunette with a weary look around her eyes gave me a tight smile and a small wave and walked down to the red Alfa-Romeo parked illegally in the white zone in front of Gump's department store. The nerve of some people.

It was almost two-twenty when I got to Chapman's office. Elaine Parker had her hair in a tight bun today. She got up from behind her desk and came out to greet me. She was wearing a saddle-colored suede jacket that had padded shoulders and tapered down to her waist and a matching skirt that stopped a couple of inches short of her knees. Brown leather boots with thick, Victorian-looking laces climbed up her legs, stopping inches below those dimpled knees.

"Come with me," she said, lightly grabbing my elbow and leading me to a doorway to the right of her desk. She opened the door with one hand, released my elbow, and waved me inside, giving me the full wattage of her big smile.

I should have been suspicious when I saw Harry Chapman behind his desk smiling so hard it looked as if he'd hurt his cheeks.

I was only a step or two inside when I was grabbed by the shoulder, whirled around, and slapped hard across the face. Losing my balance so quickly is what saved me. I stumbled, falling backward, my arms cartwheeling like a swimmer doing backstrokes, finally landing on the carpet in a thump.

The man who hit me was, forgive the redundancy again, a big Samoan. Bigger than the one who had answered Chapman's door. Bigger than an NFL middle guard with his pads on. He was wearing a khaki safari jacket, the pockets bulging. He came toward me. I reached to my hip and pulled out the S&W .32 revolver.

Big Boy sneered.

I pulled the hammer back.

"You pull that trigger of that little gun and I'm gonna stick it up your ass, mister."

I pulled the trigger, aiming a yard to his left. The bullet whizzed past him, plowing into a picture on the wall. I was too busy to pay attention then, but later saw it was one of Warhol's black Marilyn Monroe prints.

Big Boy stopped in his tracks, staring right into the barrel of my "little gun." When a gun is pointing at you, they all look big.

I looked over at Harry Chapman. His hand was drifting toward his shoulder holster.

"Don't even think of it, Harry," I said, climbing to my feet.

Elaine Parker was leaning against the closed door, eyes bulging, chest heaving, sucking in big gulps of air, like a diver getting ready to go to the bottom for abalone.

Sitting in a chair against the far wall, casual as can be, one leg crossed over the other, was a dark-haired man in a suit so pale it looked like vanilla ice cream. I moved slowly toward Harry Chapman, keeping the gun on the big Samoan.

"On the floor, Eddie," I yelled at him.

His eyes narrowed and he wiped his palms on the sides of his safari jacket, much too close to the bulging pockets.

"You know me, huh?" he said.

"Everyone knows you, Eddie," I lied. It was a shot in the dark, but it looked as if I'd found Moana Tagaloa's partner. "Down on the ground, quick."

He hesitated, giving Ice-cream Suit a questioning glance.

Chapman's desk was a beautiful piece of free-carved walnut. I put a bullet into the section between the stapler and a Danish-modern–looking red telephone. Chapman almost jumped out of his chair. Eddie's eyes squinted closer to being completely shut. You could almost hear his brain clicking. Two shots. Four left. Actually there were only three left, since I never leave a bullet in the chamber under the hammer.

"Down, Eddie. Spread them, you know the procedure." I edged over to Chapman, pulling his automatic from his fancy black-mesh nylon and Velcro holster. Since Chapman's gun was a big, sinister-looking semiautomatic pistol with a magazine that probably held close to twenty bullets, it might seem that the right thing to do was pocket my little revolver and point the bigger gun at the bad guys. Big Arnold, Charles Bronson, Nick Nolte, et al., just reach down, pull a pistol, rifle, or Uzi submachine gun off a dead villain, put their finger around the trigger, and start spraying the air with lead. Just once I'd like to see one of them grab a weapon, look at it, and say, "How the hell does this damn thing work?" The problem with semiautomatic pistols is that they're all built differently; the safeties are in different locations. Sometimes a red dot under the safety means it's on, but on another brand that signals the safety is off. There are different releases to allow you to jack a round into the chamber. For all I knew Chapman had a bullet in the chamber and all I had to do was pull the trigger. But certain models have trigger releases that have to be activated before the weapon can fire. All very confusing.

Which is why I shoved Chapman's gun under my arm and kept the revolver pointed right at Eddie.

He was dutifully lying facedown on the floor, arms and legs akimbo, fingers tapping silently against the carpet.

I took a moment to study the stranger in the chair. The bored look on his handsome features had been replaced by a scowl, which helped me recognize him: the bad-tempered tennis player at George Rochard's house.

"You," I told him. "Stand up very slowly. Then take your jacket off, even slower."

"I have no weapon, Mr. Polo. You don't have to—"

I pulled the trigger again, aiming well over his head.

"Someone's going to hear those shots and call the police," Elaine Parker said, her breathing still nowhere close to normal.

"Fine with me," I said.

The man in the chair got to his feet, his eyes never leaving mine. He took off his jacket, draping it carefully over the back of the chair.

"Now the pants pockets. Inside out."

A key ring and a very slim, black alligator wallet dropped to the floor. His pants had just one back pocket, and that contained nothing but a handkerchief.

He stood there, smoothing his yellow silk tie, examining both ends to see that they matched in length. All very calm. Very in control.

"On the floor. Next to Eddie," I told him.

"I assure you—"

"Down!" I screamed at the top of my lungs.

He gave me a disappointed frown, then sank to his knees, looking down at the carpet with disgust, probably worried it was going to ruin the crease in his pants.

Chapman's leather, high-back chair sat on rollers. I pushed it with a foot, knocking him away from the desk.

"Elaine, come on over here, sit on Harry's lap. He looks lonely." It wasn't that I was a romantic, I just figured that Chapman would have a tougher time getting out of that chair with Ms. Parker anchoring him down.

She complied with the order quickly, her breaths coming in short, nervous snorts now. Her complexion had paled. If she passed out in Chapman's lap, at least she wouldn't fall to the floor and hurt herself.

I took in a deep breath myself, holding it for ten seconds, then blew out the air, and according to Jane Tobin's yoga instructions, much of the tension at the same time, though I had the feeling I'd have to blow air the rest of the afternoon to get rid of all the tension running around in my nervous old body. I put Chapman's pistol in my waistband, making sure that the barrel was pointing away from any vital organs.

Ice Cream's jacket was a beautiful piece of raw silk. There was no label inside. The only things in the pockets were a black plastic comb, a black leather cigar case, a gold Dunhill lighter, and an expensive-looking gold fountain pen.

I stooped down and picked up his wallet. No wonder it looked so slim. Seven one hundred–dollar bills and a half-dozen twenties. No identification of any kind, not even a credit card. I dropped the wallet back to the floor. "All right," I finally said, maneuvering myself toward the exit door, "just what the hell was this setup all about?"

No one answered. I walked over to Ice-cream Suit and dug my heel into his ankle. "I have the feeling you're in charge. Let's not be so formal. What's your name?"

He raised his head a few inches from the floor. "You can call me Frank."

"Can I now? How about a last name?"

"Ummm, Lopez," he said with little conviction.

I shuffled over toward Eddie, keeping a safe distance from his canoe-size feet. He had positioned his arms as if he was about to do a push-up. I was curious as to just what was making his pockets bulge, but I felt that if I let him get to his knees to take the jacket off, he'd try something stupid, and I didn't want to pull the trigger again. I'm a terrible shot. I might start missing the walls and actually hit someone, and besides I had only two bullets left. "Don't even think about it, Eddie."

"This is all unnecessary," said the man who called himself Frank Lopez.

"I got the impression that I was in for a game of bounce Polo off the wall."

Lopez raised his head a few inches from the carpet. "Eddie overreacted. All we want to do is talk, I assure you."

"What is your part in all of this, Mr. Lopez? All I know about you is that you look like you'd be a sore loser at tennis. And anything else."

"It's difficult talking this way. Since you now know I'm harmless, would it upset you if I got back to my chair?"

"Yes, it would," I said firmly. "But you can roll over and sit up. I came here to show something to Harry Chapman, but since it appears you're the man in charge I'll show it to you."

I dropped the packet of photographs alongside Lopez. He rolled easily onto his side and sat up, arms tucked in and crossed the way they do in yoga classes. And karate classes. I backed away a few feet.

Lopez studied the pictures one by one. "Not very good, really."

"Bad lighting," I responded. "I had to take them quickly, in a bank vault. I wasn't even able to count the emeralds. But that looks like three cassette tapes. Thirty minutes a side."

"And you naturally didn't play the tapes."

"Naturally. Yet. I won't have full possession of them for another few days." I explained my position as executor of John Henning's estate.

Lopez smiled a mirthless smile. "So all of this bargaining is rather futile right now, isn't it, Mr. Polo?"

"Yes, you would have had Eddie bashing my brains in for nothing."

Chapman's chair was squeaking. Elaine Parker was wiggling on his knee as if she had to get up and run to the bathroom.

"How much are they worth to you?" I asked Lopez bluntly.

He had very long, thin fingers, the kind a concert pianist dreams about. He fluttered them. "Maybe nothing. Who knows what's on the tapes. Maybe your friend Henning was a Beatles fan."

"The tapes are labeled, Frankie. The label says 'Rochard.'

Harry-boy found the bug. We both know that there's no music on those tapes. How much?"

Lopez pursed his lips. "Ten thousand dollars."

"Wrong answer." I transferred the revolver to my left hand, then took the small Rollei camera out of my coat pocket with the right. I sighted in on Lopez and took a picture. He didn't like it a bit.

The camera is an old model; the film has to be advanced by hand. It was clumsy, but I ended up taking a half-dozen pictures of a fuming Frank Lopez, then skirted past Lopez and took a few shots of Eddie.

"Harry has no doubt told you that I'm an ex-policeman, Frankie," I said, pocketing the camera. "I'm going to have these developed, and if anything happens to me, delivered to a cop I know in homicide."

Lopez's face was a gargoyle of rage now. It was a corny old ploy: Harm me and this evidence will be turned over to the police. It was used at least once in every Republic Studio grade-B movie ever made. Corny, but effective. The threat could be real. If a man dressed as well as the supposed Mr. Lopez did and didn't carry one single piece of identification, it's a cinch he wouldn't be happy about his picture being flashed around.

"Call me when you have a serious offer on the emeralds and tapes," I said as I got to the door, taking a quick peek outside in case some of Chapman's employees had been alerted by the gunshots. All was clear. Apparently he had given the rest of the office the day off.

"Hey," Chapman yelled as I was about to exit. "What about my gun?"

"I'll leave it on the dock," I said, closing the door and sprinting past Elaine Parker's desk.

CHAPTER NINETEEN

"Bad people," I told Mrs. Damonte, holding a hand well over my head. "A big man. He could be trouble. He could come looking for me here."

Her ancient face remained impassive. "Make a big mess?" she asked.

Not long ago someone had trashed my flat, slashing the furniture and cutting up my clothing. Mrs. D. and a couple of her cronies had treated the whole affair like a pirate's picnic, wading through the debris with smiling faces while Mrs. D. quoted me prices on just how much it would cost for each item to be repaired or cleaned.

"Make big trouble. These people could have been involved in John Henning's death. If you see anyone hanging around, call the police right away, okay?"

Her head bobbed in an affirmative manner and she shut her door, only to open it seconds later.

"You didn't like the *buccellato?*"

I put my fingers to my lips, kissed them, blowing the kiss in her direction. "Fantastic. As usual."

"Yes," she agreed, closing the door again. Mrs. D. is without a doubt the best cook I have ever run across. Baked goods, homemade pastas, sauces, veal, fish, you name it, she's the tops. A culinary artist and, like most artists, upset when they do not get their deserved rave reviews.

Cooking made me think of Jane Tobin and our dinner date. I walked up the remaining flight of steps to my front door and called Jane, catching her at the *Bulletin*.

"Dinner still on?"

"Are you trying to back out?" Jane demanded.

"No, just checking. Do you know anyone on the paper who has a handle on what's going on in Colombia?"

"Nobody has a handle on Colombia, Nick. What do you need?"

After running out of Chapman's office I'd stopped at another one-hour photo-print store near Fisherman's Wharf and had four copies made of each of the pictures I'd taken of the alleged Mr. Frank Lopez and Eddie. They were darker and blurrier than the pictures I'd taken in Gene Chaput's office due to the lighting, but Lopez's face was easily visible. I put the receiver between my ear and shoulder and spread the pictures out on my desk. "I've got a photograph of a guy who may be involved in some smuggling. I'd like to ID him."

"Ben Weber's done several stories on the drug wars. He might be able to help you."

I remembered Weber's articles. He'd gone down to Colombia several times, almost got himself killed. "Is Weber around?"

"I saw him wandering around this morning."

"Okay, I'll give you the pictures tonight. What's on the menu?"

"It's a surprise. You'll love it."

My stomach got a little queasy. Surprises are for birthdays and card games.

I stuffed a set of the pictures, along with the photo store's invoice showing that four copies had been made, into an envelope, wrote Frank Lopez, care of Harry Chapman and Chapman's office address, then used the phone book to find a courier service. They quoted me a price of twenty-two dollars to make delivery this evening and said a man would be over in less than an hour to pick up the package.

I sat back and looked at my hands, grateful to see that they weren't shaking. Still, I agreed that I had earned myself an early drink.

The fax line buzzed while I was in the kitchen pouring myself a glass of wine. I carried it back to my office and watched as sheets of paper rolled slowly out of the fax machine. Seven sheets in all.

Most people or firms sending you something over a fax line

have a cover letter, showing their name, address, and the number of pages to follow. Usually the telephone number from which the pages originated and the date and time of transmission are printed on the top of each page. But not on those of my money-man genius in Southern California. The documents popped out of my fax without a clue as to where they'd originated. Untraceable. Three of the legal-size sheets listed credit information on Moana Tagaloa, his addresses, bank dealings, and credit card transactions for the past six months. Three other pages showed the same type of information on one Atuie Edward Muliaga, who was authorized to write checks on Tagaloa's business account.

Muliaga's Visa card was under the name of just plain-old Eddie Muliaga. The seventh sheet had only one figure, in the center of the page: $ 2,000. Information doesn't come cheap. I called Paul Paulsen and asked him if he could squeeze in another criminal check for me.

"I don't know if I can afford to, Nick," Paulsen said reluctantly.

"They checking up on you?" I asked with genuine concern. Paul was a good friend. And a valuable source.

"No, but I'm on a diet. You can't bribe me with fancy food."

I heaved a sigh of relief. "Your diets never last more than a week, Paul." I gave him Muliaga's full name, the addresses shown on his financial accounts, and his Social Security number.

"I'll get back to you, Nick. Oh, by the way, your other buddy, the one that died in Tahoe—"

"Moana Tagaloa."

"Right. His FBI sheet came in. I mailed it to you."

"Anything exotic, Paul?"

"More of the same. Arrests but no convictions, back East, down in Texas. He was a bad boy wherever he went."

"I have a feeling Muliaga is going to have the same package. I'd appreciate it if you'd let me know as soon as possible on this one. You know anyone in the feds that's hooked up to Colombia?"

"I try and stay away from those people, Nick. Both the feds and Colombians."

I thanked Paulsen and carried the financial sheets over to my desk. The pages were packed with all kinds of juicy information. It was another facet of the workings of a private investigator that

I owed a debt of thanks to John Henning. The police department has no access at all to credit, bank deposits, credit card transactions. The information can be obtained but only after long drawn-out court subpoenas or search warrants. The public's vision of an all-powerful law enforcement agency, with computer access to all available facts and data, is a blurred one. No one agency has a corner on everything. Each one has its own pocket of sources, and they don't like to share their goodies with anyone else.

Even the Internal Revenue Service has limited information banks, which is why those multimillionaires can counterpunch with them in court, finally ending up with a settlement a small percentage of the huge amounts owed. An IRS agent once explained it to me this way: Each and every day over two hundred and fifty billion dollars, that's billion, not million, moves in, around, and out of the country, the vast majority of it in perfectly legal transactions. Uncle Sam's sleuths have no way to keep up with the flow.

Criminal records are no better. I once sat in an office with a man I'd arrested for rape four years earlier. I ran a statewide check on him to see what he'd been up to since that arrest. What arrest? It had disappeared from computer files. Gone. Vanished. If another police officer had picked up this guy and checked him out, he'd look clean. No prior arrests. Where did the record go? Did it fall through the proverbial cracks? Or did this guy know someone in Sacramento who simply pushed a delete button on his computer and watched the screen go blank?

I started with Tagaloa's credit first. There were several addresses listed, all in Los Angeles, the last for his office on Sunset Boulevard. There were a half-dozen state and federal liens and collections, all over three years old. Since then Tagaloa's credit had been excellent. Accounts at various department stores, Hertz and Avis, all opened in the last eighteen months, all with high balances, no payment problems, the current status shown as R1, which is the top rating. They spiral down all the way to R9, which is where collections and judgments come in. So Tagaloa had been a bum credit risk a few years ago, and now he was a model account.

His Visa and American Express charges were a lot more interesting, though unfortunately the latest billings, for the past couple of weeks, weren't posted yet. Tagaloa must have died with a closet full of frequent-flier miles owed to him. He used them all: United, TWA, American, Avianca, and Aero California airlines. The charges on Aero Cal were all in the amount of $114.86 and showed the charges were made in Tijuana. I checked the desk calendar against the dates shown on the Aero California charges. All Wednesdays. The first Wednesday of the month, every other month for the past eight months. There were numerous charges for Hertz rentals, most of them in Los Angeles, all for the same approximate amount, just under sixty dollars. The dates for the car rentals and Tijuana airplane tickets were identical. Then other Hertz rentals at Tijuana, only this time the amounts were $36.15. Why would it cost more to rent a car from L.A. to Tijuana than from Tijuana to Los Angeles? I strained my eyes going over the credit card report and found the answer. Cortes Motor Hotel, Ensenada, Mexico, $54.40. This was always on the day following the purchase of the plane ticket at the Tijuana airport.

Aero California wasn't listed in the local yellow pages. I dialed 800 information and got a number down in Los Angeles. A recorded message from a woman with a sultry accent came on the line, her voice drifted over some Latin background music informing me in English that Aero California served Baja California out of Los Angeles. The sensuous voice asked me to wait for the next available operator, which I dutifully did, and eventually a voice similar to that of the recorded message came on the line.

"This is Moana Tagaloa," I told her. "My American Express card shows a charge for last month. On the sixth, in the amount of $114.86. I don't remember doing any business with you that date. Could you check, please?"

She asked me for the credit card number, which I read off the financial report. After being on hold for less than a minute, she came back on the line.

"Ah, Mr. Tagaloa. We show that you took one of your regular round-trips that day, from Tijuana to La Paz. If there is a problem, I can send you a copy of our billing."

"No, that's all right. My mistake. Thank you for your interest."

My own interest went right to Muliaga's financial report. Sure enough he had an American Express card, with identical charges of $114.86 on Aero California, and Hertz rentals in the same approximate amounts, along with a night's stay at the Cortes Motor Hotel in Ensenada. The dates were all on Wednesdays. All in the months when Tagaloa didn't make the trip.

I went through the credit card charges for both men carefully, laying out columns of air travel and vehicle rentals for each. Good old Hertz came through again. The day after the stopover in Ensenada, both Tagaloa and Muliaga picked up a car in San Diego, with rental amounts varying from thirty to forty dollars. An amount I assume would cover the short trip from San Diego to Los Angeles.

I would have yelled "bingo," but I was afraid Mrs. Damonte would hear me. Tagaloa and Muliaga made regular trips, spelling each other once a month. A drive down to Tijuana airport, a plane ride down to La Paz and back, then a night in Ensenada and a magical appearance in San Diego.

I took a world atlas down from the shelf and looked up Mexico. Baja looked like a snake lying off the mainland of Mexico, separated by the Gulf of California. La Paz was a coastal town on the southeast tip. Ensenada was near the northern border, no more than forty miles from Tijuana, and was another coastal town. The drug smugglers liked to use those sexy, streamlined, cigarette speedboats to smuggle cocaine up to San Diego and points north. Both Tagaloa and Muliaga looked as if they could capsize those skinny beauties, so maybe they used something a little larger for their expeditions.

The doorbell rang, startling me out of my thoughts and almost causing me to jump out of my shoes. I unholstered the .32 revolver, realizing that there were only two bullets left. A check through the peephole showed a skinny young man with red hair. Not Maureen O'Hara or Red Buttons or Lucille Ball red. Heinz-ketchup red. The hair drooped down to his shoulders. Thick black-lensed sunglasses mended with Scotch tape rested on his nose. His blue and white-striped shirt had the name of the messenger service stitched across the front. A Sony Walkman was plugged into one ear. He was rolling his head from side to side, and he was snapping his fingers to the beat of whatever was coming out of the Walkman.

I gave him the envelope and a check for the agreed amount, then slipped him a ten-dollar bill. "I'd appreciate it if this got delivered right away."

He pocketed the money, pointed his index finger at me as if it were a gun and said, "Fifteen minutes," then skipped down the stairs two at a time.

I went back to the reports. Tagaloa's last listed entries were from United Airlines, Avis, and Harold's Reno, the date shown was the fourteenth of the month, the day before I flew to Lake Tahoe and found Sharon Rochard's body in the hot tub.

I reloaded the .32, fiddled with Chapman's SIG-Sauer automatic until I was sure I could operate it, then took a quick shower.

I changed into slacks, turtleneck, and sport coat, then packed a small bag with a change of underwear and fresh shirt.

The phone rang as I was zipping up the bag.

"Not very bright, Nick," said the unhappy voice of Harry Chapman.

"Did our friend Mr. Lopez enjoy the pictures?"

"You're in over your head, Nick," Chapman responded harshly. "You're going to get us both killed."

"I could have been in the bay over my head, Harry. You set me up."

"Bullshit! You overreacted. All we wanted to do was talk. And deal with you."

"Eddie Muliaga has an odd way of greeting people."

"He was just going to check to see if you were carrying—" Chapman said, then quickly added, "By the way, where's my gun?"

"I left it on the dock right outside the door. I hope it didn't get knocked over into the water."

"Yeah. Sure," Chapman said in an angry hiss. "I'll bet that's just what happened."

"What did Lopez think of the pictures?" I asked again.

"You know, Polo, you're cute. Real cute. Only you're playing it too cute this time."

"Remind Lopez that I've got sets of those pictures placed in hands that will deliver them right to the cops if anything happens to me, Harry. I'm not ending up like John Henning."

There was a long pause, then Chapman said, "Is that what this is all about, Nick? You think I killed Henning? Shit, you know me better than that. I wouldn't get mixed up in anything like that."

"You're mixed up in enough, Harry. Do you know what's on those tapes?"

"Do you?" Chapman challenged.

"Conversations about emeralds and trips to Baja California. Tagaloa and Muliaga should have used cash, not their credit cards, Harry. Sloppy. What the hell, they weren't going to write the trips off on their income tax. Nobody's paying income tax on those emeralds, are they, Harry?"

Another pause, then, "He wants to meet with you again, Nick. Discuss a price. When will you have possession of the tapes?"

"A day. Maybe two. Tell Lopez and big Eddie not to bother to come to call. I'm moving for a couple of days. And remind him about those pictures."

I hung up before Chapman could respond, stuffed his automatic and the financial reports in the bag, and went to the basement for the car.

There was one thing that Harry Chapman said that rang true. He wouldn't get mixed up in a murder. I was no fan of Chapman's. Maybe there was some professional jealousy involved. Harry could be a pain in the ass, but he ran a successful and, as far as I knew, pretty clean shop. Most of the stories in the newspapers about him were highly exaggerated, no doubt thanks to Harry telling highly exaggerated stories to the reporters about recovering valuable art objects, rescuing kidnapped children, and aiding the police department in high-profile investigations. He could be accused of being a braggart, even a downright liar once in a while. But a killer, or even setting up John Henning? No. Not his style. He didn't have the temperament or stomach for that kind of work. Bugging someone's house or office, mingling with characters like Tagaloa and Lopez, yes, that would excite Harry. He liked being around the edge of danger. The far edge. When he got closer to the middle he'd start to sweat. And Lopez wouldn't like that.

CHAPTER TWENTY

JANE TOBIN HAD a surprise waiting for me. Ben Weber, the reporter who had done the series of articles on Colombia.

Weber was sprawled out on Jane's sofa, looking very comfortable. Very familiar with the surroundings. He stood up to shake my hand. He was just about my height, pushing six feet from either direction, depending on how straight he was standing. He had dark brown hair, worn in a loose, casual, uncaring style, curling over the top of his freshly laundered Brooks Brothers blue oxford shirt. One side of his mouth was hooked into a perpetual smile, as if he was permanently amused by what he saw of life through his blue eyes. His Levi's were starched and creased. I never trust guys that starch and crease their jeans. Or maybe it's just that I don't trust guys that look comfortable in Jane's apartment. His cognac-colored corduroy coat sported leather elbow patches and, like the pants, was neatly pressed and creased. A minor miracle. I can buy a brand-new corduroy coat, walk out of the store with it, bend an elbow once, and suddenly there are very noticeable lines running against the cloth's grain making the coat look as though it is ready for the back of the closet.

Weber's handshake was strong and firm. Probably from all that ironing.

"Nice to meet you, Nick," he said, his smile widening the dimple in his chin. "Jane said you had some pictures of a Colombian bad guy."

I handed Weber a copy of the photographs. He studied them while Jane came in carrying a tray with two stemmed glasses, still frosty from the freezer, filled to the brim with vodka, a small twist of lemon floating on top.

She gave me a big smile and a light peck on the cheek. She placed the tray on the glass-topped table in front of the sofa and hurried back toward the kitchen, returning moments later with a third drink. Mine. Glass unfrosted, oversize cocktail onion pierced through the middle with a red plastic toothpick bobbing on the bottom.

I gave her a smile not quite as frosty as her glass. Or Weber's.

"I don't know, Nick," Weber said, shuffling through the pictures, then dropping them on the table and picking up his drink. "He looks vaguely familiar, but I can't place him. He's nobody big in major cartels, I can tell you that, unless he's someone new. They're playing musical chairs down there so fast you can't keep up with them. What's your connection?"

"Emeralds. I think he may be smuggling emeralds into the country."

The interest drained from Weber's eyes. "Emeralds. Small stuff compared to the *talco*, Nick." He turned to Jane. *"Talco*, that's the latest lingo for cocaine." He then went into a half hour of war stories of his times in Colombia, his numerous brushes with both the law and drug traffickers when he was mistaken for being either a *pichicatero*, "dealer," or *oreja*, "undercover officer." Jane refilled his drink right in the middle of a yarn about his being run out of the country by a crooked judge. "It's unreal, Nick."

I kept trying to bring the subject back to emeralds, but Weber wasn't buying it. He went back to his adventures "in the jungle." I had the feeling that if you locked Weber and Harry Chapman in a room together they would have both died of heat prostration from all the hot air they concocted.

Weber finally looked at his watch, drained his glass, and stood up. "Got to go, Janie." He picked up the photographs again. "Can you spare one of these?"

"Sure. Help yourself."

He selected a picture and slipped it into his pocket. "I'll show it to a few guys. Something may turn up," he said, his voice level, showing he wasn't holding out much promise for positive results.

I carried the empty glasses into the kitchen while Jane escorted

Weber to the door, slipped off my sport coat, unbuckled my belt, and pulled off the .32 revolver's holster, putting the gun on top of the refrigerator.

Jane reached for an apron when she got back to the kitchen. She spotted the holstered gun on the refrigerator but said nothing. "What did you think of Ben?" she inquired innocently.

"Good dresser," I answered, rinsing out the martini glasses.

"Ah," she replied, giving me one of those "gotcha" smiles.

Jane Tobin has many, many good qualities: bright, loyal, generous, intelligent. The chink in her gorgeous armor is that she is really a lousy cook. Not for lack of trying, in fact it's almost overtrying. She tackles a recipe in the same manner a politician attacks his pork barrel in a nonelection year. Overkill. She always picks recipes that call for ingredients that no one ever has in the pantry. The kind with the dust on the top of the jars in the gourmet section of the supermarket. Tonight's started with langoustine *feuillantines* with curry sauce (shrimp and spinach miniature sandwiches covered with whipping cream and curry and I'm afraid to ask what else), followed by shiitake mushroom and potato *galette* (potatoes, mushrooms, and Parmesan cheese), and roulade of salmon (salmon hidden under piles of charred red and yellow peppers, olives, tomatoes, and, of course, balsamic vinegar). Has to have balsamic vinegar, not wine or, good heavens, cider vinegar. Who or what are the balsamics? If they ever go on strike or close down, hundreds of nouveau-cuisine restaurants are going to wither away.

We discussed the case during dinner. I cleared away the plates while she put on espresso.

We had the coffee in the living room.

Jane brought a couple of yellow-lined writing tablets to the couch. I spread the financial-data reports on the table, and we made a chronological listing of all of the trips that Tagaloa and Eddie made to Baja California.

"These charges for flights on Avianca Airlines—did you ever find out where they were to?" Jane asked.

"No. But I've got a hunch."

"Me too," Jane said, studying the list she'd made. "Colombia. Can you find out for sure?"

139

"No problem." Jane's apartment is decorated in an eclectic manner, incorporating mementos from her various newspaper assignments. The walls are studded with baseball bats, balls, a symphony conductor's baton, and pictures of Jane standing alongside or under the heavy arm of stars of movies, TV, and every sport imaginable. The telephone on the end table by the couch was in the shape of a football, given to her by an assistant coach of the 49ers after one of their Super Bowl wins. I picked up the top half of the football, called information, got Avianca's 800 number in Los Angeles, and within two minutes had the information I needed. "First-class round-trip from L.A. to Bogotá. Fourteen hundred dollars."

Jane went back to her chart and waggled her head. "I don't understand. It's so obvious when you look at the paper trail they left. Why weren't they a little smarter?"

"Every election day people go into those little booths and pull the slot for multimillion-dollar bonds to build more prisons, Jane. We need more every year because the people they're putting away aren't very bright. If they were smart, the prisons we have would be empty."

She took a last sip of her coffee, then leaned back against the cushions. "But what have you got out of this, Nick? What good has all your running around done? Are you any closer to actually getting someone charged with John's murder?"

I sank down alongside her, my hand going to her hair, running my fingers through those short, silky auburn strands. "No. Not really. I haven't got anything that would hold up in court for John's murder or anything else."

She pulled my hand from her hair, ran her tongue across my palm lightly enough to cause a tickling sensation, then said, "Maybe we ought to—"

Time for the third surprise of the night. The doorbell rang. I climbed to my feet. "If that's Weber coming back with more war stories, I'll—"

"Hey, Polo. Open up. It's me," Harry Chapman's voice yelled from the apartment hallway.

I ran into the kitchen, pulled the revolver from the top of the refrigerator, freeing it from the holster as I hotfooted it back to the living room, picked up that silly football phone again, and punched in the numbers, 9 and 1, then handed the receiver to Jane. "Keep your finger on number 1. If Chapman isn't alone, push that button and tell the emergency operator you're being attacked."

Jane nodded, her eyes tight with fear.

Even good old Jim Rockford, the most entertaining and probably most plausible of all the TV private eyes, when confronted with a situation where there was someone outside pounding on his door, possibly with a gun, would hug the wall a few feet from the door for protection. Well, a real bullet will pass through the sheetrock and lath alongside the door as easily as it will through the door itself. I lay down flat on the carpet a good ten feet from the door.

Chapman was leaning against the bell. "Come on, Nick. I know you're in there. That piece-of-shit car of yours is parked in back. Open up."

"What do you want, Harry?"

"I just want to talk, for Christ's sake. I went to your place and some crazy old lady almost blasted my ear off with an air horn."

Good old Mrs. Damonte. "Who's with you, Harry?"

"I'm alone, Nick. Come on, will you. We got to talk."

I got to my knees and reached out for the doorknob. "I've got someone here one digit away from the 911 emergency number, Harry. If there is anyone but you there when I open this door, the call will be made and your name shouted loud and clear."

"I'm alone," Chapman blurted belligerently.

And he was. I checked out the hallway, then pulled him inside, pushing him up against the wall, poking the barrel of the .32 into his ear while I frisked him. He had another automatic in his shoulder holster, a nasty-looking Beretta this time.

"Hey," Chapman protested, "I'm not losing this one, damn it."

He reached out toward his gun and I jammed the .32 deeper in his ear.

"Be nice, Harry, and you'll get it back."

I stepped away and flicked a glance at Jane. She was still standing with her finger on the phone. I smiled and she blew out her cheeks in a sigh of relief, let go of the phone, and flopped back onto the couch like a kid falling backward into a swimming pool on a hot day.

Harry Chapman looked like he'd come out of an all-night poker game as the only loser in the bunch. His hair was rumpled, his tie undone. A polka-dot pattern of blood stained both the tie and the front of his shirt.

"I could use a drink, Nick," Chapman said.

"Me too," Jane said, bouncing to her feet and heading for the kitchen.

I used the barrel of the .32 to motion Chapman toward the couch. "Sit down, Harry. How did you find me here?"

Chapman fell into the couch in a thick-bodied slump. "I know that Tobin is your steady-Eddy. I've seen you all over town with her."

"Steady-Eddy," Jane said with a disapproving look on her face. She put a bottle of Christian Brothers brandy and three old-fashioned tumblers on the cocktail table. "Steady-Eddy?" she repeated, her eyes bouncing from Chapman to me.

"It means that we are often seen in each other's company," I explained.

"I know what it means, Nick. I just think there must be a better way of expressing it."

Chapman reached for the brandy, the tip of the bottle making clinking sounds against the glass as he poured with a shaky hand.

Jane poured herself a tot and questioned me with her eyes. I shook my head and watched Chapman slurp his drink down. He wiped the back of his hand across his lips, then let out a groaning sigh.

"I'm telling you, Nick, these guys are crazy." He took a another sip of his drink, then repeated, "Crazy."

"They're your clients, Harry," I told him.

Chapman nodded to himself. "Ah, nothing personal," he said looking at Jane, "but I've got some things I've got to say to Nick. Things I wouldn't want printed in the paper, because they could probably get me killed."

Jane's back stiffened. "Anything you say here is off the record."

Chapman looked at me. "It's her apartment, Harry."

142

Chapman drained what little brandy was left in his glass. "Did you tell her what happened at my office?"

This was getting touchy. I didn't want Jane to get in the way of the mysterious Mr. Lopez and his Samoan goon. "Time for a conference," I said, gesturing for Jane to follow me into the kitchen.

"There are probably a lot of things Harry is going to say that it would be safer for you not to know."

She shook her head stubbornly. "Chapman found you here easily enough, Nick. If he can, so can someone else. You can get killed just as easily for something somebody thinks you know as for what you actually do know."

Unfortunately she was right. Chapman tied me to Jane right away, and she was probably spotted at the funeral or at Rochard's house. I'd already put her in jeopardy. "Okay, let's go see what the man has to say."

Chapman had helped himself to more of the brandy.

"Jane stays, Harry. But everything is off the record. Way off the record."

Chapman didn't like it, but apparently he didn't feel as if he had much choice. The alcohol had slowed down his speech, but his hands were still shaking.

"After you left my place, they went crazy, Nick. Blamed me for everything. Said I should have briefed them about you. You surprised the hell out of Muliaga by jumping up with that gun."

"Tell me about Muliaga."

Chapman ran his eyes around the walls as he spoke. "I don't know a hell of a lot about him. He was a partner of Tagaloa. First time I saw Muliaga was yesterday."

"But you called him, Harry. You called him in Los Angeles at Tagaloa's office."

"Yeah, yeah," he admitted. "Tagaloa told me about Eddie being his partner, but yesterday was the first time I actually met him." His eyes stopped their wandering and focused in on mine. "I've got to ask you again. When you said you saw Tagaloa at my house, you weren't kidding, were you?"

"I've seen a copy of Tagaloa's DMV photograph. It looked like the same man to me."

Chapman grimaced, his face wrinkling like a fan.

"I take it he wasn't an invited guest, Harry."

"No way."

"So he broke into your house."

"No way, Nick. You think my office is alarmed? My house is protected better than England's Crown Jewels. Ain't no way anybody could get in there without an alarm going off."

"Someone must have given him a key," Jane Tobin said. "Who would have access to a spare key and know your alarm system?"

Chapman looked at Jane, then stared at me.

"Elaine Parker?" I suggested.

"Nah, I don't think so," Chapman said, his hand going to his bloodied nose. "Well, maybe, but I don't think Elaine would do that. Why the hell would she do that?"

I had no answer to that one. "Come on, Harry," I prompted. "Tell me what happened after I left your office in a hurry."

"All hell broke loose. Then you sent those damn pictures over and Frank had a fit."

"Frank? You mean Lopez? What's his real name?"

"I don't know. I never asked. I don't want to know, believe me, I'm better off not knowing."

I suddenly realized I was still holding the .32 in my right hand and Chapman's Beretta in my left. I pocketed the .32, found the clip ejector on the Beretta, emptied it, a total of twelve cartridges making clinking sounds as they fell into a ceramic ashtray on Jane's coffee table, and after making sure there wasn't a bullet in the chamber, tossed the gun to Chapman. He stroked it as if it were a lost pet that had wandered back home, then slipped it into his shoulder holster.

"Frank's your client, isn't he, Harry?"

Chapman considered the question for a moment. "Now, I guess he is. You want the whole story?"

Jane and I nodded our heads in unison.

"About a year, year and a half ago," Harry said, "George Rochard hired me to do a security sweep on his downtown store. You know the scene, Nick. You go in with a bug detector, check all the telephones, all the walls, under the rugs, the works."

144

"Was this just at his downtown store or at all of his branches?" I asked.

"Nah, just at the downtown San Francisco store. I tried to sell him on doing all the stores, but he wasn't interested. Anyway, it's a nice little account, no problems. Until Rochard calls all in a panic. 'Get over here right away,' he's screaming. That's when I find your bug."

"Only it wasn't my bug, Harry. John Henning put that bug in."

Chapman shrugged his shoulders. "How was I to know? It was an identical handmade piece of junk to the job you did for Sunset Oil years back. I didn't know Henning. He must have been small-time. I had no idea he was working for you." He tapped a finger against his forehead. "But I recognized the bug right away."

"Henning bugged the Sunset Oil lines too, Harry."

"You got paid for the work, Nick. I saw the invoice. How was I to know you subbed out the job to Henning? Anyway, Rochard calls all hot and bothered. I'm not due to run a sweep on his place for a couple of weeks, but he wants one right now. So I go over and find the damn bug. He has a fit. Wants to know who put it in. So naturally, I come to you."

"Where was the bug?"

"Outside, at a service panel. Rochard has a system with five phone lines hooked into the business, but this was set up on his personal telephone. One line, not hooked up into the business numbers. Which was smart. If Henning hooked into the business lines, he'd need miles of tape to record all the shit that came into the store."

"You told Rochard that you were sure I had bugged his office?"

Chapman laced his fingers across his chest. "No. I mean I knew you were involved right away, soon as I see the bug, but there's no sense in solving the crime too quickly, Nick. I had no idea about the emeralds or tapes then, of course."

"You wanted to string your client along. Run up some billing hours."

"Sort of," Chapman agreed. "When I see Rochard next, this Tagaloa guy is there with him. It's Rochard's office, but Tagaloa, he's seems to be the guy in charge, you know what I mean? He's popping questions at me left and right and Rochard's just standing alongside him looking sick."

"When was this?"

Chapman tilted his head back to the ceiling. "I forget the exact date, but it was a couple of days before Sharon Rochard was killed. So I tell them I'm working on it, doing my best. Tagaloa asks me about a private eye named John Henning. I tell him the truth. I never heard of him. He tells me Henning's the guy who bugged Rochard's office."

If Chapman wasn't lying and this meeting took place two days before Sharon Rochard's death, then John Henning was already dead. I told this to Chapman.

A thin film of sweat was spreading over Chapman's forehead. "Hey, I didn't know. I told him that I had leads, and that maybe Henning wasn't working alone."

"So you gave him my name?"

"Hell, no, Nick. I just couldn't pop your name out then. Tagaloa would have known I was milking the case. Shit, you can see how much the bastard trusted me, getting into my house like that. I just said that it might be a good idea if I checked out Henning. That's when he told me Henning was dead. 'You want to check him out, you'll have to travel to hell, brother,' was the way he said it."

"You think Tagaloa killed Henning?" I asked.

Chapman's eyebrows joined in irritation. "How the hell would I know, Nick? All I know is that he seemed sure that Henning was the man who bugged Rochard's phone."

"What do you know about Tagaloa?"

"Just that he was a big, mean-looking son of a bitch that I didn't want to mess with. I didn't know who he was until he gives me one of his cards showing he's a private eye out of Los Angeles. He started taking over. Had me checking out Rochard's staff. I had my men running all over the place trying to tie one of them to the bug. Tagaloa said it had to be an inside job."

"Did it?"

"Well, you had to know about Rochard's private line, but to bug it you didn't have to get into his office. Just the service box, which is down in the basement. Anyone in coveralls could get down there with no problem."

"So that was the first time you saw Tagaloa, at Rochard's office?"

"Sure was. But the bastard almost moved into my office."

"Did you find any one of Rochard's employees who might have been involved?"

"Not really. There was a manager that Rochard had fired about a month ago. Tagaloa thought he could be the one who put in the bug. The guy moved out of town. I found him up in Seattle."

"Did you talk to him."

"No," Chapman said wearily. "Tagaloa sent his partner, Eddie Muliaga, up to Seattle to talk to the guy. Tagaloa said that after Eddie interviewed him, he was sure the guy wasn't involved. Probably beat the shit out of the poor bastard. I'm telling you, they had me running around like crazy on those employees."

Judging from what I'd seen of Muliaga, I didn't envy the poor gentleman in Seattle. "But nothing really came of your investigation on the employees?"

Chapman reached out for the brandy bottle again. "Not a thing. Then this other guy, Frank, shows up. Man, he's really spooky. Even Muliaga looks scared shitless of him. Rochard called me and said that someone was coming over and that I should cooperate a hundred percent with him. I'm telling you, Nick, those pictures. The ones of the safe-deposit box, they had this Frank going. Muliaga wanted to go out and find you and waste you right away. But Frank, he kept studying those pictures. You know what he said? He said there weren't enough. He was looking at the picture of those emeralds and saying there weren't enough. And if they weren't in this fucking box, where were they?"

"Did he say just how many emeralds there should be, Harry?"

"Nope, just kept tapping his finger on the pictures, saying there weren't enough. That and the tapes, Nick. He wants those tapes bad. If I were you, I'd make a deal with him."

"Is that why you're here, Harry? To talk me into making a deal?"

Chapman put his drink down and looked me in the eye. "No,

Nick. I'm here because I'm scared shitless. I don't want any part of these guys. They treat me like I'm some fucking flunky. Then you send those pictures and they go crazy again. Frank starts slapping me around like it's all my fault. Muliaga is drooling, just waiting for Frank to tell him to finish me off. I'm telling you, these guys are scary. I want out."

"Me too, Harry," I admitted. "Me too."

CHAPTER TWENTY-ONE

I GRILLED HARRY CHAPMAN for another half hour. He had worked Jane's bottle of brandy from an inch or so from the top all the way down to mid-label. He was babbling a bit toward the end, but I was satisfied that he had gone out hunting me on his own and that Eddie Muliaga hadn't been on his tail.

"I checked for a tail, Nick. Believe me, I checked."

Chapman was scared and had no one to turn to. No one to trust. He wasn't even sure about his secretary, Elaine Parker, so his solution was the obvious one. "I'm getting out of town, Nick. Just blowing town for a few days. I want no part of this thing. I'm not going to lose my license, go to jail, or get my ass shot off." His eyes were watering. "You believe me, don't you, Nick? I may not be a saint, but I never set Henning up. Or you either."

"You'd better keep in touch with me, Harry. We're in this together whether we like it or not. Call me at my place. If I'm not there, leave a message on the machine saying when you'll call back again."

Chapman struggled to his feet. "No way, buddy. I'm not playing games on the phone. That's another reason Muliaga wants to wring your neck. He figures you're the guy that fucked up his answering machine."

Harry had a point. I didn't want him using Jane's number, either at home or the office.

I gave him John Henning's number. "The phone's still hooked up, until the end of the month." I'd have to install a new answering machine at John's house.

Chapman didn't like it, but he couldn't think of anything better. He looked longingly at the bullets in the ashtray, so I held out the tray to him and he stuffed his pocket like a kid grabbing Halloween candy. I followed him out to his car, watching him stumble into the front seat. Maybe a drunk-driving charge would be a blessing for poor old Harry Chapman. A nice safe jail cell. I watched until his taillights were out of sight. No one took up after him. I got my overnight bag from the trunk of my car.

Jane had two steaming cups of espresso waiting by the time I got back to the apartment.

"Do you believe Chapman?" she asked.

"Yes, I think I do. He's too scared not to be telling the truth."

"So it looks like Tagaloa killed John."

"Maybe. How did he find out that Henning put the bug in Rochard's office?"

"From Sharon. It must have been from Sharon," Jane said.

"Then travel all the way to Lake Tahoe to kill her? Sharon didn't have the emeralds with her. Or at least they weren't found on Tagaloa or in his car."

"Maybe this other guy, Eddie. Maybe he was with Tagaloa, and when they got the emeralds, he killed Tagaloa. Or gave him enough cocaine to let Tagaloa do it to himself."

I held the espresso under my nose, hoping the strong, pungent coffee smell would clear up my clouded brain. John Henning's friend Laura Bradford had told me that she'd seen Henning and Sharon Rochard talking together at the AA meetings. John easily could have given her his business card then. Would she hold onto it, though? Put it away somewhere where no one would look? No one except someone like Tagaloa, who would have no regrets about going through her belongings, searching out those secret places, even with her husband looking over his shoulder.

And the emeralds, the ones the mysterious Frank Lopez was so worried about. The picture I'd taken at Gene Chaput's place showed a pretty nice little envelope full of gems. But not nearly enough for Mr. Lopez. How many were there? Who had them? How would whoever had them get rid of them? Turn them into cash?

I decided I was wasting the espresso as an inhalant and began drinking it.

"Are you back with the living?" Jane asked politely. "For a minute there you looked like you were in another world."

"Yes," I admitted, "another world. That's where I'll have to go. Uncle PeeWee's world."

I dropped Jane off at the *Bulletin* in the morning, made a quick stop at Fox Hardware on Fourth Street, purchased an answering machine, then drove directly to John Henning's house. The smell of death still clung to the walls, and I went through the routine of opening all the windows and doors.

His mailbox had collected the usual supply of unwanted solicitations as well as a couple of small checks from insurance-company clients and a gas and electric bill. No telephone bill, because Henning would not have one. At least not one from the phone company. Another trick of the trade he'd taught me was how to hook up with an independent telephone broker. All your calls are actually billed to the broker. The guy John uses, and whose services I also take advantage of, has an office in Stockton, California, which is located some ninety miles east of San Francisco. You have to use a special code before dialing out from your home or office number. A bit of a pain, and an added expense on local calls, but you actually get a break on long-distance tolls. The saving or lack there of is not the reason for using this service. What makes it useful is that if for some reason someone were to subpoena your telephone records, or if the scoundrel had a source at the phone company that could provide the information for a price, they'd end up looking at blank paper.

I made sure Henning's phone and the new answering machine were in working order, then spent a couple of hours going through the house again, doing a thorough job, checking behind and under the furniture and rugs, going so far as to pull away some rotting wallboard in the basement, looking for clues, finding nothing but dust balls and evidence that rats or mice were not infrequent visitors.

The phone ringing startled me. A cheerful voice asked to speak to the owner or manager of the firm and before I could tell her that that worthy gentleman was deceased, she informed me that her firm could supply a combination life and disability insurance package at an unbelievably low rate.

"Too late for that, I'm afraid," I said, pushing the disconnect bar, then looking at my watch and figuring it was still a little too early for Uncle PeeWee.

I treated myself to a long, late breakfast at American Chow, a fun forty-seat diner in a blue-collar area of the city that was fast giving way to interior designers who were sandblasting the old redbrick buildings and filling them with wholesale dealers selling everything from jewelry to antique furniture. American Chow was holding its own, the stools alongside me filled with a mixture of fashionably dressed men and women who would probably be insulted if you tried to categorize them in the yuppie generation, and barrel-chested truck drivers in Big Bens and hickory shirts who waited until they got home at night to shave. The harried waitresses catered to the truck drivers. They left much bigger tips.

It was after noon when I parked in back of St. Peter and Paul's Church and walked across Columbus Street to the small trattoria simply called The Cafe.

The elderly gentleman behind the bar dispensing espresso, cappuccino, and bitter Italian aperitifs recognized me, giving me a hearty greeting, designed not so much for friendship but to ensure his compadres scattered around the room playing cards that it was all right to continue the games.

He held up an index finger to signal for me to wait a minute while he picked up an ancient black telephone without a dial and spoke in a hushed tone.

"Your uncle says to come right back," he said to me in Italian after gently lowering the phone on its cradle.

The paisans kept their eyes on their cards as I went to the back of the café, knocking briefly on the door before entering.

"Nicky, come in, come in," my uncle Pee Wee called in a booming voice. He stood up from behind his desk and came out to greet me, first shaking hands and then pulling me close for a hug.

My uncle and I are almost identical in height. He got the nickname Pee Wee because his brother, my father, towered over him at six foot three. I couldn't remember the last time anyone called him by his given name, Dominic. Uncle is a handsome man, and no one ever made him angry by telling him he looked a lot like the actor Victor Mature did in his prime.

"Sit, sit," he said, pointing to a chair in front of his desk. It had been several months since I'd visited my uncle. He looked the same, immaculately dressed; pearl-gray suit, white shirt, black silk tie, white handkerchief edging out of the suit pocket. His hair was as dark as ever. Darker than mine. He used to sport a trim mustache, but somehow the mustache was getting mysteriously gray while his hair was not. The mustache was soon banished.

"You're looking good, Nicky. Very good. Staying out of trouble?"

"As much as possible, Uncle. How is business?"

Uncle's business was simple. He's a bookie. The old-fashioned, honest-type bookie, who kept a stable of lifelong, reliable customers. Being a bookie and having a vowel at the end of your name lends itself to certain speculation, but my uncle had no connections to so-called organized crime. I say so-called because unlike the well-coordinated image they present on screen, they can be an awfully disorganized group. A frightening, scary disorganized group, of course. The mob had never really gotten settled in San Francisco, probably because the city was really not much more than a small town compared with the metropolises in the East and the southern part of the state. But while Uncle Pee Wee was not "connected," he had an ear to the ground and not much went on in an illegal way without his hearing about it.

He knocked his knuckles on his desk. "Business is good, Nicky. Can I be of some help to you?"

"Yes, perhaps, Uncle. A friend of mine died. Emeralds are involved. A large amount of emeralds."

Uncle Pee Wee locked his fingers under his chin, elbows on his desk. "Stolen emeralds?"

"Smuggled. From Colombia. Raw stones."

"How many?"

"I'm not sure, Uncle. A great many."

"You have names?"

"The man who died was John Henning. A friend. A private

investigator. Not the kind of man to get mixed up in a smuggling caper."

"I knew John. A good man."

I'd forgotten that Henning had done some electronic work for Uncle Pee Wee, setting up switching devices on his phones so that when bets were called in, they went to an empty room. Empty except for a relay box that sent the call to another phone, across town where the bets were actually recorded. "A woman died also. Sharon Rochard. Her husband is George Rochard."

"The jeweler. He's a player. Not with me, but I know that he's a player. You think this Rochard was smuggling the gems in to sell at his stores?"

"Yes." I took the pictures of the man calling himself Frank Lopez from my pocket and handed them to Uncle Pee Wee. "This man is involved. I don't have a good name for him."

Uncle took his time looking at the photographs. "He does not appear to be very happy with the person taking the pictures."

"It was me."

He chuckled. "Somehow I knew that. What is his involvement in your puzzle?"

"I think he may be the Colombian connection."

Uncle Pee Wee dropped the pictures and shook his hand as if it were burned. "Ahhhh, the Colombians. They are dangerous. Like all the ones who get mixed up with the powders. It fries their brains. Tell me what you think I need to know to help you."

I told Uncle Pee Wee the whole story, bringing him up-to-date on Tagaloa's overdose just a few miles from where Sharon Rochard was found. About Chapman's involvement and my meeting with Muliaga and the man called Lopez.

"And what is it you want from me, Nicky?" Uncle asked when I was finished.

"I'd like to know if anyone has heard of a large amount of raw emeralds suddenly coming onto the market. And I'd like to get a name to go with those pictures."

He picked up one of the photographs again. "Yes, he is a key piece to your puzzle, Nicky. I'll do what I can. There is one other person in your story who intrigues me."

"Who?" I asked, mentally making a bet with myself he'd say Muliaga.

Never bet against a bookie. "The woman. Elaine Parker. She sounds much smarter then her employer."

Mrs. Damonte was waiting for me, holding an upturned broom in her gnarled hands as if it were a pitchfork.

"Man came last night. I send him away."

"Yes, he told me. No other visitors?"·

"Nopa," she said, lifting her lips a fraction, which for Mrs. D. was what passed for an agreeable smile. She twirled the broom around like a drill sergeant showing the recruits how it was done and put the business end to work on the spotless terrazzo steps.

The little digital window on my answering machine showed that six calls had come in. I pushed the rewind button, listening to that chattering-squirrel sound as the tape rewound. It took some time.

The first two calls were from attorney clients. The next was the rapid-fire explosion of push-button keys, the little beeps coming so fast that it almost sounded like one long, electronic wail. Apparently Muliaga had one of those Super Speedy Dialers, because within seconds the sound of the machine clicking on to relay its messages came on.

So Muliaga had gotten even. But since all he'd picked up was the names and telephone numbers of two of my clients, no real harm was done.

The fourth call was someone who hung up without leaving a message, the fifth, Muliaga raiding the machine again. The sixth was from Paul Paulsen.

"Hi, Nick. Your friend Muliaga's a bad boy. A half-dozen arrests, mostly batteries, no convictions. Still waiting for the FBI. Talk to you later."

I rewound the tape, opened the machine and took out the cassette, replacing it with a fresh one, dropping the old tape to the floor and smashing it with my heel, then throwing it into the wastebasket.

Poor Muliaga. If he'd waited until Paulsen called, he would have really gotten an earful.

155

I called Paul at the Hall of Justice.

"Nothing back from the FBI, Nick," he said.

"No problem. I'm having trouble with my answering machine, Paul. Better not call anything in for a while."

There was a long pause. "Trouble, huh?"

"Nothing serious."

I gave Paulsen John Henning's number. "If you get anything, leave a message there, Paul."

"Okay, check your mail. That stuff on Tagaloa should be there by now."

He was right. Mixed in with bills, advertising flyers, and a nice-size check from a client was a plain envelope with no return address and my name scribbled across it. The FBI sheet on Tagaloa was more of the same of what showed on his California criminal record; a long list of arrests—New Jersey, New York, Dallas. Tagaloa had more battery charges than a truck-stop service station. Battery, assault with a deadly weapon, robbery. And again all with no convictions.

There was one more person I wanted to run a criminal check on.

Sheriff Eric Colvin was at his desk when I called Lake Tahoe. He didn't sound overly pleased to hear from me.

"No dead bodies since you left, Polo. I hope you're not planning a trip back up here."

"Good thing you went into law enforcement rather than going to work for the chamber of commerce, sheriff. Anything new on the Rochard or Tagaloa deaths?"

There was a squeaky sound coming over the line, probably Colvin rocking back and forth in his chair.

"Rochard was a probable suicide according to what I read in the papers. Tagaloa's not my problem, Polo. I told you that. Happened the next county over."

"Want to do a little trading, Sheriff?"

The squeaking stopped. "What are you offering?"

"Tagaloa had a partner. Both in the private eye business and in his life of crime. Eddie Muliaga. Like Tagaloa, lots of arrests, no convictions."

The squeaking started up again. "Some little birdy tell you all this, Polo? Whatever, it ain't of much use to me."

"I thought you might pass it along to your neighboring sheriff."

"Did you now?" Colvin said, the squeaking once again stopping. I could picture him pulling his feet from the top of his desk. "And what little favor are you expecting in return?"

"Sharon Rochard was a showgirl in Vegas. That's where her husband met her. I'm curious if she has any kind of an arrest record."

"You know what name she was using in Vegas, Polo?"

"No. Her date of birth will be on the death certificate though."

"I know that," Colvin said angrily. "So you want me to check with the Vegas sheriff, see if they've got anything on her." He phrased it so it wasn't a question.

"I'd be interested in the results, Sheriff."

"Why's that? You told me she was a witness to an accident. A dead witness now."

"I'm just curious, Sheriff. A cop's disease. You never get rid of it."

"Well, I'm gonna get rid of it, the day I retire. All right. What's your number there?"

"I'll be out most of the day. What would be a good time to call you back?"

"Give me a couple of hours," he said brusquely, then severed the connection.

Why bring in Sheriff Colvin? you may ask. Why not just run a criminal check on Rochard myself? Getting her date of birth from the death certificate or her driver's license would be no problem. Checking California and Nevada for marriage records would no doubt give up a former name. If all that failed, I could have Jane make contact with some of the gossipy people she met at the funeral. Credit records would pull up a Social Security number, from which former names could be developed.

But Las Vegas, like lots of major cities, sometimes doesn't bother to add misdemeanors like prostitution to their computerized rap sheets, unless the prostitution arrest is connected to another crime, such as robbery or assault. The prostitution busts are kept on file in the vice squad, or sex detail, or whatever particular detail handles prostitution.

The casinos often hire beautiful showgirls to entertain big spenders after the shows. If they don't "entertain," they soon find themselves offstage. In those cases, it's the casinos themselves that pay the girls for their extracurricular performances, not the gentlemen on whom the favors are bestowed. If the customer has something to complain about, he goes right to his casino procurer, not the police. But the police often found out about what was going on from the frontline prostitutes, who don't like seeing their territory invaded and squeal to the cops on both the moonlighting showgirls and the "amateurs," bored Southern California housewives who invade the casinos on weekends for extra spending money. Arrests may not be made, but names are taken and filed away by sharp cops who figure that sooner or later that bored housewife's husband is going to finally figure out what's been going on and decide to put that hunting rifle that's been rusting in the closet to use, or that the long, tall corpse last dressed in a sequined evening gown and dug up by coyotes in the desert will turn out to be a former dancer on the strip.

So Sharon Rochard would be left to Sheriff Colvin. But not Elaine Parker. I should have questioned Harry Chapman about her last night, but my thinking cap wasn't on very straight at the time.

Uncle Pee Wee was right. She did seem to be much smarter than her employer.

CHAPTER TWENTY-TWO

I SPENT A frustrating half hour at the computer trying to pin down Elaine Parker, but nothing popped. The name was too common. Which left my financial-wizard friend in Southern California.

"The check is in the mail," I said, as soon as he grunted his way onto the phone.

"It's finger-licking good, the suit's a perfect fit, and Nixon's not a crook. Yeah, I heard them all, Polo. But I haven't seen my money, yet."

"I mailed it as soon as I got the report," I told him, digging the checkbook out of the desk's center drawer and postdating a check to him in the amount of two thousand dollars. "I just need a quickie." I read off Elaine Parker's name and home address. "Just a credit report. I'll pay rush prices."

"Rush is two hundred dollars," he croaked.

I winced and croaked back an "okay," knowing that his magic fingers would fly across his computer keyboard, breaking into credit files quicker than a José Canseco line drive reaches the bleachers.

"I'll write the check right now. Drop it in the mailbox in less than an hour," I promised.

"Good idea, Polo. And don't forget to get a check in the mail to Bank of America Visa. You owe exactly five hundred fifty-two dollars and eighty six cents. They'll kill you with interest if you don't pay by tomorrow."

My spine straightened up, and I didn't hear the click of the phone being hung up. The son of a bitch was digging through my credit files. Well, the old proverbs were coming home to roost: rotten apple, rotten tree. Lie down with dogs and you get fleas. Run behind horses and you get dust in your face and a terrible view. Sleep with strangers and God only knows what you'll end up being treated for nowadays.

I quickly made out all the necessary checks, enveloped them, and was licking the stamps when the muted ring of the fax machine went on and the financial record on Elaine Parker inched slowly out of the machine's mouth.

There was nothing exciting about her banking or retail accounts. She shopped in a lot of upscale stores, as well as the big department jobs like Macy's, the Emporium, Saks.

She had an aka of Elaine Potts. If that was her maiden name, it must have been a doozy to carry through high school. She was listed at the address on Fortuna Avenue for the past two years. Prior to that there were three Los Angeles addresses. Los Angeles, the home of misters Tagaloa and Muliaga. A connection? Or was I overreaching?

It would be nice to take a little peek into her apartment, but since Chapman had the place alarmed, I'd have to do a little creative burglaring.

I dialed Chapman's office.

"Is Harry in?" I asked innocently.

"No, he's not, is this—"

"Nick Polo, Elaine. Sorry I had to run out on you like that yesterday."

Her voice turned warm and cuddly. "I don't blame you. I just couldn't imagine what was going on. I was terrified."

"I guess the boys weren't too happy when I left."

"Oh, it was unbelievable." Her voice lowered to a confessional whisper. "They sent me home right after you ran away. I'm really frightened, Mr. Polo. Could we get together somewhere? I have to talk to you."

"Just the two of us?"

"Yes, Harry's not around. I don't know where he is." She turned on that sexy whisper again. "I'm scared, Mr. Polo."

She sounded so sincere she almost had me believing her. I tried to think of a safe place to meet her. "Do you know Stars?"

160

"The restaurant by Civic Center. Sure."

"Five-thirty okay with you?"

"I'll be there. And thanks, Nick." Her voice was husky, dripping with sex now. "I really appreciate it."

I hung up, knowing that Elaine was quite possibly involved with Lopez and Muliaga all the way up to her well-plucked eyebrows. That she may have given Tagaloa the key to Chapman's house. That she was playing Chapman for the all-day sucker that he was. That the excitement in her eyes yesterday at Chapman's office came from wanting to see Muliaga arrange my features into something resembling Mr. Potato Head. I knew all that, but even so there was a bulge in my pants that hadn't been there before she started emoting in that come-hither, dial-a-porn voice of hers.

I called the *Bulletin.* I might need moral support when I met Elaine Parker. Besides, I'd definitely need help in picking her purse.

Jane Tobin sounded full of business. "Don't have much time, Nick. Got to finish this column on capital punishment."

We had completely opposite views on the subject, so I quickly switched the conversation to another topic. "Busy tonight?"

"Yes. Staff meeting, then a dinner."

She didn't volunteer who her dinner companion was to be. I had visions of Ben Weber sweating over a hot ironing board. "Wouldn't happen to have some free time around five-thirty, would you?"

"No, I really don't Nick. Sorry. How about tomorrow? Free for dinner?"

We made a tentative date.

The phone rang just seconds after I hung up on Jane.

"Hello, Polo," Sheriff Eric Colvin said.

"Sharon Rochard have a record?"

"I talked to a fella who remembered her. Worked out of one of the big casinos, the Crystal Palace. Great legs but not much of a dancer. Did some free-lance hooking. Made most of her money taking care of the boys with the golden pens."

Golden pen was a term casinos used for the preferred customers who didn't pay a cent for their rooms, food, or entertainment, whether the entertainment was in the crowded show rooms or in their lavish hotel suites alone with someone like Sharon Rochard.

"But Sharon was never busted, huh, sheriff?"

Colvin snorted. "You kidding? Not back then. Not even now. The boys don't want any stories about prostitution in their wonderful, family-oriented entertainment centers."

"Is that what they call them now?"

Another snort from Colvin. "They try to make them look like Disneyland, for Christ's sake. Mommy and Daddy park Junior in the fun-land arcade center, then go to the adult gaming rooms and shove phony silver dollars into machines that jingle out our nursery rhymes when they swallow the coins, then set off an alarm like the *Queen Mary* coming into port when they cough up a few dollars."

"You sound a little bitter, Sheriff."

"I liked the old days better, son. You put real money, real silver dollars, into the machines, not phony coins that lose their shine as soon as the sweat of your palms hit them. The blackjack dealers dealt from one deck, not three. The felt on the craps tables might have been a little worn, but the dice were straight and honest. There may have been a little sawdust or cigar ashes under your feet instead of plush carpeting, but at least you knew you were gambling, honest-to-God gambling. People dressed up, men wore suits, ties, women evening gowns. Now they all look like they're in a fucking shopping mall searching for back-to-school bargains for the kids."

"The good old days, huh, Sheriff?"

Colvin's voice turned serious. "They were. They really were. Don't let anyone bullshit you that they weren't. You owe me one, Polo. Take care now, hear?"

Stars is one of the current "in" places and deservedly so. It's located near the city, state, and federal office buildings, and close to the opera house and Davies Symphony Hall, where everybody from Sinatra to the New York Philharmonic plays when they're in town.

It's a big, bright airy place; light walls, lots of mirrors, with a menu offering everything from a hot dog to turnip puree and fresh foie gras. The bar is a long mahogany beauty, and there are brass plaques with favored customers' names embossed on them in front of some of the stools. It has another wonderful advantage. Two double-door exits, one leading to Golden Gate Avenue in front, the other out Redwood Street, which is really a little alley in back.

I got there a little before five, cased the place, as they say on the late show, then went across the street to a coffee shop and kept an eye on the Golden Gate Avenue entrance. The wind had come up, causing discarded newspapers and sandwich wrappers to dart around like lost birds.

By five-forty there was no sign of Elaine Parker, or of Eddie Muliaga or Frank Lopez. They could have gone into Stars from the alley in back. I was just leaving two dollar bills alongside my coffee cup when a Yellow Cab pulled up in front of Stars and Elaine Parker climbed out. I waited a few more minutes. Still no sign of Lopez or Muliaga.

Parker was standing in the restaurant's small lobby, getting more than her share of stares from the boys at the bar who were wondering who would be stupid enough to stand up such a beauty for even a minute.

She had dropped the icy secretary act. Her hair was down and she was wearing a double-breasted camel hair blazer over a challis pleated skirt that went down to mid-calf over another pair of leather boots.

She stood with her head held high, ignoring the attention, finally walking in the direction of the bar. I scanned the room for Lopez and Muliaga. Still no sight of them.

I caught up to Parker when she was halfway to the bar. "Hi, Elaine. Sorry I'm late. Got tied up."

She accepted the answer with a seductive smile. "Hi, Nick." She slipped her arm through mine. "Let's sit at the bar."

She climbed onto a stool and gave me that smile again. "I'm so glad you took the time to meet me." Her purse was one of those thin, saddle leather jobs, with a long belt that hung over her shoulder.

The bartender approached. "Mind if I order for us?" Elaine asked, then turned to the bartender without waiting for my answer. "Two vodka Gibsons, up. Please."

She slid her fingers slowly along my coat sleeve. "I watched

North By Northwest, last night. For the umpteenth time. That's what Cary Grant and Eva Marie Saint were drinking on the train. Wasn't that a terrific movie?"

"Terrific," I agreed. We made small talk while waiting for the drink. More small talk while waiting for the second drink.

Parker gave the rest of the gentlemen things to think about as she slowly lowered her cocktail onion into her mouth, making a low sucking sound, cheeks hollowing in, then just as slowly pulling the empty toothpick out past those red lips. I myself paid little attention, of course, being constantly on alert for Muliaga and company.

"Have we got time for one more, Nick?" she asked, draining the last drop of the martini from her glass.

"All the time in the world," I said, signaling to the bartender. Her voice was turning into that husky growl.

"That Harry Chapman is a real prick, Nick. Taking off like that. Leaving me alone." Her fingers started another slow hike along my sleeve. "I'm scared to death. I couldn't sleep a wink last night."

"Where is Harry?"

"I don't know. He never went home last night. This morning he called me at the office, said he was out of town on a case, wouldn't be back for a couple of days." She was using one fingernail like a corkscrew, twisting it into my blazer. "Bastard isn't working on any case." Her face hardened into that efficient-secretary look for a second. "I'd know if he was working on a case."

"What about Frank Lopez and the Samoan? Where are they, Elaine?"

She withdrew her fingernail. I was happy to see there wasn't any blood on it. "I don't know, and I don't care." She sat up straight, tilting her head back, running a hand through her hair. "I'm afraid to go home. Afraid they'll be there waiting for me." Her lips extended in a thoughtful pout. "What should I do, Nick?"

Mrs. Damonte fluttered the venetian blinds of her window and gave a small cackle as I assisted Parker up the slippery slope to my front door.

Parker had insisted on one for the road. Twice. Five martinis are way past my limit, but not wanting to seem a wimp, I kept up with her. Barely.

"This is nice," Parker said once inside the door. "I just love bricks."

So did my father, a bricklayer by trade, who hated his hands to be idle, so when he had a day off, Mom suddenly found another wall bricked up.

Parker opened her arms and twirled like a ballerina into the living room, then the dining room.

I helped her out of her coat. Her purple silk blouse had oversize cloth-covered buttons. The top two had somehow come undone since we left the restaurant. She held onto her purse with both hands.

"How about another drink?" I suggested.

"Why not?" she replied, walking in a commendably steady manner over to the CD player.

Feeling like a high school kid trying to get his date drunk, I mixed her a stiff vodka, and a water over ice for myself.

Elaine was curled up on the front couch. I handed her the vodka and sat down at the opposite end of the couch. "You're not trying to get me drunk just to fuck me, are you, Nick?"

"Can it be done?"

That got me a giggle.

Her head was bobbing down to her drink, but I noticed that the amount of liquid in her glass was not going down.

"How do you like working for Harry Chapman?" I asked, taking a macho swig of my plain water.

She bulged out her lower lip with her tongue. "Harry's been a disappointment, to be honest. He promised to take me in, give me part of the company. Ten percent. And I deserve it. I've been damn near running the place for him. But I don't think it's going to happen," she added with resignation.

"Why not?"

"Harry's been acting like a complete fool. Quite frankly he's terrified of those men."

"You mean the guy who calls himself Lopez and the big Samoan?"

She went through the sipping-without-swallowing routine on her drink again. "Both Samoans."

"Ah. Tagaloa. The one that died up in Lake Tahoe."

"Yes," she agreed, unslinging her purse from her shoulder and dropping it to the floor. "Harry was scared shitless of him."

"You know, I was looking for Harry and went to his house. Tagaloa came to the door. Harry claimed he didn't let him in. How do you think Tagaloa got into the house?"

"Harry's a damn fool," she said bluntly. "He even accused me of giving that big gorilla a key. Can you imagine?"

I certainly could, but I shook my head and rattled the ice cubes in my glass. "No. But how did Tagaloa get in there? Harry must have the place alarmed like Fort Knox."

"Simple," Parker said, waving a hand as if it was holding a magician's wand. "Tagaloa had the run of our office. The absolute run. He was in Harry's office all the time. Harry has spare keys in his desk. He even borrowed Harry's car a couple of times. Harry keeps a set of house keys under his spare tire. For all I know he made a copy of Harry's key to my place."

"But why would Tagaloa bother with Harry?"

Elaine edged forward on the couch, her skirt riding up her thighs. "Because Harry could bullshit Rochard about his great hunt for whoever had bugged his office, but not Tagaloa. He figured either Harry put the bug in himself or was stringing Rochard around, stalling him. Running up a bill. Which he was. I know, because I handle the billing. You should have seen the big bastard come to the office, like it was his, not Harry's, ordering me around like I was working for him."

Possible, I had to admit. All possible. Tagaloa could have simply drawn an outline of all of Chapman's keys and had copies made. You have to go to a real locksmith to get the job done, not to one of those little metal carving machines at the front of a hardware store checkout counter. It always looks better in the movies when the secret agent presses the key into a piece of wax to get an impression, but a simple tracing on a piece of paper will do the job, and the locksmith won't even look at you as if you're a burglar or a jewel thief when you ask him to make up the new keys. It was exactly what I had planned to do with Elaine Parker's keys if I could ever get them out of her purse. "So you never saw Tagaloa or Eddie Muliaga before down in Los Angeles."

Her eyes narrowed.

"That's where their office was. And you lived down there too, didn't you?"

Her expression sobered. "How did you know that?"

"Harry mentioned it," I said casually. "Big town, L.A. No reason for you to have met them."

"None at all," she agreed. "The law firm I worked for didn't handle the type of work that those two did."

Again, possible. She could be telling the truth.

Her voice got husky again. "I liked the way you handled yourself at Harry's office, Nick." She put her drink down on the coffee table, reached over and undid my tie, pulling it past half-mast, using those long fingernails to start undoing my shirt buttons. "You had them scared. Really scared. Me too." Her nails began scratching right circles on my chest. "I have a confession to make. I wet my pants when you started shooting."

"So did I," I responded in a reasonably clear voice, as her head dropped to my chest and her tongue began exploring. "God, I'm hungry," she said.

Dinner was a mushroom omelet. Dinner was also quite late. We left a trail of clothing: blouse, skirt, shoes, pants, tie, pantyhose, all the way from the couch in the front room toward the bedroom, with frequent stops, clawing at each other on the hallway carpet, oblivious to the rug burns that showed up on elbows and knees the following morning. I could imagine Mrs. Damonte following our crashing progress from her flat below. I made a careful examination of Elaine Parker's legs: They were long, willowy, perfectly tapered at the ankle, very strong, and amazingly flexible. I could not determine whether or not they were hollow, but they certainly seemed that way as she continued belting down wine when we finally went to the kitchen to do something about dinner.

Elaine kept topping up my glass with Chablis while I got the omelet and toast going. She was wearing my old denim apron. Just the apron. Certainly not for Julia Child, but on Elaine Parker it was a real fashion statement. She kept up a line of chatter about wanting to leave Harry Chapman, to go to someplace more "progressive." I gave her a quick tour of my one-room office, just to show her how unprogressive I was.

"You should think about expanding, Nick, you really should," she cooed into my ear, the ever-present bottle of wine poised above my glass.

Peering down the top of Elaine's apron made certain forms of expansion inevitable.

She was gone when I struggled into the land of the living in the morning. The blurred image of the digital watch on the stand next to the bed said it was 7:22. I was in no condition to argue with it. The bathroom mirror told me more about how much liquor I swallowed last night than I wanted to know. I gulped down the first few gallons of water that sputtered out of the shower faucet, then let the cold spray hit me full face for a while. It didn't help clean away the cobwebs. My wonderful male macho plan of drinking Elaine Parker under the table and making copies of her keys had backfired, to say the least. While I was out cold, she had the run of the flat. I barefooted it into the office.

I should have known Elaine was too efficient to take off without leaving a note. There it was, centered on the computer screen:

THANKS FOR THE GREAT TIME, NICK
CALL ME LATER

Everything else looked in the same seminormal state it usually did. Nothing really out of place. There wasn't anything in the computer files relating to Henning or the emeralds, so if she got in there her efforts were wasted.

A half-dozen manila folders sat in a plastic upright holder between the computer and the copy machine. One of them held the financial records on Tagaloa, Muliaga, and on Ms. Parker herself. Those would have interested her.

I got a pot of coffee going, then went back to the bathroom to see if it was worth taking my life in my shaky hands by shaving. "Stupid son of a bitch," I shouted at my sorry-looking reflection.

CHAPTER TWENTY-THREE

HE WAS SOAP OPERA handsome, with waves of graying hair, big brown sadder-but-wiser eyes, and cheeks that dimpled deeply when he smiled. His eyes flicked over me, doing a very professional examination in a matter of seconds, taking in my best dark-blue blazer, pin-striped shirt, heavy silk knit tie, and highly polished loafers. It was the fifty-dollar watch on my wrist that was his tip-off. No Rolex sale to this turkey.

"May I help you, sir," he asked, his voice very civil, his eyes already looking toward the doors at the couple entering the store. The gleam in his eye told me that they must look promising.

"Yes, I'd like to see George Rochard." I handed him my business card.

"Mr. Rochard is quite busy this morning, sir. Perhaps one of our salespeople can help you."

"No. Give Rochard the card. He'll see me."

His face seemed to freeze. "One moment, please, I'll see if Mr. Rochard is available."

I killed time by wandering around the store. It was a study in contrasts, old elegance to modern schlock. Showers of crystal hung from antique chandeliers suspended from the high, frescoed ceiling. The carpet was one of those dizzingly busy orange-yellow-brown patterns you see in movie theatres. The glass and bleached-wood display cases were in a horseshoe shape, with the higher-priced baubles and beads at the front, the flanking cases holding everything from pearls, jade, and gold and silver trinkets to wafer-thin Swiss watches, charms, tiepins, gold-framed sunglasses designed by Porsche so that your glasses and car match, and pocket-size liquor flasks. A white, silk-covered arch stood over one section featuring wedding rings.

The counters and glass shelving against the walls were filled with Oriental vases, Hummel figurines, crystal ashtrays, and knickknacks.

The soft piped-in music in the background had been performed by a symphony orchestra under orders to make Gershwin sound boring.

The salesman who'd greeted me at the door coughed politely while I was trying to read the tiny price tag on one of those slim gold watches.

"Mr. Rochard will see you now, sir," he said in a tone cardinals use in introducing Protestants to the Pope.

Rochard's office looked as if it was more in keeping with his father's wishes: Persian carpets and coffered ceiling. One of those priceless-looking crystal chandeliers was centered over a mahogany desk whose wood matched the wainscoted wall. A half-dozen sturdy Queen Anne–style chairs circled the desk. There were two phones on the desk, both off-white plastic: one a business-style affair with buttons for a half-dozen lines; the other, one third the size. Rochard pointed at one of the chairs with his pipe.

"Sit down, Mr. Polo. I wasn't expecting to see you again."

"Does that mean that you didn't think I'd survive your playmates?"

Rochard's face reddened. "Certainly not. I'm not quite sure just what you're up to, Mr. Polo, but I want you to know——"

"I've got your emeralds, George," I said, wiggling my fanny into the stiff, ungiving upholstery.

Rochard tapped the stem of his pipe against his teeth and tried to look unconcerned. "My emeralds?"

"Maybe they're not yours, George. Maybe they're"——I snapped my fingers rapidly——"uh, what's his name? Your houseguest. Dark-haired chap. Plays tennis. Hangs around with big Samoan private investigators."

Rochard stalled for time by pulling a leather tobacco pouch from his desk drawer. He filled up, toasted the bowl of his pipe with a match, and puffed clouds of smoke in the air.

"Fernando warned me that you would be prying into my affairs," he said between puffs.

Fernando. At least I had half a name, though I'm sure Fernando-Frank-Lopez had dozens of them.

"Fernando and his goons have been prying into your affairs too, George. I think that Mr. Tagaloa killed your wife."

Rochard bolted from his chair, pushing his pipe at me, his expression showing that he wished it were a gun. "How dare you come in here like this and make a statement—"

"Knock it off, George," I said harshly. "You're not an idiot. You must have had ideas about your wife's death. Awfully convenient of Tagaloa to shoot himself full of cocaine right after Sharon died. Maybe he was celebrating. Celebrating a big payday. A big payday from you."

Rochard's face went slack, as if all the bones had suddenly been removed. "You, you don't know what you're saying." He started to sag. I got him by the shoulder and settled him back in his chair.

"I—I would never harm Sharon," Rochard said, lacing his fingers under his chin.

"Even if she wanted out? Wanted a divorce? Community property rights are pretty cut and dried, George. She'd get fifty percent."

"Of what?" Rochard scoffed. "You're right. I'm not a complete idiot, Mr. Polo. Sharon and I signed a prenuptial agreement before our marriage. It was drawn up by a very competent attorney. If she left me, she left with nothing. If things don't change soon, there will be nothing."

"You're in the middle on this, aren't you, George?" I said, patting him on the shoulder lightly. "In over your head."

"The emeralds," he mumbled. "They want the emeralds back." His hound-dog eyes looked as if they would burst into tears at any minute. "Do you really think they killed Sharon?"

"Yes, and a friend of mine. John Henning."

"I know nothing of a John Henning."

"He's the man that put the bug in your phone here," I said, pointing at his desk. "Maybe we can work something out, George. I can get you the emeralds. I can get you off the hook. But I want something in return."

Rochard waved a tired hand, like an old man without enough energy to swat away a mosquito. "I can't pay you. I'm overextended now. Business has been terrible. The branches simply aren't working out. That's why I—"

"Jumped in bed with Fernando and the Samoan boys," I said, finishing the sentence for him. "There's something I don't know, George. Something I have to know. How were the emeralds stolen?"

Rochard stared into the bowl of his pipe for several seconds, no doubt debating with himself just how much to tell me.

"I can help you on this, George," I prodded. "Get you out of it alive. Get Fernando and his boys off your back."

"Can you really get the emeralds? I'll pay you for them. It'll take a while, but I'll make it worth your while."

"I can. If you don't believe me, check with your boy Fernando."

"From my car," he finally said with a martyred look. "They took them from my Jaguar."

"Give me some details, George."

"We'd set up meeting places, but usually if the deliveries were to take place in San Francisco, they were made right at the parking lot. I park every morning at the garage on Grant Avenue. I have a reserved spot. When there was a delivery, I'd be notified of the day and time. The emeralds would be put in my car's trunk, I'd carry them back to the store."

"Notified by who? Tagaloa?"

"Usually. Or his partner."

"They had a key to your car's trunk?"

"Yes. Only this time when I got there, the trunk was broken open. The emeralds were gone."

"When Tagaloa notified you, how did he do it? How did he make contact?"

"He telephoned the day before."

"Telephoned you here?"

"Yes, always at the office. Always on my private line." He tapped the stem of his pipe against the smaller of the two phones on his desk. "That's why I had the line put in, so none of the employees would have a chance of overhearing our conversations."

"The whole shipment of emeralds was taken?"

"Yes, all three hundred." Rochard nervously ran a finger between his collar and his neck. "A mixture of one- and two-carat stones. Plus a few large ones. Very large emeralds."

"How large?" I asked.

"There were several in the three- to five-carat range."

I let out a low whistle. "What kind of money is Fernando claiming you owe him?"

Rochard cleared his throat, like a man with a cold coming on. "An even million dollars."

A nice round figure. And that was before Rochard had them cut and polished.

"What did Tagaloa say when you told him the shipment had been stolen?" I asked.

"He was furious. Didn't believe me. He had already returned to Los Angeles."

I remembered the multitude of air travel on Tagaloa's credit charges.

"I told him the Jag's trunk was broken into," Rochard continued. "He still didn't believe me. He said it had to be an inside job. Had to be. He said if it wasn't me, it had to be someone who overheard our conversation. I told him that I had the office telephone lines checked every month. He had me call Chapman. I got him to come right over. Chapman found the bug in a matter of minutes."

"Then what happened?"

"Tagaloa flew back up to San Francisco. He didn't much trust Chapman. He thought he might have been involved. Chapman said he thought he could run down whoever put the bug in the phone. Something about it being an out-of-date piece of equipment."

Good old Harry. "And Tagaloa went along with that?"

"Reluctantly. He questioned the staff. Everyone in the building who might have had access to the phone—the sales staff, accountant, janitors, everyone."

"What about your wife?"

"I told him it couldn't have been Sharon. There was nothing in it for her."

Except the fact that she recognized she was on a sinking ship, maybe.

"Did Sharon know about your private line?

"Yes," Rochard said wearily. "She knew. She didn't come to the office very often. Maybe every couple of weeks. We'd go out to lunch, shopping. She used my office for some personal calls. She liked calling me on the private line, not going through our switchboard."

"When did this Fernando come into the picture?"

The question seemed to confuse Rochard.

"When did you first meet Fernando?"

"Over a year ago." Color was returning to Rochard's face. "I think I've said enough, Mr. Polo. If you really can get me back those emeralds I'll pay you for them. It will take a little time, but if you can be patient—"

"Forget it, George. You help me on this and you get back your emeralds for free. No money involved. All I want is information."

"No money," he said skeptically.

"Not a cent. Just information. Now tell me about Fernando."

Rochard's eyes returned to the bowl of his pipe. He must have thought it was a crystal ball. "I don't understand your motives." His eyes raised and met mine. "I don't trust your motives."

"What have you got to lose, George? You don't get those stones back, you're a dead man, one way or the other." I let my eyes wander around the room. "The best that could happen is that you'll lose all of this, the stores, the house, the Jag, everything. The worst is that you'll have a couple of bullets neatly placed in the back of your head. These boys play rough, George. You should have known that when you hooked up with them."

Rochard dropped his pipe in an ashtray and leaned forward, elbows on the desk, hands steepled as if in prayer. "It was a mistake. Easy to say now. But I was desperate. It seemed like an easy way to bail myself out from some business mistakes."

"Hot emeralds. Who approached you?"

"Fernando."

"And how often were you getting shipments?"

174

"At least every other month. Sometimes more often."

"Were they all about the same size? Same number of stones?" I asked.

"Approximately," Rochard answered. "Sometimes bigger, sometimes smaller. This one was the biggest yet."

"How did you get rid of them?"

Rochard's voice turned hard, professional. "There's never a problem selling good-quality stones. It's all in timing the market, when to sell, and I know the market as well as anyone," he boasted.

"Fernando's last name, George. What is it?"

He hesitated, licking his lips.

"You're in this far, George. Give it to me."

"Vasquez. Fernando Vasquez."

"That his real name?"

"I really don't know. Now what about my stones? When do I get them back?"

"Who do you think stole them, George?"

"Not Sharon," he said stubbornly. "It wasn't her."

"Where did you meet Sharon, in Las Vegas?"

His eyes came to life. "Who told you that?"

"It was some of her friends at the funeral. They mentioned she had worked in Las Vegas."

"What has that to do with my emeralds?"

"Nothing. I'll get back to you as soon as possible, George," I said, standing up and pulling a page from Harry Chapman's book by flashing my holstered gun.

The sight of the weapon must have brought terrible images of Fernando Vasquez and Eddie Muliaga to Rochard's mind.

"What—what if Fernando finds out what I've told you?"

"He won't find out from me, George. Just hope that he didn't have your office bugged."

Rochard's hand reached out to the telephone as if it were a bomb that could go off any second.

CHAPTER TWENTY-FOUR

I USED ONE OF those open pay phones where you have to hold one hand over your ear to fight off the street noises. This one was right in front of a Gucci store. I checked my answering machine. There was one brief message: "Nicky, call me."

Uncle Pee Wee was always short and to the point, and very careful of just what he said on the telephone. He was also sure that his side of the phone wasn't bugged when he used it.

I dialed the number for The Cafe.

"Nicky, where are you calling from?"

"A pay phone, Uncle. On Post Street."

"Good. They can't bug every pay phone in town."

Not every one, but the feds had recently caught one of Uncle's competitors by tapping the phone booth he used on a too-regular basis outside of one of his favorite drinking establishments.

"Some news," Uncle Pee Wee said. "The jeweler you mentioned. He has been losing rather heavily to some people in Las Vegas."

"Do you know how heavily?" I asked.

"No, but they seem nervous. And they don't usually get nervous unless things go into six figures. I may have something for you on the emeralds later."

"Someone has heard something?"

"Yes, but nothing definite yet. Just that there may be stones available, at a very discounted price."

"The man from Colombia, Uncle. I have another name for him. At least a name he uses. Fernando Vasquez."

"I'll look into it. Call me later. Ciao."

"Ciao, Uncle," I said, hanging up the phone and wishing I'd made the call before my meeting with Rochard. Six figures. Anything from a hundred thousand to nine hundred and ninety-nine thousand. Something like the annual income of the well-dressed ladies and gentlemen parading in and out of Gucci's.

I dropped another quarter and called the answering machine at John Henning's house. There were no messages from Harry Chapman.

Tailing jobs in a car are difficult. It's so easy to lose your quarry at a stop sign, or at a sudden turnoff on a freeway. It's difficult when your quarry doesn't think he's being tailed. When he's expecting it, it's impossible. And I was expecting. I spotted the blue sedan three blocks after pulling away from the curb near Rochard's office. He was doing all the right things—staying back a half block, keeping a few cars between us. I made a series of slow turns, forgetting about the blue sedan and looking to see if he had company. He was alone. A one-car tail job. The worst. I almost felt sorry for him.

I took the scenic route home, pulling into the driveway and running up the front stairs. I peeked through the shutters and watched the blue sedan climb up Green Street toward Mason. Minutes later it was coming down the hill. One of Eddie Muliaga's beefy arms was hanging out the driver's-side window.

I changed into jeans and a dark-blue T-shirt, got two cold Anchor Steam beers from the refrigerator, and went out looking for Muliaga. He had the sedan wedged in front of a fire hydrant across from Capp's Corner, a restaurant well worth a visit on your next trip to San Francisco.

I approached the car cautiously, hands extended away from my body. Muliaga glowered at me from behind the car's windshield.

"Where's Fernando?" I asked him.

"Somewhere else," he answered gruffly. He had both of his massive hands wrapped around the steering wheel. He flicked an eye at the beers in my hands.

"Peace offering, Eddie. Let's talk."

I took his grunt for an affirmative answer and handed him a

bottle of the beer. He kept his eyes on me as he chugalugged the beer down, his lips making a suction-popping sound when he pulled the empty bottle away. He tossed it over his shoulder to the back of the car.

"You gonna drink the other one, Polo?"

"I guess not," I said, handing him the second bottle. He only drank half of this one in one sitting. He wiped his lips with the back of his hand, then said, "What you want, asshole?"

I squatted down so I was eye level with him in the car. "Tell me about Manny Tagaloa."

"He's dead."

"Why?"

"He was stupid, that's why. I told him plenty, don't take that shit. It's gonna kill you. Dope is for suckers. He wouldn't listen."

"So now you get his share, right, Eddie?"

He took another swig of the beer. "You want to deal, Polo? How much?"

"What good's money when you're dead, Eddie? Why did Tagaloa kill Rochard's wife?"

He rolled the bottle of beer across his forehead, then wiped away the dampness with a dirty handkerchief. "Manny don't kill her. If he killed her he'd do it by fucking her to death, not holding her head underwater."

"Maybe he held her underwater in the hot tub while he was screwing her."

Muliaga got a kick out of that. He pushed his head back and laughed, mouth open, showing more yellow metal than some old-time prospectors saw in a year of panning for gold.

"Or maybe you held her under while Manny was in the throes of passion."

He drained what was left of the beer and tossed the bottle behind him. I hoped the rental agency dinged him for the damage to the car's upholstery.

"You like to push, don't you, Polo? You can get hurt that way." His shotgun-shell fingers began drumming on the steering wheel. "We got no reason to kill the Rochard woman. No reason at all."

"But Manny Tagaloa went up to Tahoe to see her?"

"Did he?"

"Yes. Why, Eddie?"

"Maybe to talk. Easier to talk to her when she's away from her husband. Find out what she knows about the emeralds."

"And maybe she was a bad listener, huh, Eddie? Maybe you and Manny didn't like her answers."

His voice turned hard. "No reason to kill that woman. Understand?"

"What was the reason for killing John Henning, Eddie?"

The drumming fingers stopped their movement, and Muliaga dropped his hands to his lap. "You ask stupid questions, Polo. We don't kill nobody. I don't kill nobody never. But I think I'd be willing to make an exception for you."

I stood up so I could keep an eye on Muliaga's hands. "Someone killed Henning."

"He your partner, Polo? Tough. I lost a partner too. Real tough."

"You don't seem too broken up, Eddie. Guess you'll have to handle all those trips to Colombia and Baja California by yourself now. Ever get wet on those boat trips from Ensenada to San Diego?"

He pushed open the car door and climbed out onto the street. "I'm getting tired of waiting for those emeralds, Polo."

I backed away and pointed an index finger at Capp's Corner. "There are three cops I know having lunch in there now, Eddie. I'd hate to break into their mealtime."

His arms were swinging slowly alongside his body, as if they were anxious to make a move toward my throat. "You gonna push too far, Polo. And I'm gonna make you pay. Why don't you give me my emeralds? That way you make some money and I won't have to hurt you."

"Tell Fernando if I get hurt, he won't get all of his emeralds. All two hundred and fifty."

Eddie's arms stopped swinging and he wrenched the car door open. He got behind the wheel, stabbed the accelerator, and the motor growled. "Thanks for the beers, Polo. I'll pay you back for them. Believe me, I will."

I watched until his taillights disappeared into a maze of traffic on Powell Street.

* * *

"A virgin mary?" Jane Tobin inquired in a sarcastic tone.

"Good for you," I said, taking a swallow of the plain tomato juice. "Lots of vitamin C."

Jane leaned sideways on her barstool and peered into my eyes, the whites of which early in the morning had somewhat resembled the color of the drink in my hand.

"Do a little celebrating, last night, did you, Nick?"

"Pining away for you all night. How was dinner?"

"All right," she said, taking a sip of her sidecar, an old-fashioned drink that went along with the restaurant's decor. We were sitting at the curved bar at Asta's, a restaurant named after the Thin Man's dog. (All right, trivia buffs, I know that the Thin Man was actually Clyde Wynant, and not Nick Charles, but the sequence of follow-up movies has made Charles and the Thin Man one and the same.)

Two large-screen television sets ran continuous replays of all the Thin Man movies, with the sound off, while music from Duke Ellington and Glenn Miller spilled out of the speakers. This was the one where a young, gangly Jimmy Stewart is the bad guy. They had done a nice job in giving the restaurant a 1930s flavor with art deco light fixtures, black-and-white-striped stools and chairs, large vases filled with full-blooming orange-tipped birds of paradise. The bar itself was highly varnished pressed wood chips with a maroon trim. "Recycled wood," the bartender, a good-looking chap in one of those white-button waiter jackets told us. "Everything you see has been made from recycled products." I hoped he didn't mean the food.

On the screens the real Asta was scurrying around an enormous living room, and Nick and Nora, dressed in silky pajamas, were chasing after him.

"How goes the hunt?" Jane asked.

I gave her a brief rundown of my meeting with George Rochard, splicing in the information I'd learned from Uncle Pee Wee.

"Rochard's really between the proverbial rock and hard place, Jane. He's sweating blood to get the emeralds back so he can pay off his gambling losses and keep Fernando and Muliaga off his back."

180

"But what does it boil down to, Nick? What have you found out about John Henning? Who killed John?"

"Not-Rochard. Though I wouldn't dismiss him as a suspect for his wife's murder. If he thought she'd been double-crossing him, he might have killed her. He met Sharon in Vegas. He owes a fortune to the casinos. Maybe he found her playing around with some of her old boyfriends. Everything seems to point to Tagaloa as John's killer."

"Why kill John if the emeralds were still missing? What was the gain in killing him?"

Her logical reporter's mind was in high gear: who, what, when, where, why, and how, the six classical questions.

"I don't know," I admitted. "They were probably more worried about the tapes Henning had gotten from the wiretap on Rochard's office."

"So you think John told Tagaloa about the tapes, about Sharon Rochard hiring him, and that's why Sharon was killed? But then why not go after Sharon right away?"

I hate it when she's so damned pragmatic.

The bartender informed us that there would be a half hour wait for our table. "You can eat at the bar right away if you wish."

Jane wished. The menu was right up her alley. Imported wines were listed as "From the Continent." All of those exotic jars and cans in Jane's cabinet were actually used by the chef. She ordered grilled green-lip mussels with saffron pasta and red pepper fennel sauce. Would Nick and Nora order blue-lip or red-lip mussels? No way.

My stomach was just starting to come back to normal, but I decided to play it cautious and order a steak sandwich and another virgin mary, while Jane ordered a glass of domestic champagne at five dollars a pop.

"Why don't you just go and give all the information you have to the police, Nick?" Jane said while a waiter started arranging plates, napkins, and utensils in front of us.

It was a good question. I didn't have a good answer for it. "It just doesn't fit, Jane. Something's missing. Besides, if Tagaloa did kill John, then he was doing it on orders from this Fernando character. Or Tagaloa's partner, Eddie Muliaga, could have been the one who did John in. Maybe there's a double cross involved, and Muliaga has had the emeralds all along."

I had spent the afternoon going over Tagaloa and Muliaga's credit card trips. There was nothing that showed Muliaga was up in San Francisco at the time Henning was killed, but Los Angeles is just 389 four-lane freeway miles from San Francisco. "Tagaloa accidentally offing himself doesn't sit well either, though according to the sheriff he was an accident waiting to happen—overweight everywhere except his nasal passages. Bad heart, clogged arteries, perfect candidate for an overdose. Eddie Muliaga said he warned Tagaloa about using dope."

"Do you believe him, Nick?"

"Eddie is no Einstein. He makes his money with his muscles and misguided guts. It doesn't take much of an imagination to see him handing Tagaloa a syringe overloaded with high-grade coke."

"Do you want me to ask Ben Weber if he knows this Fernando Vasquez?"

"I doubt that's his real name, but sure. Ask Weber. Will you be seeing him soon?"

She ignored the sharp tip of my pointed question.

Up in TV land William Powell was crawling around on a carpet, with Asta sniffing at his heels. It looked as if he had discovered a clue. I stared down into my virgin mary. Maybe I had too.

I dialed Nevada information from the restaurant's pay phone and got the listing for the Crystal Palace, the casino that Sharon Rochard had worked for. I placed the call on my credit card. I was transferred to four different people before I got the answer I needed.

I then made a local call to Uncle Pee Wee.

"Your Mr. Fernando Vasquez is a man of mystery, Nicky. No one I know has heard of him," Uncle informed me.

I wasn't surprised about that. Lopez-Vasquez wasn't the type of character who would give the George Rochards of the world his real name.

"About the emeralds," Uncle said. "I may have something for you there. There was a sale of uncut stones. At a very low price."

"Where?"

"Here in San Francisco."

"Do you know the buyer, Uncle?"

"Yes, but I can't give you his name, Nicky. You know that."

"Can you get in touch with him?"

"Yes," Uncle Pee Wee answered cautiously.

"Ask him if the seller looked like this." I gave Uncle the description, and he told me to call him back in half an hour, which turned out to be just enough time for Jane to finish her dinner and a dessert order of a banana-cherry Betty, a concoction of warm bananas and ice cream topped with warm cherries.

CHAPTER TWENTY-FIVE

I WONDERED IF they would have waited for me all night, or if they would have come pounding through the door. Jane pleaded an assignment in the early morning hours necessitating a trip to Fort Bragg, a scenic coastal town some 180 miles north of the city. "Someone from the paper" would be picking her up at five in the morning.

I was tempted to bring in Ben Weber's name as that someone, but since we both made it clear that our relationship was in Jane's words, "open to other options," I didn't pry. A gentleman to the end. Perhaps a surly, grouchy gentleman, but a gentleman no less, I escorted her to her front door, where we exchanged good-night kisses and promises to call each other tomorrow.

I had left my Ford parked behind Jane's convertible in her carport. Muliaga's dark-blue sedan had me blocked in. I started to backtrack up the stairs when I first saw the car, but Eddie Muliaga's hands grabbed me from behind, his fingers digging into my elbows.

The mysterious Fernando stepped out from the backseat of the sedan. No ice-cream suit this time; Fernando was dressed for nightlife in a silk, cobalt-blue suit. A long white scarf was draped across his shoulders, the ends reaching down to the bottom of his suit jacket.

Harry Chapman followed Fernando from the back of the car, his movements slow and awkward, looking like a much-used full-back struggling out of bed the morning after a championship game. Chapman must have a terribly high cleaning bill. The last time I saw him there was blood spattered across his shirtfront and tie. He was dressed a little more casually now, beige slacks and a light green cotton shirt. It would take a lab analysis to determine if there was more blood on his outfit this time than last.

One eye was closed and there was an open gash over the other eye. Coagulated blood had stopped the wound from dripping more blood onto Harry's clothes.

Fernando walked over briskly, his eyes glistening as though he was laughing at a private joke.

Muliaga was digging his fingers into my elbows so hard my arms were going numb.

"Mr. Polo," Fernando said, flashing his teeth at me. "So nice to see you again." He flicked his eyes at Muliaga. "You can release him. Make sure he's not armed this time, eh, Eddie?"

Muliaga gave me a professional pat-down, taking the .32 out of its holster and stuffing it into one of his safari jacket pockets.

Fernando twisted his neck around so he could see Harry Chapman. "Come here, Harry, say hello to your friend."

Chapman walked with his arms straight down, like a prisoner. "Hi, Nick," he said, wincing, as if talking caused him pain.

Fernando wrapped an arm around my shoulder as though we were old buddies reminiscing about our college days. "Without good old Harry, we wouldn't have known that you'd be likely to stop by at your girlfriend's place. Right, Harry?"

Harry nodded his head forward, arms still hanging straight down; he looked like a puppet with just one string attached.

Fernando took a handkerchief from his back pants pocket and wiped down the fender of my car before nestling his hip cautiously against it.

"That is a very pretty woman, Miss Tobin." He brought his fingers to his lips and made a kissing sound. "Full of the juice of life. I'm sure she photographs well. You may not know it, Mr. Polo, but Eddie is an excellent photographer. He is very—persuasive in getting his models to pose exactly the way he wants them to, aren't you, Eddie?"

Muliaga dug his fingers deeper into my elbows. "Yeah, sometimes they take a little coaxing, but they always end up doing what I want them to."

Fernando moved up close, his face inches from mine, "Perhaps when Eddie is through taking pictures of Miss Tobin, we could make an exchange. The photographs, all the photographs, and the negatives of those unfortunate pictures you took of myself and Eddie for those of Jane. Jane, that is her first name, isn't it?"

I could smell his breath. I could smell his after-shave. His legs were spread apart, his groin an absolute bull's-eye for my knee. But with Eddie Muliaga right behind me, Fernando knew I wouldn't even give it a try. His eyes mocked me, then he swiveled away, his scarf swaying behind him, a bullfighter turning his back on the beaten bull.

He turned his taunting ways on Chapman, grabbing his cheek and pinching it, shaking the flesh so hard that the loose skin rolled like shock waves across his Adam's apple. "Yes, good old Harry."

"Okay, Vasquez, Lopez, whoever the hell you are. You'll get your photographs. Now do you want to make a production out of showing just how tough a guy you are or do you want to get your emeralds back?"

"Both, I think, Mr. Polo."

"I'll get the stones for you. Or at least tell you where they are."

"All of them?" he asked quickly.

"All except the three that are in John Henning's safe-deposit box. I can't get at those for a couple of weeks." His face first showed confusion, then anger. "The picture I showed you of the emeralds was a phony. Taken in a jeweler's office. A few stones, the bag stuffed with paper. The tapes in the pictures were phonies too. Blanks. Any tapes that Henning did have were destroyed by his killer."

The confusion was gone. Nothing but anger now. Before he could tell Eddie to start to rearrange my vertebrae I said, "I didn't know where the stolen emeralds were then. I do now."

"Where?" he demanded.

"I'm not positive. But I know where to look."

"I'm not a patient man, Mr. Polo. What little patience I have, you've used up."

"By tomorrow morning. You'll have the stones or know who has them."

"I could make you tell me right now," he threatened.

I twisted my neck and snuck a peak at Muliaga. He looked as though he was out of patience too. "Not here, Fernando. You're used to operating in your country. I start screaming now and a half-dozen people will call the cops, including Jane Tobin, who, in case Harry didn't tell you, is a reporter. A newspaper reporter. You know the kind of connections they have."

With that face Fernando should avoid poker games. Confusion was back on his puss. He changed expressions like rubber masks. He had to be confused if he thought that a good citizen would call the cops even if I did get off a shout for help in the time it took for Eddie to shove one of those baseball mitts he called hands over my mouth. Several screams, maybe. Combine the screams with a few gunshots, probably. An interruption in their cable-TV service, absolutely.

"I'm going to need a little help in getting the stones back," I told Fernando.

"Eddie will go with you."

"No, one look at Eddie and these people will bolt. I'll take Harry."

Fernando leaned back against my fender. He didn't bother with the hanky wiping this time. "I don't think that will work."

"What have you got to lose? You can always find us."

He ground the toe of his Italian moccasin against the oil-spotted carport floor.

"What is your price?" he finally asked.

"Ten percent."

"Wholesale?"

"Wholesale," I agreed. "But remember, that jeweler I mentioned saw one of the stones I swiped from John Henning's safe-deposit box, so I know what wholesale really is."

"It really is a lot of money, Mr. Polo."

"Listen," I said, putting some anger in my voice. "I'm not going to haggle with you like some goddamn field hand down in Colombia. You're here in San Francisco. You pay ten percent of what they go for wholesale here, otherwise it's not worth my effort."

"Is it worth your life?" he responded.

"Fernando, you may be good at smuggling emeralds out of

your country. For all I know you may be a good shot, a hell of a golfer, and give a great massage. But when it comes to bluffing, you ain't worth a shit. Kill me and your whole scheme blows up in your face. You'll have to find some other tunnel to get your stones into the country. I traced your buddy Eddie here and his partner traipsing in and out of Baja. I've got dates, times, receipts, for the airplanes they used, the motels they stayed at, and I know what boats they used from Ensenada. If I just wanted to get you off my back, I'd have turned the information over to the cops already. Just one cop knocks on George Rochard's door and he'll start singing louder than Judas Priest." The name from one of the cassettes in the glove compartment of Jane's convertible had suddenly popped into my head.

That look of confusion settled on Fernando's features again.

"It's a rock band," Muliaga piped in.

So much for his musical taste.

Fernando signaled Muliaga with a jab of his chin. "Let him go, Eddie."

"Where can I reach you?" I asked Fernando.

He pursed his lips before saying, "Mr. Chapman has been kind enough to provide us with a key to his house."

Eddie Muliaga touched my arm, as lightly as a bird. "You fuck around with us, Polo, and I'm going to take those pictures of your girlfriend. If it takes years, I'll get those pictures."

His eyes were the calm, clear eyes of a psychotic. I believed him.

"Thanks, Nick," Harry Chapman said in a shaky voice.

"Don't thank me yet, Harry. If my hunch about the emeralds is wrong, you're back on the Colombian's shit list."

I kept the car crawling along between fifteen and twenty miles an hour. The slower you drive, the easier it is to spot a tail. I drove aimlessly around the Marina District until I was satisfied that Muliaga wasn't following us.

"How the hell did they get hold of you, Harry? I thought you were going to stay out of town, keep in touch with me."

"Yeah," he mumbled, his words distorted by his fingers probing his mouth for loose teeth. "I called Elaine. Something new came in. Big case. Needed my input."

"So you came back and our friends were waiting for you."

"Yeah. The big ugly Samoan grabbed me coming out of my office."

"Was there a big case that needed your attention?" I asked.

"Uh-huh. Surveillance case in Monterey. Couple of weeks' worth of work. Uh, Nick. I'm sorry about dumping on you and the Tobin woman."

"Looks like you didn't have much choice, Harry." I parked in front of my flat and killed the engine. "So Elaine Parker didn't set you up."

"I don't know, Nick. I'm not sure about her. What do you think?"

"I think you should either give her ten percent of the business or get rid of her, Harry." I felt no remorse about advising Chapman on the fate of Elaine's employment. If he did fire her, she'd land on her dainty feet, another job, better prospects, more money. If not in her chosen profession as a businesswoman, then as a product sampler for a distillery.

Chapman followed me up the stairs. The movement of venetian blinds showed that Mrs. Damonte was on the job.

As we went past her door Chapman said, "That crazy old lady with the air horn live here all the time?"

Chapman would long remember his first encounter with Mrs. D. Something about having an air horn blasted in your ear that sticks in your memory bank. "All the time, Harry. Better security than all those electronic gadgets you have sprinkled around your house and office." I pointed him toward the bathroom. "Clean up, then we've got work to do."

I rummaged through my closet and got a clean pair of slacks and a shirt for Chapman. He had washed and crisscrossed some Band-Aids across the gash above his eye. A close look showed that he was probably going to have to get some stitches put in. He upturned a palm, showing me a single tooth, the root showing fresh blood.

"So loose I pulled it out," Chapman explained.

"Consider this a gift from the tooth fairy," I said, tossing him his SIG-Sauer automatic.

"You told me it went into the bay," he said, his hands enthusiastically caressing the gun.

"Everybody lies to you, Harry. There's a clean shirt and pair of pants for you on the bed. Get changed; I'll put on some coffee."

My clothes fit Chapman pretty well. With the automatic stuck in his waistband and the bandages on his face, he looked like someone you wouldn't want to mess with. Looks are deceiving, but if he played his part right, he'd do just fine. Harry swished the coffee around carefully in his mouth, flinching when the hot liquid hit a nerve.

"Got any brandy?"

"Gallons of it, Harry. But none for you. Not now. Later we may celebrate with a bath in a tub of Courvoisier. But for the rest of the night, we both have to be very sober. Very alert."

CHAPTER TWENTY-SIX

WE SLIPPED IN THE door just before closing time. The place was almost empty. Harry headed for the men's room. There were two stragglers at the bar. Audrey was wiping down tables.

"Where's Winky?" I asked her.

She straightened up and blinked her thick lashes until the contacts focused in. "Oh, it's you," she said, with little enthusiasm. "He's in his office. You want me to tell him you're here?"

"Don't bother. I know the way."

The cooks and waiters were going through their cleanup chores. José, the punk who had pounded me to the pavement in front of the restaurant, was working the sink, his sleeves rolled up, scouring away at a stack of dishes.

A huge metal stockpot was simmering away on the stove. It smelled so good I took a quick peek. The pale brown liquid was filled with chicken bones, cloves of garlic, clumps of leeks, and bunches of parsley. The parsley bunches still had those metal twisty-bands the supermarkets use wrapped around them. I patted my stomach and tried to remember if Jane or I had ordered soup the night we ate there.

José spotted me and stepped back from the sink. The hot-water faucet was attached to a long rubber hose. He held the faucet out toward me.

"How's your buddy Bomber Jacket doing?"

He scowled back at me, dropping the hose to the floor, wiping his hands on his apron. One of the other workers shouted something to him in Spanish, and he bent down to pick up the hose, his eyes never leaving me. He spat on the floor, then went back to his sink chores.

Winky Harris was at his desk, working away at a computer, the amber-on-black screen showing row after row of numbers. His deeply tanned forehead was wrinkled in concentration.

"Aren't you afraid you'll get skin cancer?" I said loud enough to startle him.

He swiveled around in his chair and glared up at me. "What the fuck do you want, Polo?"

"I see you never got around to firing José. I guess good dish-washers are hard to find."

He balanced on the end of the chair as if he was going to jump up and run out at any moment. I closed his office door behind me. "I should have figured you out earlier, Winky. I just couldn't fit you in. But once I put you in the picture, there was nobody else."

"What the fuck are you talking about?" he asked again.

"I heard you sold the stones real cheap."

His tan seemed to pale a bit, but it was probably my imagina-tion. "What the fuck—"

"—am I talking about?" I finished the sentence for him. "The emeralds. Didn't get a real good price, did you? Panic selling is never a good idea. Should have waited awhile." I pointed a finger at the computer screen. "Business that bad? Need a quick cash infusion? You and George Rochard should get together and cry on each other's shoulders. The restaurant business must be tough. So many places going under. I'll give you a tip, Wink. Wash the parsley and take off the twisties before you put it in the stockpot. Gets rid of that metallic taste."

"I don't know anything about any emeralds. You're crazy. Get out of here."

He started to rise from his chair, and I hit him as hard as I could with a right hand. He fell back into the desk, knocking over the computer screen and the telephone. He got up, massaging his chin. "You've gone too far, asshole," he said. "This time I'm calling the cops and having you busted."

"Go right ahead," I suggested. "You're going to have to talk to them pretty soon anyway."

He continued to rub away at his chin. I hoped it ached half as much as my knuckles did.

"What do you mean, talk to the cops?"

"I mean you'll want to explain to them how you killed John Henning and Sharon Rochard."

His eyes gauged the distance from me to the door, then raked up and down my sport coat to try and determine if I was carrying a gun. I flipped open my coat just enough so that he could see the butt of the .38 revolver, the one I usually keep in the car's headrest.

"You must be drinking too much, Polo." He tapped a finger against his temple. "You're going crazy in the head."

"No, I don't think so. Getting Henning to come here was a mistake. This wasn't his style. Poor old John sucking away at a virgin mary while Sharon slugged down the tequila. Why would Sharon Rochard bring him here, such a public place? She knew he was a recovering alcoholic. Why would she flaunt the booze in his face?"

Harris sat back down on his swivel chair. "Who knows what one drunk will do to another one?"

"You're the one who told her to bring John in, weren't you, Winky? Because of the wiretap. The tapes he made. You were worried about old John. He'd listened to those tapes. Maybe even made a transcript of them. Is that why you purged his computer?"

Harris shook his head slowly from side to side, his eyes glancing up at the wall clock. "Maybe a psychiatrist could help you with your problem, buddy, cause I don't have a clue as to what you're talking about."

"John had one fault. At least it was a fault to someone like you. He was honest. He could figure out from the tapes that Rochard was in the smuggling business. That there was a big shipment of emeralds due. You were worried he'd go to the cops, weren't you? Did he tell you that's what he was going to do? Or maybe you just couldn't take the chance. So Henning had to go."

His eyes flicked up to the clock again. It was after two in the morning. Closing time.

"I'm just guessing on a lot of this," I said, "but the way I figure it, it was Sharon Rochard's idea to begin with. Sharon was no dummy. She earned her living out of the casinos in Vegas. She had to have street smarts. She could see her husband's business was going down the toilet. But she'd signed a prenuptial agreement. If Rochard went bust, she'd get nothing. Unless she got out quick. Meeting Henning at that AA meeting, learning what he did for a living, must have seemed like a sign from the heavens to her. So she hired Henning to tap Rochard's phone. She probably knew about the emerald smuggling for some time. She must have been keeping a close tap on Rochard's operation. Or maybe she was just trying to catch poor old George at something—anything. Hanky-panky or phony business deals. Anything to give her an edge. Whatever, the shipment of emeralds must have been a bonus. All those emeralds. How was she going to get them? She'd need help. She needed someone she could trust. Someone she knew from the old days. Like a bartender in Vegas. A bartender who had his hands in more than the till. A bartender who set up high rollers with pretty women with big league curves, cover girl skin, and spike heels rounded at the back. You. Winky Harris. Introduction specialist. Sounds better than pimp, doesn't it? I called the Crystal Palace in Vegas. Talked to a couple of your former coworkers. They said to say hello to you, wish you luck with your restaurant."

"You're babbling, Polo. Not making any sense."

"Oh, it makes sense, all right. Sharon couldn't write Henning a check for his services, because old George was probably keeping a close eye on her expenditures. And she couldn't hand him her Visa card, so she paid him with emeralds. Or more likely gave them to John as collateral. She'd come up with the cash later. Were the jewels she gave Henning from the ones you stole from her husband's car? Or were they ones she'd swiped earlier, on her visits to his office when she came to shop and go to lunch with dear old George? That was a nice touch of yours, by the way, banging up the Jaguar's trunk. Did the two of you pull it off together? Sharon opens the trunk with a key and then you do a little breaking and entering with a crowbar after the emeralds were already in your pocket. Very nice. But you couldn't trust Henning, could you Winky? He might have made backups of the tapes. Might just go right to the police with the emeralds Sharon had given him. John was old, not in the best of health. How did you get him to drink all that bourbon? He was a vodka man. Just pour it down his throat? Stick the gun against his head and make him drink? Was it straight from the bottle or did you cut it down a little for him with some water? Or ginger ale. John liked ginger ale."

Harris folded his arms across his chest and leaned back in his chair. "You're crazy, Polo. The police would never believe your crazy story. Even if they believed your bullshit, there's no proof. Nothing."

"No, you were careful. Very careful, I'll give you that. And that job on Sharon Rochard. That was a masterpiece. You knew where she was. You must have driven up to Lake Tahoe right after I left your place. Was it the booze again? Getting her drunk must have been a lot easier than it was with John Henning. She loved the sauce. So you just let her suck it down and then held her under. Did Sharon struggle much? Even if she was drunk out of her skull, you'd think she put up some kind of a fight. That last fight for life. Or had you kicked all the life out of her by then?"

Harris leaned back in his chair until his head was facing straight up at the ceiling. "Don't you read the papers, Polo? Suicide. Sharon committed suicide. And so did this Henning guy. Both suicides. The cops have no interest in their deaths because they know they weren't murdered." He dropped his head and gave me a lopsided grin. "You're the only one with these crazy ideas. And no proof. Get the fuck out of here."

The door burst open and José stood there, a large chef's knife in his hand. I pulled out the .38. It didn't seem to make much of an impression on José. He held the knife in front of him as if it was a switchblade, his fingers wiggling along the knife's black wooden handle.

"Careful, José," I said backing away until I bumped into the wall. José was no more than six feet away on the left, Winky Harris even closer.

"José and his buddy Bomber Jacket were supposed to do a little more to me than just rough me up, weren't they, Harris? Serious hospital time. Maybe never coming out of the hospital. Knock me around and dump me somewhere. Just another little uptick on the victims-of-grievous-assault list. In this town, another mugging doesn't get much notice."

"You're full of shit, Polo," Harris said, edging his legs in front of the chair so he could get to his feet in a hurry. "But you're also a pain in the ass. You shoot my employee here, it's you who will be going to the cops. I don't like assholes like you pushing me around. So we're going to teach you a little lesson." He rattled off some rapid Spanish to José.

I cocked the gun and pointed it at José.

"You'll get the first one in the stomach, José."

Harris slid open his desk drawer. The butt of an automatic was there, within inches of his hand. "You'll get off maybe one shot, Polo. Maybe you hit José, maybe you don't. But we'd get you. Either with the knife or this gun. We'd get you for sure."

He had a point. And so did José's knife. "Then I'd be dead, and you wouldn't have to worry about the murder charges?"

Harris chuckled. It was a deep, dirty chuckle, the kind you'd imagine terrorists let out when they read in the paper just how many people were killed by their bombs.

"You got shit, Polo. Shit. You couldn't make any of that stick."

He had another point. "Now, Harry," I shouted.

Chapman slammed his automatic into José's back. The knife clattered to the floor. I guess Harry wanted to give back for the beating he took earlier. He took it out on José, slamming the butt of his gun against the back of José's head, not once, but several times.

I kicked the desk drawer closed just about the same time Harris's hand was snaking toward it. He pulled back his fingers and yelled.

Standing over the unconscious José, gun in hand, banged-up face, Harry Chapman did indeed look like a rough character.

"Do you know this man?" I asked Harris.

"No," Harris barked out, continuing to shake his fingers.

"He's from Colombia, Winky. That's Colombia, South America, where they find emeralds in the ground."

Harry was enjoying his role playing. He slapped the automatic against the open palm of his hand and just glared at Harris.

It wasn't my imagination now. Harris's dark hide was turning

196

paler by the minute. "He wants his emeralds back, Harry. He wants them bad."

"I—I don't have them, I tell you. I—"

"You sold them, didn't you?"

"I—"

"Didn't you!" I shouted loud enough to startle myself a little bit."

"Yes, I—"

Harris was having a hard time finishing a sentence. His eyes were following the movement of the gun in Chapman's hand.

"Where's the money, Winky?"

Harris waved a hand at the upturned computer screen. "There. Into the business." He looked anxiously at Chapman, started to say something, then just shook his head and looked at the floor.

I reached over Harris and took the gun from his desk drawer and slipped it into my pocket. "Was it worth it?" I asked him. "Killing Henning and Sharon Rochard, just to keep this dump going?"

"You don't understand," he moaned. "Everything I've got is in the place. Everything. All those years of kissing ass in Vegas, scrounging for a buck. I've got something here. I just needed a break. When Sharon brought me that tape, I—I just had to—" His voice trailed off into an indistinguishable mumble.

I pushed Chapman away from the door. He followed behind me, out to the bar. Audrey was sitting on a stool, one long leg crossed over the other.

"What's keeping Winky?" she asked.

"He's tied up, Audrey. Maybe you'd better go home without him."

"How tied up?" she asked, sliding gracefully off the stool.

"Bad. Real bad."

"I knew it," she said. "He's been acting like a goddamn prince the last couple of days. I knew it was too good to last."

She walked past us toward Harris's office. I went behind the bar and fished among the bottles until I found a bottle of Hennessy V.S.O.P. cognac. I filled two balloon snifters halfway and handed one to Chapman. "You earned this, Harry."

Chapman raised his glass and ducked his mouth to it.

I took a small sip, swirling the cognac around my teeth and tongue as if trying to wash out a bad taste.

"What now?" Chapman said.

I reached for the phone. "I tell Fernando what happened to his emeralds."

"I'm not sure of everything that's going on, Nick, but will this get me off the hook?"

"Off the hook and back swimming free, Harry."

I had Harry dial his home number and thought about Winky Harris. Harris was right about one thing. There was no proof against him. Nothing to pin him to either Henning's or Sharon Rochard's death. The cops hate opening old suicide cases. They wouldn't look very deep no matter what I told them about Harris's motives. The money he got for the emeralds could be explained away as a business loan. The cases were closed, the bookkeeping completed. Why make more work? Once Harris got over his fear, once he realized that I had no proof, that any semi-good attorney would have a field day if the district attorney even tried to charge him with murder, he'd get his courage back. Then he'd think about the mysterious man with the automatic weapon and the bashed-in face. If he was so tough, why was his face bashed in like that? It would take more than an overacting Harry Chapman to scare him again.

My last call from Asta's to Uncle Pee Wee was the clincher. While the buyer would never drop a name, the description I'd given Uncle Pee Wee—male, forties, sinister looking, black hair, deep suntan, was right on. But what was the penalty for selling stolen emeralds? Emeralds with no legal owner. Winky could say that they were his, that he won them in a card game. No one, certainly not Fernando or Muliaga, would come forth and say, "Hey, those babies were mine." The police would start asking a lot of questions, the same type questions reporters ask: who, where, what, when, why, and how. Questions better left unanswered by the likes of Fernando and Muliaga.

Whoever answered Chapman's phone did so without saying a word.

"With whom do I have the pleasure of speaking?" I said.

"Always a wise guy, huh, Polo?" came the guttural tones of Eddie Muliaga.

"What would you do to the guy that killed Sharon Rochard, stole your emeralds, then sold them dirt-cheap just to keep his business afloat?"

"Kill the motherfucker," Muliaga said calmly.

"That's what I figured," I said, breaking the connection. "You can go home now, Harry."

CHAPTER TWENTY-SEVEN

THE POUNDING ON the front door brought me out of my nap. I rubbed my eyes and heaved myself off the couch. Jane Tobin looked fresh and perky and her voice was full of good cheer.

"How was Fort Bragg?" I asked, as she went by me and took her normal route to the refrigerator.

"Great. We got back hours ago." She opened the refrigerator door, her nose wrinkling in disapproval when finding no aluminum foil–wrapped care packages from Mrs. Damonte's kitchen. "I've got good news, Nick. Ben Weber has identified that photograph of yours. The guy from Colombia."

"A man of many talents, Mr. Weber," I remarked without a decibel of good cheer.

"I thought you'd be excited. Ben went through a lot of trouble for you."

"He did, huh? How did he stumble across this information while he was whale watching?"

"Whale watching? What are you talking about? There are no whales in Colombia."

No. But whale watching is one of the required tourist attractions off Fort Bragg. "Weber's in Colombia?"

"Sure," Jane said, settling into a kitchen chair. "He left the other day. The morning after you met him at my place. I just got off the phone with him."

"Oh," I responded cleverly. It's amazing how much good cheer you put into one word.

She handed me an envelope. "All the information's in there."

I dropped the envelope on the table and went to the refrigerator and pulled out a bottle of Korbel brut champagne.

"Are we celebrating something?" Jane asked as I got two tulip-shaped glasses from the cabinet over the sink.

"I guess you could say that." I stripped off the bottle's wire cap and thumbed out the cork. It ricocheted across the room.

I filled our glasses then told Jane about what took place at the Jefferson Park restaurant in the wee small hours of the morning.

"Winky Harris did it? He killed John Henning? You're sure?"

"Yes. He killed John. And Sharon Rochard too."

Jane's face turned serious. "You've got to go to the police now, Nick. You've got to."

"Already taken care of. I spent a long couple of hours with Inspector Bob Tehaney this morning." I reached for the envelope Jane had brought, started to open it, then decided against it. I didn't need another name to add to the Frank, Fernando, Lopez, Vasquez collection. By now he was probably halfway back to Colombia, getting ready to screw the peasants out of more emeralds. "I'll give this to Tehaney."

"Well, what's Tehaney going to do now?" Jane demanded. "He must have enough proof now to arrest Winky Harris."

"I don't know about proof. But he's certainly got enough information to bring him in for questioning. His only problem may be finding Harris. We went to the restaurant and his house. No sign of him."

"What about the Colombian and the Samoan. What's his name?"

"Eddie Muliaga. Gone too. We checked at Harry Chapman's house. Chapman said they took off as soon as he got home and told them about Winky Harris."

Jane held her champagne glass in front of her eyes and studied the bubbles for a moment.

"Where do you think Harris is?"

"I don't really know, Jane. I don't really care. He'll pop up one of these days. If he doesn't, it means that Muliaga got to him before the police did. Either way, he's a loser."

Her green eyes went back to watching the champagne bubbles. "You know who I kind of feel sorry for? George Rochard. He's lost everything, hasn't he? His wife, and now the police will be all over him because of the emerald smuggling. He'll lose his business too, won't he?"

"Probably. He's another loser." I picked up the envelope containing the Colombian's real name and tapped it against the kitchen tabletop. "But that's what happens when you jump into bed with guys like this and Eddie Muliaga."

She moistened her lips with the tip of her tongue, then looked up at me, her green eyes sparkling. "Speaking of jumping into bed with guys, did you really think that I was up in Fort Bragg with Ben Weber?"

"No. Never. He's not your type."

"Oh, really. And just what is my type?"

I reached for the champagne bottle. "The type that takes you out for expensive dinners all the time. Let's try Asta's again. I've had good luck there."